NEXUS CONFESSIONS:
VOLUME TWO

NEXUS CONFESSIONS: VOLUME TWO

Edited and compiled by
Lindsay Gordon

Always make sure you practise safe, sane and consensual sex.

First published in 2008 by
Nexus
Thames Wharf Studios
Rainville Rd
London W6 9HA

www.nexus-books.com

Typeset by TW Typesetting, Plymouth, Devon

Printed and bound in Great Britain by
CPI Bookmarque Ltd, Croydon CR0 4TD

ISBN 978 0 352 34103 7

1 3 5 7 9 10 8 6 4 2

Contents

Introduction

Who can forget the first time they read a reader's letter in an adult magazine? It could make your legs shake. You could almost feel your imagination stretching to comprehend exactly what some woman had done with a neighbour, the baby-sitter, her best friend, her son's friend, a couple of complete strangers, whatever . . . Do real women actually do these things? Did this guy really get that lucky? We asked ourselves these questions, and the not knowing, and the wanting to believe, or wanting to disbelieve because we felt we were missing out, were all part of the reading experience, the fun, the involvement in the confessions of others, as if we were reading some shameful diary. And when Nancy Friday's collections of sexual fantasies became available, didn't we all shake our heads and say, no way, some depraved writer made all of this up. No woman could possibly want to do that. Or this guy must be crazy. But I bet there are reader's letters and confessed fantasies that we read years, even decades ago, that we can still remember clearly. Stories that haunt us: did it, might it, could it have really happened? And stories that still thrill us when the lights go out because they have informed our own dreams. But as we get older and become more experienced, maybe we have learnt that we would be foolish to underestimate anyone sexually, especially ourselves.

The scope of human fantasy and sexual experience seems infinite now. And our sexual urges and imaginations never cease to eroticise any new situation or trend or cultural flux about us. To browse online and to see how many erotic sub-cultures have arisen and made themselves known, is to be in awe. Same deal with magazines and adult films – the variety, the diversity, the complexity and level of obsessive detail involved. But I still believe there are few pictures or visuals that can offer the insights into motivation and desire, or reveal the inner world of a fetish, or detail the pure visceral thrill of sexual arousal, or the anticipation and suspense of a sexual experience in the same way that a story can. When it comes to the erotic you can't beat a narrative, and when it comes to an erotic narrative you can't beat a confession. An actual experience or longing confided to you, the reader, in a private dialogue that declares: *yes, if I am honest, I even shock myself at what I have done and what I want to do.* There is something comforting about it. And unlike a novel, with an anthology there is the additional perk of dipping in and out and of not having to follow continuity; the chance to find something fresh and intensely arousing every few pages written by a different hand. Start at the back if you want. Anthologies are perfect for erotica, and they thrive when the short story in other genres has tragically gone the way of poetry.

So sit back and enjoy the Nexus Confessions series. It offers the old school thrills of reading about the sexual shenanigans of others, but Nexus-style. And the fantasies and confessions that came flooding in – when the call went out on our website – are probably only suitable for Nexus. Because like the rest of our canon, they detail fetishes, curious tastes and perverse longings: the thrills of shame and humiliation, the swapping of genders, and the ecstasy of submission or domination. There are no visiting milkmen, or busty neighbours hanging out the washing and winking over the hedge here. Oh, no. Our readers and fantasists are far more likely to have been spanked, or caned, feminised into women, have given themselves to strangers, to have dominated other men or women, gone dogging, done the unthinkable, behaved inappropriately and broken the rules.

Lindsay Gordon, Autumn 2006

Walk on By

It wasn't my ideal job. Let's face it, spending eight hours a day in a dingy, dusty basement with only racks of files and the odd spider for company isn't at the top of anyone's list of ambitions. But I'd finished my degree over a year ago and still hadn't managed to find a permanent job. If it hadn't been for the odd bit of temping, and occasional handouts from my parents (always accompanied by disapproving shakes of the head and lengthy enquiries about my future prospects), I'd have been living on the street.

As it was, I had one tiny room in a shared house and I still took my washing home to mum once a week. It wasn't much, but it was mine and at least I didn't have to worry about my little sister rushing in every time I decided to have a wank. And, let's face it, wanking was about the only sex life I had these days. Well, I was hardly a good prospect, was I? Anyway, I'd always been really shy around girls and, what with my somewhat unusual sexual preferences, it seemed easier not to even bother. I wasn't a virgin, but you could hardly call me experienced. And when it came to my more specialised appetites . . . well, those had always been strictly confined to my fantasy life. I'm sure there were girls who got off on having their feet worshipped and didn't mind a bit parading around in nothing but high heels, but let's just say I'd never met one of them.

Anyway, as I said, it was hardly my dream job; frankly I couldn't think of anything more boring, but there was rent to pay, I owed thousands in student loans, and I was beginning to dread going cap-in-hand to my parents every few months. It was time to stand on my own two feet and, if that meant working in a musty old cellar, then it had to be.

The job itself was simple enough. My employers, one of the City's oldest firms of solicitors, were only just moving into the computer age. The basement housed their archives. It would be my job to retrieve and file wills and trust documents and title deeds and, in quieter moments, to design a computer program to catalogue everything in the archive. This was no mean feat; some of the papers had been there since Victorian times. But, to tell you the truth, I relished the challenge and for a shy, gauche young man like me, working alone suited me down to the ground.

It was pretty dark and spooky in my basement. The overhead lights did little to relieve the gloom, merely creating shadows and adding to the sense of decay. What's more, the dust and crumbling paper exacerbated my asthma and I spent most of the day red-eyed and sniffling. Hardly appealing, so, when you think about it, it was probably a good thing that I worked alone.

But I'd only been there half a day when I noticed an unexpected, and most welcome, fringe benefit. The basement was essentially one huge rectangular room. On the floors above, the building had been divided into separate, smaller rooms but my domain had never been partitioned. One side of the room faced the street where there were windows to let in light. I hadn't paid much attention to them at first, beyond thinking that they wouldn't allow me to see much of the world. The windows were at eye level and only about a foot high. What would normally have been the windowsill on the outside was the pavement.

Towards the end of my first morning I heard a clip-clop sound coming from outside and looked up to notice two sets of women's feet walking past. Both women were wearing high heels of the type worn by office workers. One of them wore plain black court shoes but the one closer to me had on chocolate-brown suede shoes with a series of narrow straps across the instep. The other one wore ordinary, dark nylons but the woman in the brown shoes was wearing sheer, seamed black ones with the Cuban heel just visible at the back of her ankle where the shoe ended. I was pretty certain that her nylons, unlike her companion's, were probably stockings and I couldn't help my mind wandering a little farther up her leg to that inviting and mysterious zone between stocking tops and underwear.

As the windows ran the whole length of the building, from the vantage point of my desk I was able to watch then walk the full length of the building. Once they had passed me, their heels clacking against the pavement, I could see them from the rear and got a lovely view of stocking seams running up the backs of two shapely calves. My boring unappealing job suddenly seemed a lot more exciting. As the two women disappeared out of sight I realised I was holding my breath.

Needless to say, that night in my room, I relived that moment in minute detail. Running over in my mind the sound of the steel-tipped stilettos clip-clopping against the paving slabs. The curve of their insteps, the subtle gleam of light on their nylon-clad legs. Either one of them would have been enough to bring me off but it was the woman in the brown shoes with the old-fashioned seamed stockings who really excited me. I don't know why, but for some reason I always imagined that women who dressed that way were dominant and demanding. In my imagination they wanted nothing more than to have me kneel at their feet, gazing up at their magnificent stockinged legs. Maybe, if I was lucky, I might even get to lick the leather and run my tongue slowly along the length of the cruel, slender heel.

From then on, I woke up every morning eager for work. I took to going in early to catch the office girls walking past on the way to their own jobs. I knew that, if I let it, my new obsession could interfere with my job so, ever the professional, I disciplined myself, rationing my voyeurism to my free time.

I got into the habit of buying two slices of toast and a cappuccino in the sandwich bar opposite then sitting by the basement window while I ate my breakfast. At nine o'clock I'd sit at my desk and wouldn't look out of the window again until lunch-time which, needless to say, I ate at my favourite seat where I had the best view. It wasn't easy, but I was paid to work, not to look out of the window, and I couldn't ignore my responsibilities. And, with something to look forward to, I was able to channel all my pent-up energy and excitement into my work and even began to enjoy it.

I soon developed favourites. I could even identify them from the sounds of their footsteps as they approached down the street. There was a woman who passed by very early every morning who always wore rather slutty shoes that were somewhat scuffed, the leather on the heels curling slightly like banana peel. Though my view was restricted to the knees down, I felt I could tell a little about their characters from their legs and feet. The woman with the tarty shoes was short and a little chubby. Her calf was full and rounded and she always wore black, very shiny tights of the kind, I knew, that contain a high proportion of Lycra.

She always wore impossibly high heels that meant she was practically walking on tiptoes. She had half a dozen pairs of shoes, which she alternated. Most of them were unusual colours: crimson, green, yellow and pink. She always walked slowly and sometimes she looked as though her feet hurt and I concocted the fantasy that she was a street girl on the way home after a hard night. I was probably completely wrong. She could have been an office girl for all I knew, or even a high-court judge with terrible taste in shoes, but in my imagination she was a tart with a heart going home to a fry-up and a warm bed.

Did she do it in punters' cars, I wondered? Did she peel down those shiny tights and just bend over in an alley? Or maybe she had a room with a maid to show in the clients and a bowl of condoms on the bedside table where she stripped off completely and let them do whatever they wanted provided they had the money to pay. I couldn't help wondering how much she would charge if you asked her to keep her shoes on.

There was another woman whose shoes were always shiny and immaculate and clearly expensive. She rushed past as if she were terribly busy, talking into her mobile phone so loudly I could hear every word. I imagined that she was a recruitment consultant or estate agent whose income depended on commission and she was ruthless and focused in her pursuit of clients.

Was she the sort of woman who'd like to dominate a man at the end of the day? Would she lift her foot and run her spiked heel down my torso and threaten to grind it into my testicles if I wasn't a good boy? Or maybe she preferred to let go in her free time and allow someone else to take charge. One day she hurried by in a pair of square-toed, kitten-heel black slingbacks and I noticed that she had a hole in her tights. I longed to finger her pale skin through the gap and touch her naked flesh with the tip of my tongue.

Needless to say, sitting by the window looking at a parade of gorgeous female feet going by got me rather hot and bothered. But no matter how horny it made me, I had a strict rule that I'd wait until the evening to relieve my pent-up arousal in the comfort and privacy of my own bed. Even though nobody would ever know about it, somehow, wanking in a dank basement seemed just too seedy and desperate.

After a while, I even came to enjoy the frustration. Fuelled by my arousal, my work had never been better and, when I finally allowed myself to come, reliving the parade of shoes that had passed by the window that day, it was never less than spectacular.

By far my favourite was the woman I had seen on the first day in the brown suede shoes. She had an elegant, languorous way of walking that reminded me of a catwalk model. Something about the rhythm of her steps told me that her hips swayed as she moved and it wasn't difficult to picture her buttocks swinging from side to side, hypnotising me.

She usually passed by just before nine and seldom went home before six. Most lunchtimes, she walked by my window while I was sitting at my vantage point eating my sandwich and came back just before I returned to work. On the days when she didn't, I imagined she was indulging in some stuffy business lunch, forced to be polite to clients she couldn't stand. At least I hoped she couldn't stand them because, by this time, I'd developed quite a crush on her.

It was crazy, I knew, because, in reality, I knew nothing about her other than that she had expensive taste in shoes and favoured old-fashioned hosiery, but fantasies never hurt anyone and, since they were the only sex life I had, I intended to enjoy them to the full.

She seldom wore the same footwear twice. She owned several pairs that I recognised as Manolo Blahnik and Jimmy Choo, so I guessed she was – if you'll pardon the pun – well-heeled. Though her choice of shoe was never slutty, they were always exotic and individual. She favoured tall, slender heels which showed her arched instep to its best advantage and made her calves seem even more shapely. She liked suede and buttery, sensual calfskin and shoes made from silk. There was a crimson pair fastened by ribbons around the ankle and a dark green beaded pair with the same iridescent sheen as a fly's wing.

No matter what shoes she chose she always wore sheer, traditional nylons. In my fevered imagination I pictured her sitting on her bed each morning, taking a flimsy stocking out of the packet and rolling it down in readiness. Then she'd put her scarlet-painted toes into the stocking's shaped toe and gently ease it up her perfect legs. She'd fasten the top to her suspenders – attached, in my imagination, to the bottom of a frothy black corset (unlikely, I know, but, hey, it was my fantasy so why not) – and turn her back to a full-length mirror to check if her seams were straight.

I couldn't help picturing myself naked on my knees looking up at her legs and tracing the seam with my eyes, and then my fingers, from where it began at the heel with its dark step-shaped pattern and up the

7

curve of her calves and thighs. At the top there was the circle where the seam ended just under the dark welt of the stocking-top. If I was lucky, maybe she would bend over and treat me to a glimpse of plump lips beneath the globes of her buttocks as she slid her knickers up her legs. Well, I could dream, couldn't I?

When I pleasured myself at home after a long day at work, it was this woman who fuelled most of my solitary fantasies. I christened her Dita, after Dita Von Teese, the exotic and glamorous wife of Marilyn Manson. Was she a high-class escort or a high-powered businesswoman? Whatever she did, I knew it was lucrative. Occasionally I might catch a glimpse of the bottom of a dress or a skirt and these too were expensive and tasteful.

It occurred to me, of course, that I could go outside and get a proper look at her. After all, I knew her routines; it wouldn't be difficult. But, tempting though that was, part of me felt as though doing so might break the spell. Maybe she had a face like a bag of spanners, though I doubted it. But even if she was every bit as gorgeous as in my imagination, if I saw her for real, somehow I knew it would ruin things. Part of the appeal was that I'd never seen the rest of her. Because I'd never seen her face, because I didn't know if she was blonde or brunette, well-endowed or flat-chested, I was free to create whatever fantasy I chose. In my mind, she was perfect and who would want to tamper with perfection?

One evening, I was sitting on my stool by the window looking at the parade of legs and feet on their way home from work. The five o'clock rush to the tube station was long over. I'd have gone home myself ages ago only I was waiting for Dita to go past. I knew she was at work today because I'd already seen her trot past in the morning in impossibly high black patent shoes with a metal heel and a fine strap around her slender ankle. They were what I'd heard other blokes calling 'Fuck me' shoes, and they certainly worked on me.

I wanted to catch another glimpse of them, to imprint them on my memory so that I could have a really delicious, slow session at home. I'd almost given up – maybe she'd gone home in a taxi or was out at a business meeting and had never returned to the office – when I heard a familiar clip-clop approaching along the pavement behind me. I stood up and turned round to get a better look. She was walking along with another woman, whose footwear seemed dowdy and ordinary by comparison. As they drew level with me they stopped and turned to face each other. They were obviously deep in conversation and wanted to finish talking before they went their separate ways.

The other woman was telling Dita about a disastrous blind date she had been on. The story seemed interminable, with every moment and facial expression needing discussion or explanation and Dita sounded sympathetic and interested even though, to me, the woman seemed desperate and self-delusional. Dita was standing with her back to me and I realised that if I pushed my face right up against the glass I could see a little more of her. I stood on tiptoe and squashed my face up against the cold dirty window. I could hardly believe it; I could see up her skirt! She was wearing a knee-length pleated skirt which flared out from the hips, allowing me an excellent view. She was indeed wearing stockings; I could just see a glimpse of milky thigh and dark silk-clad bottom.

It was more than flesh and blood could bear. In spite of the rule I'd set myself I couldn't resist moving my hand to the front of my trousers and fingering my erection. Even through two layers of fabric, it felt fantastic. I drank in every detail. I noticed that one of her stockings was slightly twisted above the knee so that the seam veered off to one side rather than neatly bisecting her thigh. They were slightly creased around the ankle and I longed to lick my fingertips and run them up her legs from ankle to knee as I had seen women do to pull up sagging stockings.

My view up her skirt was restricted by the glass. Ideally I'd have liked to be further forwards but the window was in the way and I had to make do with the occasional glimpse of thigh and panties. Up close, her shoes were a work of art. The bottom part of the stiletto heel was shiny, cold steel and the slender strap around her ankle was fastened with an ornate buckle. They were impossibly high, arching her foot and emphasising the curve of her instep. I was in heaven. Maybe I should ease down my zip and give myself just a little manual assistance? I was the only person left in the office except for the security guard who'd rung down earlier to let me know that I was the last to leave. Who would ever know?

I pulled down my fly, thrust my hand inside and quickly located the opening at the front of my boxers. I gripped my rigid cock in my hand and squeezed. I didn't know how long it would go on for; she might tire of her friend's narrative and bid her a quick goodbye before trotting off towards the tube station and out of my field of vision. I intended to make the most of every second, to drink in every tiny detail and commit it to my memory so that, when she'd gone, I'd be able to close my eyes and recreate it while I brought myself to a well-deserved climax. And I had no doubt that the earth would move so violently that it would be off the Richter scale.

I was so involved in enjoying the view and stroking my engorged cock that I wasn't paying attention to their conversation. They kissed goodbye and the other woman trotted off across the road. I assumed that Dita too would move on, but she was fumbling through her pockets as if she'd lost something, then she opened her handbag and began to look through it. Maybe she's lost her tube ticket, I thought. Well, it wouldn't take long to find, so I stepped up the pace of my wanking and pressed my face so hard against the window that my nose was flattened and the glass steamed up every time I breathed out.

Dita found what she was looking for and closed her handbag with a snap. I must have been so disappointed that she'd be moving away that, without realising, I let out a little sigh of disappointment. But I was so completely involved in my manual manipulations that I just stood there with my face pressed up against the glass looking up her skirt.

It didn't even occur to me that she might have heard me until she turned suddenly and said, 'Who's that? Is there someone there?' Of course, I realised instantly that she'd heard me, but I couldn't risk making any more noise, so I just stood there on tiptoe with my hand inside my trousers and my nose flattened uncomfortably by the window. Maybe if I stayed very quiet she'd go away. I couldn't think of anything worse than being caught in the act. I mean, how sad was that? I couldn't imagine any woman understanding my dirty little secret. Fantasies were one thing, but I didn't fool myself that my current situation was anything other than sordid.

Dita was looking around, trying to find the source of the sound. I dared not move, so I just prayed that she wouldn't look down.

'There's someone there, I know there is, I can hear breathing, panting . . .'

Instantly, I held my breath, but it was too late. She turned round towards me and bent down. Before I had a chance to move away I found myself looking directly into her dark-brown eyes. I could hardly pretend I just happened to be looking out of the window as my nose was splayed by the glass. I moved my face away, hoping that it looked less sinister but didn't even think that this would mean that, from her position above me, she'd be able to see down the front of my body to where my hand was firmly thrust inside my open fly.

I saw her eyes narrow in recognition and then anger.

'You stay there, young man. I'm coming in.' She stood up and trotted off towards the door.

I was in absolute turmoil. I had no idea what to do. Strictly speaking, the security man wasn't supposed to let anyone in after hours but I didn't doubt that she'd be able to win him round. I zipped up my trousers and put on my jacket. There was no back way out of the offices, but if I went up in the service lift I could pass her in the lobby and she'd have no idea it had been me looking up her dress. I prayed she wouldn't recognise me and headed for the lift.

I pressed the button and watched the illuminated numbers which signalled its descent from the floors above. The wait seemed interminable. When the doors finally opened I was confronted with the sight of Dita, very angry and very beautiful, standing in the lift. Her long dark hair was caught back in a velvet ribbon. She was wearing a tailored jacket and a white linen blouse. At her throat was a velvet choker with a single teardrop-shaped pearl dangling from it. Her lips were painted a dark crimson and her eye shadow was smoky and exotic.

'Well, well, trying to make a quick getaway, eh?'
She stepped out of the lift.

'What? I don't know what you mean.' Maybe if I
could bluff it out she'd let me go. It could have been
anyone at the window; there was no reason that it
should have been me.

'Oh come off it, Peeping Tom, I recognise you.
And, even if I didn't, you've got dirt from the glass
all over your nose.'

My hand flew to my face and I realised, too late,
that I'd given myself away.

'I . . . I'm sorry,' was all I could manage to say.

'Not as sorry as you're going to be. Now, do you
mind telling me what this is all about? Do you make
a habit of spying on women while you have a wank?
You nasty little voyeur. What do you think your
employers would make of that?'

'Please don't tell them.' I couldn't keep the panic
out of my voice. I needed the job and who would ever
give me another one if I was sacked for masturbation
and voyeurism? 'I'll do anything. Anything you
want.' I supposed it was desperation that made me
say it and, as soon as the words were out of my
mouth, I realised how ridiculous they sounded. I ran
my fingers through my hair and hung my head. 'I'm
really sorry; I've been completely stupid. I need this
job, please don't report me. You've got every right to
be angry and I realise you've got no reason to show
me any mercy, but I can't lose my job. Please.'

'You should have thought of that before you got
your cock out.' She was standing with her hands on
her hips and, though still angry, I could see that she'd
grown curious.

'Actually, it wasn't really out . . .'

'Do you think that matters? Is this any time to split
hairs? You were spying on me – looking right up my

13

skirt, I expect – and masturbating. Don't you think you owe me an explanation?'

'Yes, you're right. I do . . .'

'I'm listening. And bear in mind that the quality of your explanation is what determines whether or not I go to your employers so you'd better make it good.' She was looking directly at me. Her face was stern and unbelievably beautiful. Part of me longed to obey her. I'd have done anything she wanted, yet shame and fear had made my tongue thick. But if I didn't try to explain I'd be in even bigger trouble. I took a deep breath.

'It's just that I've never told anyone my secret before. In fact, I don't think I've even said it out loud. I don't know where to begin.'

'Why not start with why you were looking at me.' Though her voice was authoritative her expression had grown gentler.

'OK. I'm a . . . what you'd probably call a shoe fetishist.' I looked into her dark, liquid eyes trying to gauge a reaction, expecting shock and disapproval. Instead I saw only curiosity and interest.

'Retifism, interesting. Go on.'

'Not just shoes, but feet and legs. I've always had it, as long as I can remember, but I've never told a soul until today.'

'Is that a pun? "Sole"?' She smiled at me, and for the first time I saw amusement in her eyes.

'Not an intentional one. When I came to work here I quickly discovered I had a fantastic view of women's feet as they walked by. Not just women, of course, but I'm not interested in the men, obviously.'

'A heterosexual pervert. I can't tell you how reassuring that is.'

'You're laughing at me now.'

'Can you blame me?'

'I suppose not.'

'So you spend your day wanking at the window?'

I shook my head.

'No, it's not like that at all. I just look. And not even during working hours, just lunchtimes and before and after work. I wank at home, I've never done that here before, I swear.

'If that's true, what was so different about tonight?'

'Well ...' I'd never felt more embarrassed but I had no option but to explain myself. 'You stopped just where I was sitting and I realised that if I stood on tiptoe and pressed my face against the glass I might be able to see up your skirt ...'

'I see. You're a dirty little boy, aren't you?'

I assumed the question was rhetorical and, in any case, my burning cheeks had surely provided her with an answer so I looked down at my feet and hoped for the moment to pass. Either that or for the floor to open up and swallow me down into the bowels of hell where I so obviously belonged. She put two fingers under my chin and lifted my head until I was looking straight into her eyes. In spite of myself, the physical contact and her dominating manner made my cock begin to swell.

'I asked you a question. You're a dirty little boy, aren't you?'

'Yes, I am. I'm a dirty little boy.' My voice was small and ashamed. It took all my effort to meet her gaze yet, in spite of my humiliation my cock was expanding and, if she noticed, it would only be compounding my sin. Without thinking, I clamped my right hand over my crotch, covering the evidence. I was so focused on concealing my shame that it didn't occur to me that covering it up would make it all the more obvious.

'A very dirty boy indeed, it would appear.' She let go of my chin and her hand moved to my wrist, pulling my hand away from my groin. She pressed her palm over my genitals. Her fingers explored their contours for a moment while she satisfied herself of my arousal. 'You said you'd do anything if I promise not to report you. Do you mean that?'

I nodded.

'Anything, whatever you want. I can't afford to lose this job.'

She crossed her arms and looked me up and down. Her eyes conducted an unhurried appraisal of my body.

'Tell me . . . I don't know your name?'

'Rob. Rob Newton.'

'So tell me, Rob. Do your little shoe fantasies include kneeling at a woman's feet and obeying her every whim? Do you crave humiliation and pain? Maybe you long for her to put on her sexiest shoes and walk all over you, or press her spiked heels into your flesh? Is that what you dream about, Rob?'

I was far too excited to answer but I guess my face and, more importantly my cock, had given me away. I could only nod in agreement and she began to smile, a slow, wicked grin that aroused and frightened me in equal measure.

'OK. Is there anywhere in this catacomb where we can find a quiet corner? We'd hardly want to be observed through the window, would we? No voyeurs, though that would be poetic justice.'

'Yes, behind the shelves at that end, it's completely private.'

'Then what are we waiting for? Lead on.'

It was impossible that this glorious creature intended to give me exactly what I'd dreamed of. Yet it seemed that was exactly what she had in mind. Emboldened by the realisation that she found the situation as arousing as I did, I felt brave enough to make a request.

'Would you ... Would you mind awfully going first? Only I've been dreaming of watching your arse sway as you walk for weeks.'

She laughed.

'Why not? Which way is it?'

'Between those racks to the right as far as you can go then turn left. We'll never be seen.'

'OK.' She turned and walked off. As I suspected, she was every bit as beautiful from the rear. She had a pert, apple-shaped arse and a narrow waist. She walked slowly, deliberately undulating her rear for my benefit. 'The last row there, on the left?'

She turned the corner and disappeared out of sight. I followed on like a lap dog at its mistress's heel.

'Well, it's hardly the Ritz, but it will do, I suppose. Now, Rob. Shall we begin?'

I could only nod in reply.

'I'd like you to take off all your clothes, please.'

I didn't even think of disobeying. I stripped off, putting my clothes on a trolley nearby which we used for transporting the files. Soon I was naked except for my boxers and my socks and shoes – the floor was far too dirty to go barefoot. The front of my underwear was tented by my erection and stained dark with pre-come. I could feel her appraising eyes on my body. I gazed back, emboldened by her obvious arousal. Her breathing had grown shallow and rapid and her lips were puffy and dark.

I peeled down my boxers and dropped them on top of the pile of clothes.

'Good. Very nice. Much more sculpted than I would have imagined. I assumed you were a desk jockey, but you're actually quite muscular.' Her voice had grown deep and breathy.

'I go to the gym twice a week.' I was unbelievably proud and excited that she found my body attractive.

'And it shows. Now. Get down on your knees and lick my shoes. They've grown dusty in this filthy basement and we can't have that, can we?'

I couldn't get to my knees quickly enough. I was down on all fours in seconds, my naked arse pointing at the ceiling as I bent my head to lick her shoes. The dust from the floor got up my nose and made me cough, but I didn't care. I licked her shoes as if my life depended upon it. She leaned against one of the shelves for support and lifted her foot, indicating that I should lick the sole.

I cleaned the dirty underside of her shoe with my tongue. It was gritty and smelly but, to me, it tasted like the finest caviar. I closed my eyes and licked. My cock was rigid, lying flat against my belly. From time to time I let out a little grunt of pleasure and excitement as I cleaned her sole. It was divine; a dream come true. If it was all that ever happened between us I would count myself the luckiest man alive.

'Good. Now, I want you to suck on my heel, that's a good boy.'

I took the spiky heel into my mouth and slid my face up and down as if I was sucking a cock. I could feel the cold metal tip pressing against my tongue as I moved and it felt dangerous and unbelievably arousing. She began to move her foot, fucking my mouth with her steel heel.

I was unbelievably excited by now; my cock painful. I was moaning, gasping and spluttering. I closed my eyes and allowed her to abuse my mouth with the stiletto and I couldn't have loved it more if her heel was a cock and my mouth was a willing pussy. It felt shameful and humiliating and strange, yet on another level it was completely right, natural and desirable. It was all I wanted, for her to use me in any way that she chose.

'Enough.' She removed the heel and I felt as though I'd had my pocket picked. I looked up at her as she reached under her skirt and removed her panties. 'Put your jacket on the floor for me to lie on.'

Under normal circumstances I'd have baulked at the suggestion that I soil a jacket that I'd just had dry cleaned, but I whipped it off the trolley and spread it out on the ground like Walter Raleigh laying down his cloak for his Queen. She lay down on it with her thighs spread and her skirt bunched up around her waist. The sight of that six inches of creamy thigh above her stocking tops, leading up to a neat trimmed pussy, was almost more than I could bear.

I longed to take my cock in my hand and plunge it in her up to the root and fuck her so hard she screamed. Yet I was conscious that I'd promised to do whatever she wanted, that we were here for her pleasure not mine and I dared not move a muscle until I had received my orders. She used both hands to spread her lips and I saw the dark rosy moist interior of her glorious pussy.

'Lick that. And don't stop until I tell you.'

I didn't need telling twice. I shuffled forwards, positioning myself between her spread thighs. I lowered myself onto my elbows and pressed my face against her crotch. I could smell her arousal and a hint of some exotic perfume. Though I wasn't very experienced, I'd always prided myself on my cunnilingus skills. I ran the flat of my tongue along the length of her slit. I dabbled it at her opening. I slid it downwards and explored the area between her two secret holes before probing at her tight rear opening.

She gasped. She was holding her lips open, spreading herself for my eager tongue. I explored every millimetre of her beautiful cunt. She moaned and wriggled throughout my exploration, leaving me in no doubt that she found it as arousing as I did. My cock was drooling pre-come onto the dusty floor. My balls were hard and tight and riding my shaft.

I moved my attention to the hard bead of her clit and pushed back its tiny hood with the tip of my tongue. She gasped in appreciation and began to rock her hips. I lavished the sensitive nub with long strokes, each of them eliciting a little moan of pleasure. I slid two fingers into her hot tight cunt and fucked her slowly as I licked.

Her thighs were trembling and taut. Sweat filmed her body, making her skin gleam. My cock ached. I reached between my legs with my free hand and took it in my fist. I began to pump it slowly, co-ordinating my movement with the rhythm of my mouth moving against her hot pussy.

I began to concentrate on her clit, circling my tongue around the edge and occasionally flicking it across the sensitive tip. I was fucking her with two fingers, crooking them inside her to stimulate her G-spot. I knew I'd found it because she arched her back and began to whimper.

I wanked myself steadily, my hand wet with my own juice. Her cunt was so slick and slippery that, from time to time, her fingers lost their grip and had to be repositioned and somehow I found that unbelievably arousing. I was sucking hard on her clit by now, taking it right into my mouth and occasionally even nibbling on it.

I was working her G-spot at the same time, circling my fingers inside her. The effect on her was electric. Her whole body was taut and tense and she was moaning and gasping. I could tell that she was on the brink of orgasm, riding that moment where arousal reaches a pitch and finally, finally tips over the edge into climax.

My hand was a blur on my cock. I could have come at any minute, but I was biding my time, waiting for her. I wanted to time my release with that incredible moment when her body would spasm and her clit would dance in my mouth and I'd feel her cunt contracting around my fingers.

She was in a world of her own, lost in her own arousal. Her hips pistoned, grinding her open crotch against my face. She was making sharp little mewling noises – sobbing almost – in response to the sensations my tongue was creating.

My cock was rigid. I was covered in sweat and dust and the floor was hurting my knees but there was nowhere else I would rather be: the taste of her cunt in my mouth and my cock in my hand.

By now, she was practically screaming. Her hips rocked urgently. I licked for all I was worth. She lifted both legs and rested her feet against my back. Her cries reached a pitch of excitement and her whole body stiffened. She was coming. I pulled down hard on my foreskin, finally allowing myself to climax.

I felt her heels pressing into my flesh. She raked them down my back, not hard enough to hurt, but I could definitely feel it.

I kept my mouth clamped over her pussy and rode out her orgasm with her. My cock pumped out jism onto the dusty floor. Some of it landed on my jacket and the idea of soiling it only added to the excitement. She seemed to come forever, her clit in my mouth and her scratchy pubes pressing up against my nose. When it was over, I lay down beside her and held her in my arms. I was covered in dust and I was pretty sure that there were cobwebs in my hair but I couldn't have been happier.

'Did you enjoy that, Rob?' she asked finally, her voice sleepy and satisfied.

'Fantastic. How was it for you . . .' I looked at her. 'Do you know, I don't even know what your name is?'

'Why don't you just call me Mistress?'

And I have, ever since.

– *Rob, London, UK*

Victim of Circumstances

I'm not really an exhibitionist. I'm just a victim of circumstances.

It started the Saturday before last. My husband's best friend and workmate, Tim, was scheduled to turn up and watch THE MATCH, while helpfully removing the beer cans from our fridge. I could gripe a little here and ask why men need to watch football matches in twos or threes? Or why they never watch 'a match' and it always has to be THE MATCH, in capitals and with a definite article?

But it's not in my nature to bitch and moan.

For the afternoon my home would be transformed into a beer-smelling playground of expletives, farting and loutish cheers. Rather than fight the inevitable entropy of manliness, I'd decided to simply take a shower, and then go into town and indulge in some retail therapy. If Ron could behave like a conventional stereotype there seemed no reason why I couldn't follow his example.

But that Saturday started like something from the corniest of corny sitcoms. Because the shower was running, I didn't hear the doorbell. Because I didn't know Ron had let Tim into the house, I didn't bother covering myself as I went from the bathroom to our bedroom. And because Tim was headed up the stairs, he got to see me *absolutely naked*.

There was a moment where I could have sworn my heart stopped beating. My cheeks turned bright red but I'm fairly sure Tim was not looking at my face. I was standing like a rabbit caught in the glow of oncoming headlamps. My bare breasts – washed, scrubbed and looking distinctly perky – were exposed and trembling for him. The triangle of my pubic bush – only just trimmed and with the short dark curls still bejewelled by shower water – was there for him to see.

Tim stood at the top of the stairs between me and my bedroom door. His jaw hung open. His eyes were wide with amazement. And then he began to grin. 'Wow,' he whispered. 'Sharon!'

I rushed past him and slammed the bedroom door closed.

As though reciting the punchline for the sitcom script I had just been part of, Ron called up, 'I don't know if the bathroom's free or not, Tim. I think Shaz might be taking a shower.'

I lay shivering on the bed, not sure what had happened and confused by my body's responses. I was embarrassed, I was angry, and I was maddeningly horny. Those first two responses didn't cause me any confusion. Tim seeing me naked was humiliating. And Ron, not thinking about me in the shower and simply letting his friend bound up the stairs, would have irked any woman. But I couldn't understand why I was so aroused.

I closed my eyes and the image came back to me. Tim was staring at my naked body. His gaze feasted on my bare breasts, then lowered to glimpse the triangle of my pubes. I wondered if he had seen anything more. I'd trimmed the dark hairs short in the shower and it was not unusual for the grooming to make my labia grow more obvious. This isn't a confession where I admit to touching myself up in the shower (although the massage spray does have a distinctive pulse). But I was petrified that Tim might have seen my pussy lips.

No. I wasn't petrified. That's the wrong word. Half of me was devastated that he might have seen so much. But the other half was very excited. Considering the spreading warmth that swept from my loins, I knew exactly which half was excited.

My thoughts were in overdrive. I wondered if I should tell Ron what had happened, or if that would make my humiliation worse. I couldn't imagine him being angry because of the incident. But I could easily picture him adding to my shame by turning the story into a crass little anecdote for all his workmates and drinking friends.

That thought killed the idea of sharing the experience with Ron.

And I was anxious to find out if Tim was aroused by what he had seen. I don't know why his opinion mattered to me, and his exclamation had said more than a single syllable can usually manage. But I needed to know if the sight of my bare body had given him an erection, if he'd had difficulty peeing after seeing me, and if the sight of my nudity now occupied a special place in his thoughts.

I was tempted to touch myself while I remembered the moment. I was already undressed. Considering the ferocity of my arousal I don't think it would have taken more than a finger against my clit and I would have reached a climax. But I couldn't let myself do it then.

Instead, I got dressed, quickly tidied my appearance, and then hurried out to the shops. I called goodbye to Ron, not daring to enter the lounge where he sat in front of the TV with Tim. My husband grunted back an unintelligible response.

Tim shouted, 'It was good seeing you, Sharon.'

His words turned my cheeks scarlet.

The memory of that Saturday stayed with me for most of the week. Each morning, when I showered, I remembered that was what I had been doing prior to Tim glimpsing me naked. Before I dressed, I stood in front of the bedroom mirror and critically analysed the view Tim had enjoyed. My breasts are full and round. They are pale enough so a starburst of pale-blue veins can be seen beneath the flesh. Arousal hit me each time I remembered Tim had seen those veins. My nipples are only small, even when I'm excited, but the areolae are huge, dusky-pink circles. My small nipples grew stiff whenever I thought about Tim looking at me, and the areolae turned dark purple, the crinkled flesh turning taut and glossy.

Throughout the days, the memory plagued me like an obsession. Every evening, when Ron and I retired to bed, I mounted him with a passion we hadn't enjoyed since before we got married. And, even when he was satisfied and snoring heavily, I could only drift off to sleep with my hands pressed against my crotch and my thoughts fixed on that moment when Tim had seen me naked.

By last Friday I thought I was over the stupidity of the distraction. It was early morning, Ron and I were both about ready to set off for work, and our conversation was snatched in those exchanges we made between visiting the bathroom, bedroom and kitchen. He asked if I had plans for the weekend. I said I wasn't sure yet. He told me Tim was calling round on Saturday to watch THE MATCH.

A fist of arousal punched me in the stomach. If Ron had been watching me I'm sure he would have seen my response. He called a goodbye at that point and disappeared out of the house. Which left me with ten minutes alone to finish getting ready for the day, after I'd fingered myself to orgasm.

The Friday dragged past in a sick haze of lurid thoughts. Not only was I remembering the previous Saturday, I was now anticipating what could occur as the next one approached. Was Tim genuinely coming round to watch THE MATCH? Or was there something else at our house he wanted to see? Last time he had seen me naked by accident. How was I going to face him after that? Would there be a danger of it happening again? And, if there wasn't, how could I shape events so it did happen?

I shook myself out of the fugue on Saturday morning. It was senseless to obsess about something so trivial. I was jeopardising too much (my reputation, our marriage and Ron's respect) to risk throwing it all away by flashing myself at Tim.

Like a junkie trying to distance myself from the source of my addiction, I planned to escape from the house well before THE MATCH began. I got up early, showered and dressed while deliberately not thinking of the excitement I enjoyed from being viewed naked. I hurried out of the house just as Ron was getting up. I pecked him on the cheek, told him to call my mobile if he needed me, and then scurried off to the garage, delighted I had made this break from my obsession.

Once again, I became a victim of circumstances.

I was still in the garage three hours later, fuming at a car that wouldn't start and cursing my own stupidity. The electrical fault could have been dealt with if I'd been concentrating on Friday. I'd dimly noticed one of the dashboard lights was flashing as I drove to and from work. But my thoughts had been so tied up with arousal I hadn't taken any notice of what the light meant.

Tim and Peter turned up while Ron and I were still struggling to make the damned thing start.

My stomach churned. My cheeks turned scarlet. And I couldn't meet Tim's gaze or properly respond to his questions.

'Car not working?' Tim asked. 'Can I take a look at anything?'

My eyes grew wide when he said that. I told Ron I was going inside to clean up after a morning spent grubbing around inside a dirty engine. He told me he, Peter and Tim would sort the car.

An hour later, when I'd finished cleaning and changing, I heard the gutsy roar of my motor's engine. The boys gave a hearty cheer, congratulating themselves on their manliness, and I groaned with frustration that my plans to escape had been thwarted. It was now too late to run out of the house. And while Ron, Peter and Tim had been labouring under the bonnet of my car, I'd had time to dwell on the nearness of all three men and fantasise about situations where Peter and Tim could see me naked. The ordeal of Friday, where I had been locked in a constant haze of excitement, paled next to my thoughts during that day.

I speculated about Peter's unexpected appearance. I couldn't remember if Ron had mentioned that he would be visiting and wondered if Tim had encouraged him to join them for the afternoon. It was easy to picture Tim telling Peter what he had seen and my pulse raced as I imagined the two men discussing me. I expected Tim would have exaggerated the entire incident and, if I'd touched my pussy while I thought about that, I would have screamed with the release.

When Ron called up to the bedroom to say the car was working, I came to a bold decision. I put on a flimsy blouse: not transparent but not particularly concealing. And I put on a very short skirt. I didn't bother with bra or knickers. Then I went downstairs as the three of them settled in front of the lounge's TV.

My heart raced fast enough to make my head pound. Hurrying through to the kitchen, snatching tins of beer from the fridge, I tried to show less haste and more decorum as I stepped into the room and handed out drinks.

I mumbled something nonsensical about wanting to thank them for repairing my car. I can't remember the exact words. Ron's concentration was fixed on the TV as a pair of chuckling pundits narrated the build-up for that day's game.

Tim's attention was fixed on my breasts.

I hadn't fully fastened the blouse and, when I lowered myself to pass him his tin, I knew I was showing a good expanse of cleavage. His grin grew wide. In my mind, I could almost hear him whisper the word, 'Wow!'

Daringly, I smiled for him.

Peter seemed equally appreciative when I passed him his tin and I noticed both guests were watching me when I settled myself in a chair with my own drink.

It's hard to explain how naughty I felt. My husband sat close enough to touch. The two men were virtual strangers. And I was casually flaunting myself at them. With my legs pressed together I suppose I looked fairly innocent as I tried to follow the football match. But, when I parted my thighs slightly, I knew I was giving Tim and Peter an unfettered view of my bare sex.

Their responses were almost like pantomime reactions. If either of them had been cartoon characters they would have had their eyes standing out on stalks and huge, dripping tongues lolling from their mouths.

I parted my legs further.

After all the arousal of the past week my labia were large and obvious. Even in the grey shadows beneath my skirt I figured they would be noticeable to the astute gazes of Peter and Tim. But, just to be certain, I parted my legs that little bit wider.

Peter's grin was broad enough to split his face in two.

Tim casually stroked himself through his pants. For the first time I noticed the fat bulge that pushed at the front of his jeans. Aside from revelling in the pleasure of being viewed and exposing myself, I had wondered if I was truly exciting Tim. The sight of his erection was my first indication that he was genuinely aroused.

I gasped. To cover my surprise, and so Ron didn't suspect what was happening, I spilled some beer over my top and acted as though that was what had caused my exclamation. The liquid turned the fabric transparent. When I glanced down I saw that what had only been suggested before was now on full display to all three men.

'I'd best go and get changed,' I murmured.

'Waste of good beer,' Ron declared, without glancing at me. No one was listening to him.

As I left the room I heard Tim say, 'I need to pop upstairs for a moment.'

The words brought me close to panic. I'd just been flashing myself at the man, deliberately showing him the most intimate secrets of my body. And now he was following me up the stairs. I didn't know whether to hurry up or slow my pace. My heart had been pounding before. Now it thundered.

Tim was by my side on the landing before I could come to a decision. 'Do you know how hot you look?' he asked. 'Do you know how badly I want you?'

I shook my head. 'We can't do anything, Tim,' I told him. And, as desperate as I was to satisfy myself, I intended to stick by the statement. 'I'm faithful to Ron. You can look, but you can't touch.'

He accepted the situation with a blink. His response was instantaneous. 'Can I look some more?'

I answered with equal haste. 'Get down on your knees if you want a close-up view.' Another wicked idea shot into my mind and, before common sense could tell me it was insane, I added, 'You can get your prick out and wank if you want.'

He did not need any more encouragement.

I tore off my skirt and stood wearing only a beer-sodden blouse. Tim was on his knees in front of me, stroking a thick erection that looked on the verge of spurting. I tried to meet his gaze but his eyes were fixed on my pussy. When I reached down and started to stroke myself, I watched him roll his fist up and down the length of his hard prick.

We were outside the bathroom door, in just the right place so that we wouldn't be disturbed should either Ron or Peter decide to follow us up. I moved so I was standing inside the bathroom, and Tim was on his knees on the small landing outside.

Deciding to give him the best show possible, I sat down on the toilet seat and splayed my pussy lips wide apart.

His eyes shone with approval.

I stroked my fingers against the glistening wetness of my hole, teasing the flesh, stretching the lips and touching lightly against the pulsing throb of my clitoris.

Tim stroked faster. I watched his fist engulf his shaft, squeezing so tight the glans turned purple.

Following his lead, realising there was little time available to us, and trying to cram as much into the few moments we had, I pulled my sex open and rubbed vigorously against the pulse of my clitoris.

Tim's eyes were massive. He devoured me with his gaze. His hand became a blur as it stroked briskly back and forth along his length.

The swell of a climax built inside me. Its power was made phenomenal by Tim's lascivious interest and my own pleasure at being watched. As my hips bucked towards the teasing fingers of my own hand, I came close to losing my precarious position on the lavatory seat. Trying to make the show complete for Tim, I wrenched open my blouse and revealed myself naked, sitting before him, and masturbating furiously.

He rolled his eyes and his hand worked more swiftly.

I continued to tease myself, not sure how much longer I could continue before the pleasure burst from my pussy.

The mood was almost broken when Ron's voice trailed up from downstairs. 'What's taking you so long up there, Tim?'

Tim grinned at me and called down, 'I'm just coming.'

I almost giggled. If I hadn't been watching his shaft spurt a delicious ooze of spunk, I probably would have spoilt the moment and laughed out loud. Instead, because it was so exciting to watch his eruption, I felt my own orgasm take hold. I plunged my fingers deep inside my sex and clutched the toilet seat with the other. The climax shook its way through my body. I trembled against the seat, spent and satisfied. When I looked at Tim I saw he was still milking the last droplets of semen from his shaft. A small sticky pool lay on the bathroom's lino in front of him.

As I knelt down to wipe it up with a wad of toilet paper I told him, 'This won't happen again.'

He grinned. 'It was good enough for me that it happened this once.'

'I'm serious,' I warned. 'If Ron found out, that you'd watched me ... I mean seen ...' I couldn't complete the sentence because it was too humiliating to say the words. Instead I said, 'If Ron found out, he'd be very upset.'

'Ron won't find out,' Tim promised. 'And if you don't want it to happen again, it won't happen again.'

And, while his words did give me some reassurance, they didn't put my mind totally at ease. Part of it is because I know Peter and Tim will talk. But part of it is because I want it to happen again.

THE MATCH is on again next Wednesday evening, and I know Peter and Tim are coming round to watch it with Ron. It's crossed my mind that if Ron gets held up at work, delayed in traffic, or if his car leaves him stranded at the office, I might have to entertain Peter and Tim alone in his absence. The thought makes me sick with excitement and dread. I can picture an ignored football match in the background while Peter and Tim stroke off to the saucy strip show I do for them. It's a recurring fantasy that grows stronger every time I allow myself its indulgence. The stripping is a small part to begin with. In the most recent version of that daydream the stripping has become incidental.

Twice now, I've stopped myself from texting a message to Tim. I want to ask if it's likely that Ron's car might not get him back from work on Wednesday evening. It might be wiser to phone the question through to Tim, so he can properly understand what I'm saying. After all, I don't want Ron to suspect he's been deliberately delayed. It would be much better if Ron simply thought he was a victim of circumstances.
    – *Sharon, Sussex, UK*

33

Figging the Brat

In the interest of honesty, I have to own up. I confess that I was crafty and manipulative but she started it. Turnabout is fair play.

It started the bright summer morning that I called my dear friend and long-time rival, Cynthia. I asked her, 'It's been a while. Why don't you come for dinner on Thursday?'

'For overnight, Justine?'

'Of course. It's hardly worth the drive, otherwise.'

'Is my Babs invited?'

I licked my lips in anticipation. Deliberately sounding doubtful, I said, 'Sure. No problem.'

Babs is Cynthia's 'brat'. She's not a naughty child in the usual sense. For a start, Babs is delightfully nubile and nineteen. Like me, Cynthia is a dominant woman who prefers 'innies' to 'outies'. Unlike me, she likes her girls to be – brats. Brats act up to earn the spankings they crave. I find that a bore. *My* pets earn their tannings by being good. When *I* slap a bottom, I do so with love, never out of anger, even pretended anger.

Babs has cinnamon curls, a petulant face and a pouty round bottom that just *begs* to feel the weight of my palm. Cynthia liked to dress Babs in drastically cropped tops and extreme low-rider boy-cut shorts made of clinging fabrics, the better to show off her long lean midriff and the curvaceous cheeks of her plump little bum.

Babs was a brat, but she was a succulent one.

'Sevenish?' Cynthia asked me.

They arrived at ten to eight, a little earlier than I expected. Cynthia's body was draped in a flowing ankle-length black cotton dress, with a coarse enough weave to show the pink of her skin. It was button-through, with just three buttons. The highest came below and between her nipples. The lowest fastened directly over her pubes. Each twist of her body displayed the inner curve of a soft little breast. Each step she took flashed her thighs to well above the tops of her lace-top black stay-up Dim nylons.

Babs was in pale-blue satin – a military-style jacket that was cropped high enough to show off the rounded undersides of her breasts and shorts ab-breviated enough to display the lush half-moons of her bottom.

While Babs unloaded the bags from their Mercedes, Cynthia and I kissed hello briefly, but with busy wet tongues. She likes to play a game of trying to arouse me enough that I'll lose my composure. I enjoy that. I arouse easily but I *never* lose my composure.

I poured arid Beefeater martinis for us adults and something sweet and only mildly alcoholic for young Babs. Cynthia crossed her knees to let one elegant leg project through the open front of her dress. 'Where's your girl?' she asked me.

'Switzerland. Finishing her Masters.'

'You must be lonely.'

'I keep myself amused.'

'Even so.' She looked thoughtful. I guessed she had something in mind but I was content to wait to find out what.

I kept the meal simple – T-bones, Portobello mushrooms, broiled yellow tomatoes from a local grower, hot baguettes straight from my oven, with a nice crisp Hillebrand Estates Merlot. I believe in drinking the *vin du pays*. I poured Babs a third of a glass of wine. Being a brat, she likes to be treated like a child in some ways and as an adult in others. When it came to drinks, she considered herself all grown up.

When she saw the portion I'd poured her, she stuck out her lower lip and reached for the bottle. I told her, 'No!' Her hand snatched back like I'd whacked her knuckles with a ruler. Cynthia looked at me as if she wanted to protest at my disciplining her protégée but she bit her tongue. She gave me another look later, when I asked, in a commanding voice, if Babs would clear the table. Babs complied but with sulky pouts, exaggerated swaying of her young hips and lots of unnecessary clatter.

They were up to something. Babs was never that obliging. Cynthia hated anyone else telling her brat what to do. When they thought I wasn't watching, they exchanged secret glances. Cynthia nodded at Babs, unaware that I had noticed.

Babs said, 'I'm bored!'

I told her, 'You may watch television in the library, or there are lots of books if you'd like to read. Some have pictures.'

'Don't wanna!' Babs stamped, hard.

I looked at Cynthia, interested to see where this charade was leading.

'Do as you're told,' she said.

'No, no, no! Won't, so there!'

Cynthia pointed to a spot on my blackened random-pine floor, close to her feet, and demanded, 'Come here!'

Swaggering, but with an obviously faked fearful look on her face, Babs obeyed. Cynthia reached up and over with her left hand, grabbed Babs by her hair and tugged the girl down over her left thigh. Babs squealed, kicked and flailed her arms, but quite ineffectually. Cynthia was deft, I'll give her that. Her long lovely right leg went up and over, trapping Babs behind her knees. Cynthia's left hand secured Babs's wrists. A swift yank pulled the girl's shorts down to the middle of her thighs, leaving the twin pink mounds of her bottom naked and elevated.

'Can I get you something?' I asked Cynthia. 'A cane or a strap or something?'

'My hand will suffice.' Her palm rose and fell with a resounding clap that betrayed a cupped palm, making more noise than was necessary.

I watched Babs's punishment with some enjoyment. The slow blossoming of the girl's cheeks made a pleasant enough sight but I was more interested in Cynthia's face. She has a vulpine cast to her features that I find quite erotic. The act of spanking accentuated the feral quality of her features, suffusing them with lust.

Once in a while, Cynthia and I had kissed and occasionally caressed in what we pretended was a casual way but it had been years since we'd tried anything serious, sexually. We each found the other's body attractive. The problem was our minds. Domme-on-Domme just doesn't work. I hadn't forgotten the way her nipples felt between my fingers, though, nor the sweet aroma of her pussy.

I wondered, watching her smack her brat's firm little bottom, whether her sex was seeping and, if so, did it still smell like scorched butterscotch.

She was watching me, watching her spank Babs. I was supposed to get turned on by their little exhibition, and I was, but I didn't let it show. The slaps fell into a steady rhythm, each blow landing low, on the undersides of the girl's bottom, right cheek, left cheek, then directly across the pretty plumpness of her sex where it was compressed backwards between her teenage thighs. I counted under my breath. By the time Cynthia got to 70 Babs's sex was oozing. Her squeals and protests had stopped. She was wriggling and panting, with little grunts from time to time. Cynthia was biting her lower lip in concentration. She has a very bitable lower lip, short, full and fleshy, in contrast to the long taut line of her upper one.

Babs wasn't my kind of submissive but I had to give her credit. She could take it. The cheeks of her bum were mottled blue and scarlet. If it had been me delivering her spanking, I'd have been considering ending it while she could still walk.

Cynthia counted, 'Ninety-eight, ninety-nine, one hundred!' Three fingers of her spanking hand formed a dagger, which she plunged into her victim's squishy quim.

Babs arched and flailed her head from side to side. Half a dozen progressively deeper thrusts tipped her over the edge. Gulping and shuddering, she climaxed.

Cynthia gathered her brat up into her lap, cuddled her and crooned words of praise, 'Such a brave girl! I'm so proud of you,' and the like. My friend's mouth nibbled over her victim's cheeks, feasting on the tears that saturated them. Their mouths found each other, Cynthia's devouring, Babs's slack with surrender. The girl snuggled lower, nuzzling, popping Cynthia's top button. A pair of sulky lips sought and found the dark-brown cone of a nipple and suckled, pumping the tidbit in and out of her mouth.

Much D/S behaviour is ritualistic. I recognised the little exhibition that followed as a well-practised sexual rite.

Cynthia crooned, 'Who's my very best baby girl, then?'

Babs released the swollen morsel. 'Babs is?'

'And does Babs love her Auntie Cynthia?'

Her use of 'Auntie' was interesting. Those two aren't related. A 'Mistress and brat' relationship often involves age-play. It seemed that in their case there was an element of mock-incest as well. How complicated! I *much* prefer my own brand of D/S – I'm the Mistress. My lovers are my slaves. You can't get much more straightforward than that.

Cynthia said, 'Show Auntie Cynthia how much her Babs loves her, then.'

Giggling, Babs slithered from Cynthia's lap, awkwardly, for her shorts still restricted her legs. She slid down between her Mistress's parted thighs to curl up on the floor between her feet. Cynthia eased her pubes forwards and undid her lowest buttons to finish undoing her dress. Looking at me, she asked, 'If you don't mind, Justine?'

'Not in the least. Please go ahead.' I didn't feign disinterest but nor did I allow my expression to change. Babs is a noisy eater. I once had a Great Dane that could devour a bowl of stew with less slurping and slobbering than Babs lavished on Cynthia's pussy. After about ten minutes, Cynthia's thighs clamped on Babs's cheeks. Her fingers dragged her brat closer by her hair. She humped at her face a few times and emitted a long soft sigh.

Cynthia gave me a sly look, up from under her long lashes, searching for some sign of my arousal.

I asked her, 'Coffee, Armagnac, or both?'

Babs went up to bed at eleven. Cynthia and I stayed up to discuss who was fucking whom and whether a mutual friend's entry would do well at the upcoming Toronto Film Festival. She hadn't adjusted her dress. Cynthia's pubes and thighs, still glistening with Babs's saliva and her own spending, were blatantly on display. Perhaps I was supposed to suggest she button up. Perhaps I was supposed to be overcome by her body's erotic beauty and fall to my knees in worship. Whichever was expected, I did neither. If ever anything was going to happen between Cynthia and me, it'd be on *my* terms, not hers.

It was two in the morning before Cynthia got around to the topic she'd been edging towards all night. 'I love your house,' she said. 'It's so spacious, but, with your girl away, you must be lonely, no?'

Of course she loved my house. Who wouldn't? It was built in 1808, post-and-beam construction, sheathed in clapboard and trimmed with gingerbread, with a wrap-around covered porch. I'd modernised it before moving in, so it's well insulated, with three-and-a-half bathrooms to complement four bedrooms. My location is ideal, for me. It's a mile north of Derry Road, just below where a ravine cuts into the face of the Niagara Escarpment. I'm sheltered on two sides by cliffs a hundred and fifty feet high. My land is densely wooded. There's a quarter mile of curved driveway to get to the house. I'm secluded, which is important to me, but I'm only an hour from Toronto, which is very handy.

'I'm off checking beans for a month, come Tuesday,' Cynthia told me.

She deals in coffee futures, so she's always zooming off to Brazil and Colombia and so on to check on how next year's crops are coming along.

I said, 'Nice. Is Babs looking forward to the trip?'

She frowned and leaned forwards, making the most of her small breasts. 'I'm visiting twenty-two plantations in thirty days. You know what they say, "She who travels alone travels fastest."'

She paused. I waited.

'I won't be taking Babs.'

'No?' I relented enough to ask her, 'Who's going to look after her for you while you're gone?'

'I was hoping . . .?'

'Me?'

'Would you? She'd be good, I promise.'

'No, she wouldn't. It isn't in her nature.' I frowned and made a little moue, as if thinking. 'Very well, she can stay with me while you're gone, but she'll be subjected to *my* kind of discipline.'

Cynthia nibbled her lower lip. 'You wouldn't be *too* severe?'

'I promise you, Cynthia, you won't find a mark on her when you return.'

The next day, after lunch, when my friend and her girl-toy had left, I drove my Range Rover down into Burlington, to Fortinos, to stock up on groceries. I keep my freezer and pantry full but I don't usually stock much in the way of sweets and I wanted to be a good hostess, even to a brat. As well as sweets, I selected the juiciest oranges, the reddest apples, a variety of exotics, such as dragon and star fruit, and picked out the largest, gnarliest, juiciest piece of ginger root I could find.

Cynthia delivered Babs on the Monday afternoon. For a change, the girl's abbreviated top was a white cotton shirt, worn with a striped tie. Instead of shorts, she wore a tiny tartan kilt. I had to admit that she made a ravishing 'naughty schoolgirl'.

She made to carry her bags upstairs.

'Leave those for later,' I told her.

'Huh?'

'Don't grunt. I'm going to go through your things. While you're in *my* house, *I'll* decide what you wear.'

'But . . .'

'Those are the rules. If you don't like them, I can call Cynthia to come and pick you up.'

'Cynthia likes me to look nice.'

I picked up a phone and started punching numbers.

Babs swayed her hips and toed the floor but she whispered, 'I don't care.'

'Good. Supper is at seven. Until then, you may play upstairs. I have a playroom on the third floor. The tall cabinet is unlocked. Take a look inside.'

I couldn't resist watching her mount the stairs. There wasn't even a thong under her kilt. That reinforced my suspicions. Cynthia had set Babs on me, to seduce me, perhaps with the idea of creating a Domme/Domme/Brat threesome. I've nothing against threesomes, but not in that configuration. Babs was cute and Cynthia was lovely. I'd really enjoy them, but only on *my* terms.

As I went through Babs's cases, editing her wardrobe, I wondered how she was enjoying my playroom. It's quite dramatic. The floor is blackened pine. The walls are stark white rough plaster, with some exposed beams. The furniture is black, heavy and leather and includes some benches with straps attached and a spanking stool I'd bought at the previous year's Toronto Sex-hibition. I'd have loved to have seen her face when she opened the cabinet. It's seven feet high and four wide, stocked with canes, crops, tawses, cats, paddles and every variety of 'percussion' I've ever come across. Considering Babs's penchant for being spanked, its contents likely had her drooling with anticipation.

I believe in the 'carrot and stick' method of training, even when the promise of 'stick' is the carrot.

Babs came down promptly at seven with a dreamy look in her eyes. I could almost hear her brain work as she tried to think how best to get me to use some of my toys on her eager bottom. Being a brat, she chose precisely the wrong method.

'I'm not eating this crap,' she said of my paella.

'Then you may go up to bed.'

'Huh?'

'I've told you not to grunt. If you aren't going to eat your supper, go to bed.'

Her lower lip protruded and trembled. 'When I'm bad, Cynthia punishes me.'

I raised an eyebrow and lifted a forkful of rice and lobster to my lips. Babs stamped her feet on the floor and thumped the table with her fists. By the time I'd scooped up the last succulent sliver of pork from my plate, she was blue in the face and sobbing uncontrollably. While I was fetching my mango sorbet from the kitchen, she disappeared upstairs. At midnight, I went up and peeked into her bedroom. She'd cried herself to sleep. Her pillow was sodden. The bedclothes had worked down to let one perfectly globular breast loll exposed. My fingers reached for its pink button, but I pulled back. All in good time. Anticipation is half the pleasure.

At eight the next morning I ground a measure of Blue Mountain coffee beans and laid half a dozen strips of bacon in a frying pan. The aromas of freshly ground coffee and sizzling bacon make effective alarms. Babs came down just as I was splashing bacon fat over a pair of eggs. She was dressed in a cropped singlet and the towel she'd knotted around her hips.

'Dirty towels go in the hamper upstairs,' I told her.

'You took away my shorts,' she accused me. 'All of them. All I have is tops.'

'And running shoes, for when we go out. Babs, if I'd wanted you to cover your bottom, I'd have left you the clothes to do it with. I've decided you will be naked from your waist down for now.'

'But I'll be embarrassed.'

'I've watched you take a spanking on your bare bottom and listened to the obscene noises you made when you gobbled Cynthia's pussy.'

'Even so.'

I shrugged.

'Please, Justine?'

'Are you begging me?'

'You can't make me go around like this.'

'Ready for breakfast?'

She blinked at my non sequitur. I waited. She said, 'I'm famished.'

'Then lose the towel and sit down.'

She sat at my kitchen table so that her lower half was hidden and then tugged the towel away but it was close enough to obedience that I allowed it. I piled my plate with bacon and eggs and presented Babs with the paella she'd left the night before and that I'd warmed up in the microwave.

'I . . .' she said.

'What?'

'Nothing.' She toyed with her paella until she'd tasted a couple of mouthfuls and then wolfed the rest down.

'Good?' I asked.

'Mm, I guess.'

'Sometimes it's nice to try new things, new ways.'

'Cynthia likes me just the way I am.'

'I understand.' I picked up my plate. 'If you've finished, we'll go for a run. Get your running shoes on.'

'But . . .?' She looked down into her naked lap.

'It's secluded. No one will see you, except me.'

Trying a new tack, or so I imagined, Babs gave me

45

a sly flirtatious look and asked me, 'Did you like it, when you watched Cynthia spank me?'

In all seriousness, I told her, 'I was impressed. You took it very well.'

She blushed. 'Could your girl have taken a hundred like that?'

I frowned. 'Don't try to compete with my Lila. Be the best *you* can be.'

'But . . .'

'Runners, now!'

Sulking, and with one hand covering her pubes, Babs met me on the back porch. I took off at a slow lope. I wanted her to overtake me. She did so with a sidelong grin that wasn't quite a sneer.

As each foot impacted the ground, the corresponding cheek of her bottom quivered. Babs had a pair of matching dimples, one each side of the pad at the base of her spine, that winked at me alternately. I let her set the pace, keeping back far enough to enjoy the view.

After about a mile, the twisting trail came to a glade with a smooth fallen log and a stand of new-growth willow.

I told her, 'Take a break.'

Babs sank onto the log, breathing easily still. I took a clasp knife from the pocket of my jeans-shorts and wandered over to the willows. When the girl saw the switch I'd cut, her eyes widened and glazed over, the way masochists' eyes always do when they see that sweet pain is imminent. It's as if half their intelligence dissolves.

'Run,' I said.

Less coordinated now that her mind had gone fuzzy, she lurched to her feet and made off down the path. I trotted after her. She gave me a backwards glance that was more wistful than fearful. Not to disappoint her, I gave her bottom a diagonal slash. Babs yelped but she didn't accelerate. In that state, a submissive can't conceive that a torment could be escaped.

Each four strides, I laid the willow wand across her lush young flesh. It wasn't possible to make a neat pattern with both of us running, but I confined my blows to her bottom and upper thighs.

Runners can get a high from the endorphins that extended exercise produces. A good spanking produces the same endorphins. By the time we got back to my house, Babs was glowing and mindless. In that state, a submissive has no will. I could have used her any way I wanted but I contented myself with having her do jumping-jacks on the veranda while I gave her a few more strokes. It's more fun if you play your fish before you land it.

When she was sweaty enough to make her singlet cling nicely, I sent her up for a shower. Her intelligence returned enough that she gave me a strange look before obeying, as if to ask why I wasn't taking advantage of her willing subservience. I let her wonder. She'd be more malleable in the long run if she became confused and perhaps unsure of herself.

I laid out crackers and preserves, with fresh butter and paté and some cheeses. After lunch, I got the Scrabble set out. She played quite nicely, even though I quickly drew a hundred points ahead, until I played 'Qwerty' on a triple word square. She challenged. I passed her the Scrabble dictionary. Once she found the entry, she swept the board to the floor, scattering tiles everywhere.

I tuned Babs out and took up my current book, Michel Faber's *The Crimson Petal and the White*. She put the TV on and cranked up the volume. I put headphones on and let Leonard Cohen and k. d. lang protect my ears. Later, when I went to the kitchen for a slice of game pie, there was a peanut butter jar in one sink, with a knife in it, a raspberry jam jar in the other sink, with a fork in it, and cracker crumbs all over the counter. At some point in the evening she must have gone to bed because when I went up at midnight she was already asleep.

I lay in the next morning, to give her a chance. When I went down at ten, the kitchen had been cleaned up, imperfectly, but cleaned up, and the Scrabble had been picked up and put away. Babs was sitting at the kitchen table, looking as demure as a girl who is naked apart from a crochet shrug can look.

'Please may I ask a question, Justine?'

'Certainly.'

'Don't you think I'm pretty?'

'Very.'

'Then why . . .?'

'Haven't I fucked you?'

She blinked at the word 'fucked' and nodded.

'Since you've been here, you've been good for a while, then – not so good. Good girls deserve love. Girls who aren't good have to wait until they *are* good.'

She wrapped a leg around the leg of her chair. 'When I'm bad, Cynthia punishes me and that makes it all right. Then we make out.'

'And you like that?'

She nodded.

'You like to be punished?'

'Yes.'

'Because you like to be spanked.'

'Yes.'

'When we went running, were you naughty?'

Her 'no' was hesitant.

'But you got whipped.'

Babs licked her lips and nodded. 'I didn't understand.'

'Do you now?'

'No.'

'The way it is with me and my Lila,' I explained, 'is that she does whatever I want, whenever I want.'

'Like . . .?' She pushed her tongue out and vibrated its tip.

'Yes, like that, or like anything else I require of her. She's obedient and I reward her. Like you, she enjoys being spanked. That's her treat. She gets it, often.'

Babs's eyes lit up. 'Often?'

'Usually, by the time her bottom has healed from one spanking, she's earned another.'

'Without being bad?'

'Without being bad. If she's *very* good, I have extra treats for her.'

'Extra?'

'Like being allowed to choose anything she likes from the playroom cabinet.'

Babs went dreamy.

'Or a figging,' I continued.

'What's that?'

'Maybe you'll find out.'

'If I'm good.'

'Yes, if you are very good.'

Babs dropped from the chair onto her knees and crawled towards me. 'I can be *very* good,' she said, licking her lips.

'No,' I told her. 'That's not how I want you to be good. Just be a sweet obedient girl, OK?'

And for the rest of the week she was. Babs helped around the house, ran with me without being rewarded with a switch, read quietly when I wanted quiet and kept her needs under control. The closest she got to sex was one night when I peeked in on her bedroom and caught her beating a pillow with a crop while fingering herself.

'Ever felt one of those on your bottom?' I asked.

She jumped and dropped the crop. After a moment's confusion, she lowered her eyes and confessed, 'No.'

'Would you like to be?'

'No. It's scary.' She shivered. 'You're not going to . . .?'

'You needn't worry. I won't crop you, not unless you beg me to.'

'Beg for it? I wouldn't do that.'

'We'll see.' I gave her a warm smile. 'You've been a good girl all week, Babs.'

She looked up at me. 'Does that mean . . .?'

'Tomorrow afternoon there'll be some treats for you. Now get to bed and go to sleep. It's going to be a very strenuous day for you tomorrow.'

After breakfast I sent her upstairs to bathe and primp. While she wallowed in perfumed water, I took my ginger root from the fridge. Using a very sharp knife, I cut out a straight section of about six inches, then peeled and whittled until I had a smooth cylinder of raw ginger wood about as long as a cigarette but twice as thick, ending in an unpeeled bulb.

I took a quick shower and got dressed. I like to present myself in an attractive way. I sprinkled talc all over and then rolled mid-thigh black latex boots up my legs. My choker matched. I considered opera-length gloves and perhaps a floppy picture-hat but decided those would be too formal.

When I listened at Babs's bathroom door, she was still splashing. I knocked and told her, 'The playroom, ten minutes, naked.'

She joined me in eight, looking timid, with an arm across her lovely young breasts and a hand shielding her pubes. Her eyes widened when she saw me naked for the first time. 'You're lovely, Justine!'

'I'm not going to fuck you unless you ask me to,' I told her. 'If I do something to you that you can't stand, you must ask me to stop. Understood?'

Her face went blank while she absorbed my words but then cleared and she nodded. 'Is it going to be – very bad?' she asked.

'As bad as you can stand, but no worse.'

'Oh.'

'Well?'

'Well what?'

'Are you going to ask me?'

'Oh – yes. Please?'

'Please what?'

'Please fuck me, Justine.'

I smiled. 'There, that wasn't hard, was it?'

She shook her head.

'I want you on your back, on the daybed.' It's a simple piece of furniture – a seven-foot square of padded black leather with a matching roll for a pillow.

Babs sashayed to the bed, swinging her hips, and draped herself on her back with her arms stretched above her head and one coy knee lifted. I looked her over slowly, eating her up with my eyes. What a tasty morsel she was! I savoured every curve, every long lean line, every dimple and crease. I took my time, letting her relish my obvious admiration but protracting it until the intensity of my gaze started to make her feel uncomfortable.

She began to fidget. I told her, 'Get hold of your legs behind your knees and lift them up to your ears.'

She obeyed, shivering. It's one thing to allow yourself to be admired while you pose prettily. It's quite different to lift and spread, blatantly displaying your sex and anus to close scrutiny. I gave her long enough for her shame to sink in, then put my left hand on her upturned bottom to hold it in place and further spread its cheeks.

'What?' she asked.

For a reply, I took my fresh-carved piece of ginger root – my 'figg', and presented its end to the crinkled pink dimple of her anus.

'Justine?' There was apprehension in her voice.

'In Victorian days,' I explained, 'gentlemen of a certain persuasion used this method to discipline housemaids.' I pressed just firmly enough to part her pucker.

'But what . . .?'

'It's ginger root. I don't need to lubricate it, or you, because it oozes its own oil.' I pushed. Half the cylinder sank into her rectum.

'I've had things put up my bum before,' Babs declared.

'I'm sure you have. You might find this different, though.' My fingers twisted and they applied more pressure, screwing the figg deeper, until the bulb at its end nestled against the girl's anus.

'Is that it?' she asked, sounding almost disappointed.

'We'll just leave it there and see, shall we?' I pulled her legs down and arranged them, thighs parted, on the leather. Climbing astride her, I knelt with one shin trapping each of her thighs firmly but not painfully. My hands positioned her wrists above her head, crossed, and held them there.

Babs looked up at me, arched above her, and licked her lips. 'I'm helpless, aren't I?' she asked with a nervous giggle.

'Yes, you are.' My free hand stroked her cheek,

then her neck, and wandered down to toy with the delicate button of one pale nipple.

Babs's eyes hooded. She sighed and arched to press her breast into my hand but suddenly froze. Her eyes widened.

'Your bottom?' I asked.

'That – um – thing. It's cold.' She frowned. 'No – it's warm. It's very warm.' Her hips wriggled. 'It's like – like it's glowing or tingling or something.'

'Painful?' I asked.

'No, not painful. It's hot, like your mouth after curry, but . . . Oh – it's spreading.'

'Spreading?'

'To my pussy's lips. To my clit. Oh, Justine, it's . . . It's burning me up. Justine, I can't stand it! It's like an itch, a lovely horrible itch! I'm so *fucking* horny! Do me, Justine! I'm going crazy! Do something to my pussy. Fuck me! Do me somehow, anyhow!'

Grinning, I gently parted the sopping lips of her pussy and laid the tip of my index finger on her throbbing clit. Babs humped up, desperate, but as she writhed at it, my finger retreated, maintaining contact but never pressure.

'No,' she whimpered. Her arms fought my imprisoning hand. Her head flailed from side to side. Sweat beaded in her cleavage. The sweet musk of her sex filled my senses. Her labia were purple and engorged, dripping nectar.

'Please, please, please,' she begged. 'Make it stop or take me over the edge! This is torture! Do something, anything!'

In my most solicitous voice, I asked her, 'Would the crop help?'

'The crop?' She thought for a moment, still gyrating her hips beneath me. 'Yes, the crop! Beat me, Justine, please?'

'Are you sure?'

'Fuck yes! Yes, please. *Anything!*'

I released and flipped her. Pinning her down with one hand in the small of her back, I snatched up my crop and laid precise lines across her cheeks, above and below where the knob of the figg protruded from her anus. After six, she was taut as a wire, quivering with tension, ready to explode. I plucked the figg out, flipped her again, thrust two ginger-oiled fingers into her pussy to her G-spot, clamped my thumb's ball on her clit and worked her flesh vigorously.

I really enjoy that, squeezing a girl's pubic bone, crushing her two most sexually sensitive areas against it, one from each side. I gripped hard and shook her lower torso in my sadistic grip.

It took Babs four gut-wrenching climaxes to come down from her lust-high. I let her sleep for a half hour before rolling her onto her back and straddling her head. My hips lowered until the lips of my pussy were kissing the lips of her mouth. Babs sighed, inhaled, and lapped up.

Later, after we'd both been aroused and slaked again, she asked me, 'No more figging, please, Justine?'

'No more, ever?'

'Well, not for a few days.'

'Very well.'

'Unless I ask for it, of course.'

'Ask?'

'Beg, I mean, Justine.'

'You're learning.'

She blushed and lowered her eyes. 'Thank you, Justine.'

On the day that Cynthia was due back, I had Babs wear nothing but the bottom half of a pair of eau-de-Nil satin pyjamas. I spent better than two hours playing with the girl's nipples. By noon they were tender, proud, dark and swollen, unlike their usual pink buttons.

Cynthia arrived wearing a bush hat and a slub silk safari suit with a micro-skirt and knee boots by Ferrier and Carmichael. She has a certain style, that one. I left Babs back in my lobby, in shadow, and opened the door.

'How is she?' Cynthia blurted. 'Has my bratty baby been too much for you?'

'By no means,' I assured her. 'She's been an absolute angel.'

Cynthia frowned. 'Where is she then?'

Without raising my voice I said, 'Come and give Cynthia a nice big kiss hello, Babs.'

Babs sauntered by me with some care. Her pyjama pants were tied low around her hips. One false move would have had them off her.

Cynthia's eyes widened. 'Why are you dressed like that?' she demanded. 'You know how I like you to dress.' She rounded on me. 'What have you done to my Babs? Have you spoiled her?'

With a wry grin, I told her, 'I told you she'd be subject to *my* discipline, and you agreed. I promised you that you wouldn't find a mark on her, and I kept my word. Show her, Babs.'

Simpering, Babs sucked her tummy in. Her pants slithered to her feet. She stepped out and did a little pirouette, displaying pristine pink skin from her head to her toes, except for her engorged nipples.

I said, 'She's a darling girl, now, Cynthia. Aren't you going to give her a kiss?'

Cynthia hissed at me, speechless for once.

'Well, someone should greet you with a kiss, so I guess I'd better.' I took a step towards her. She raised her hands defensively. She's pretty strong for so

55

slender a woman but I'm stronger. I took her wrists in my hands and doubled them up behind her back, dragging her in close. She resisted my kisses at first but she's a horny bitch and the chances were that she hadn't been laid for almost a month. Her lips surrendered, reluctantly at first, but then with abandon. While I ravished my friend's mouth, Babs obeyed the instructions I'd given her earlier. She knelt behind Cynthia, put her hands up her skirt and tugged her panties down to her ankles.

'What is she doing?' Cynthia squeaked into my mouth.

'Relax.'

Babs unwrapped the figg I'd prepared, twice as thick and half again as long as the one she'd enjoyed, and worked it up into her erstwhile Mistress's bottom.

'What?' she gasped. I didn't respond. 'It's cold,' she complained. 'No – it's kind of warm. Tingly. What on earth? Oh – that's . . .'

'When you're ready to surrender to me, absolutely, I'll put an end to your torment,' I told her.

'Never! You can't . . . Oh fuck! Oh my . . .' She sagged in my arms, straddling my thigh and humping at it.

I let her. It wouldn't help and the figg had only just started to work.

– *Justine, Ontario, Canada*

Car 371

'You know, you are a very pretty lady.' His accent was thick and he rolled his Rs. 'That's why I always come when you call,' he said.

'Oh, thanks,' I said, barely paying attention as I continued to primp in the back of the taxi.

I was becoming agitated by how slow he was driving, but I guess it was to be expected when he was clearly distracted by the view in his rear-view mirror as I adjusted my cleavage. I was on my way to see Marley again. She was a woman in her late 40s whom I had met on the chat line. She had moved here from Trinidad a couple of years earlier with her husband who she referred to as 'Money Bags'. She admitted to being with him for the financial stability, and because 'when you're pushing fifty, you need a husband'! She was bi and I was her new dirty little secret. I had been with her twice before and found her to be a lot of fun both in and out of the bedroom. She loved to get all dressed up and go bar-hopping and end the night at the local motel eating each other out, and, so far, each time that we had gotten together, she had brought me a gift.

'Sexy girl,' the Indian driver slurred while eyeing me in his mirror.

I just smiled, wondering if he knew what I was up to that evening – maybe he could sense how horny I was. My cunt was already on fire just thinking about Marley and her beautiful big black tits.

As we pulled up to her house, I was surprised to see her husband in the driveway; it was obvious he had just arrived home. 'Shit! Keep driving!' I yelled out to the cabbie.

'Why? What happened? Where do you want me to go?' he asked confused.

'Just stop up ahead for a minute,' I barked, upset that I might not get my fix for the night. 'I'm sorry. Just keep the meter running, please, I need to wait here for a bit.'

'What are you waiting for?' he turned to ask.

'It's a long story. Can we just wait – please?' I said, trying Marley's cell phone.

There was no answer, but I was so horny that I wasn't going to give up so easily. I decided to wait a while in case she called back or in the event that her husband left. We waited there in darkness for over half an hour, and my increasing disappointment was obvious. The driver continued to compliment me and make sexual innuendos. I had to give the man kudos; he was older, quite heavy and had the tiniest little eyes under his large glasses – definitely nothing to look at. Each minute that passed without a call from Marley, the more pissed off I became, and the driver's incessant grilling was not helping.

'What did you have to do here that was so important that we have to wait so long?' he asked for the umpteenth time.

'I was supposed to hook up with somebody, all right?' I snapped. 'I've wanted to see this person all week and now it's not gonna happen, so my entire night is wasted!'

'You know what I like to do to feel better?' His eyes grew beady.

'No. What?' I asked, still frustrated.

'I like to go get a motel room with a young girl,' he said.

Amazed by his brazenness, I asked, 'Didn't you say earlier that you're married?'

'Yes. So what? It makes me appreciate my wife more,' he insisted.

'Yeah, OK. Where do you get these young girls?' I asked, not really believing that he was capable of finding sex.

'Usually they are girls like you. I meet them here, and they know that I am a nice man who can make them feel good, so they come with me to motels. Sometimes, if they need some money, I give them something . . .'

'Oh, so they're hookers.' I smirked.

'No, just nice girls like you. Sex feels good, and I make good sex. I can make you feel good too. Let's go to a motel and I will show you,' he said, very seriously.

I looked at him for a moment: his large pursed lips, big hands and the beads of sweat that were forming along his brow.

'OK, let's go,' I said.

'To a motel?' he asked nonchalantly.

'I didn't say that. Let's leave here – I'm getting cold,' I said, actually contemplating having some kind of sex with him in my desperate state.

'Come sit at the front, closer to the heater,' he said.

I knew that making sure I was warm wasn't his only agenda, but I got out and moved to the front. As I slid into the car, my coat caught underneath me, opening and revealing a glimpse of my legs and my indecently short skirt.

'Drive back to my place, please,' I asked, deciding that I couldn't possibly go through with it.

He stared at my legs for a moment before finally saying, 'I will not charge you the fare if you let me touch your beautiful legs.'

I'm not sure if it was so much the free ride – that had gotten quite costly after sitting outside Marley's for so long – or if it was something to take the edge off the evening's disappointment. I had been so horny all day thinking about having my cunt licked. I looked at him and nodded, and he quickly moved his hand to my thigh. He squeezed the flesh and let out a moan, then slowly began inching his hand up my leg, moving the skirt with it, until my panties were showing.

'OK, that's enough,' I said, only I didn't push his hand away.

'Please, Miss, just one more minute. You are so sexy,' he pleaded, squeezing harder.

'Fine.' I tried to sound uninterested even though my cunt was beginning to tingle.

His big hand continued kneading my meat, and each squeeze was followed by a groan or deep breath. I watched as his hand inched closer to my cunt and I didn't protest.

His fingers began toying with the trim of my panties. He ran his finger between the edge of the elastic and my skin and, as his fingers began to make their way under the fabric, he looked at me as if waiting for a go-ahead. I made eye contact with him briefly and went back to looking down at my lap, wanting him to continue. My cunt had been aching to be touched all day, and I was at the point that I didn't care who touched it.

His other hand pulled my panties to the side, revealing my swollen lips that were already glistening wet. He used his big middle and index fingers to rub my slit, pressing hard while looking for my clit. I spread my legs a bit further apart causing his fingers to slip in between. When he hit my clit I couldn't help but gasp and push my crotch against his hand, it was feeling so good. He rubbed my clit softly, as if trying to tease it, and then leaned in to kiss me.

'No kissing!' I hissed, completely repulsed by the idea.

'Can I see your breast?' he asked.

'OK,' I said, feeling bad for having yelled.

He watched hungrily as I pulled the neckline of my sweater down and my bra cup with it, revealing my tit. My nipple hardened the moment that it felt the chilly air in the car and, without hesitation, he took it in his hands and brought it to his mouth. I didn't even have time to protest before he was lapping away at it sloppily with his big lips. My cunt continued to soil my panties. He licked and sucked my nipple and then pulled at my top until my other tit was exposed as well.

His mouth alternated between both boobs causing my insides to flutter and my clit to get so hard that it hurt. He stopped for a second, startled by the lights of a passing car, but I pushed his head back to my bosom. I didn't care that I was in that cab, with my tits out in plain view. Getting off was all I cared about. I reached down and started to rub my clit while watching his mouth slobbering about my tits. The way he moaned and groaned while taking in my flesh really turned me on – he was desperate for me and I loved it!

When he noticed me rubbing my clit, he seemed to go into a frenzy, pushing his face even harder into my chest, and squishing my tits between his pudgy fingers. He had to be as horny as I was. I closed my eyes and leaned back into my seat and fingered my hole hard and fast. I was close to coming when I heard him moan really loudly and looked over to find him stroking his cock furiously.

'Touch it. Touch it!' he commanded, grabbing hold of my hand and plopping it down onto his hard dick. It was short and chubby, and the head was wet and sticky. I tried to pull my hand away, but he kept a firm hold on it and made me stroke it, and at the same time resumed sucking on my nipple.

I could feel his cock growing and pulsing in my hand, and soon my repugnance contributed to my arousal. The entire thing was so dirty and disgusting, and yet such a turn on. I kept pumping his cock with my fist and his moans intensified. I thought he was surely on the verge of coming when he said breathlessly, 'Let's go to a motel. Please. Please. I want to fuck you. Please, I can give you so much pleasure!' he begged.

I almost considered it, but decided against it. I was horny and didn't want to stop to go look for a room. I also had no desire to spend more time with him than needed. I was close to getting my fix and didn't need a bed to get it.

'No, just move the car over there,' I said, pointing at the park across the street.

As he drove, I resumed giving him a hand job, until we were parked. 'Let's go into the back,' I said, anxious to finally come.

We jumped in and out of the car quickly and, once in the back seat, I pulled my skirt right up and held my panties completely off to the side so my swollen cunt was right there, ready for him to do as he pleased. 'Hurry up,' I insisted.

With one swoop, his trousers went down, and he kneeled between my legs, holding his stump that was surrounded by a large mound of black hair that I hadn't noticed earlier.

He held his cock and slapped it about my wet tuft, trying to find my hole. The feel of his cock against me caused my insides to shudder. Frustrated at not being able to find my hole because of the awkward angle, he used the other hand to spread my lips apart, hurting me with his roughness. His head finally pushed its way into me. I hadn't realised how thick his cock was until it filled me. Our crotches pounded together, and I could hear the sound of his balls slapping against me. His cock started to vibrate inside me, and his thrusts grew closer together, until he began to cry out in a language that I didn't understand. I wanted him to hurry up and come so I could too, so I fucked him even harder, squeezing my cunt and gripping his dick hard.

He pulled out of me and I thought he was going to blow his load over my cunt, but instead he straddled me, grabbing my hair and bringing my face up to meet his cock. I didn't even know what was happening until I felt his come shoot on to my face. I wriggled, trying to get free of his grip, while his cock kept spewing his milk until it was dribbling down my cheeks and chin.

'You stupid fucker!' I screeched. As I went to get up, he moved back between my legs and grabbed my hips, pulling my body up towards him. His tongue pushed into my hole and began darting in and out quickly and, instead of pushing him away, I grabbed his head, holding it even harder against my pussy, finding just the right spot. As I tilted my head back, feeling the walls of my cunt begin to quiver, the come that he had shot on my face began to slide into my mouth, causing me to gag. He didn't care and continued to work my clit with his tongue. The sensation was enough to drown out everything else, including the cold goop that had made its way down my throat, and I finally came – and hard.

The moment the throbbing within subsided, I immediately jumped up. 'Let's go,' I commanded, pushing him towards the front.

He didn't say a word as he put his cock back into his trousers and got settled back in the driver's seat. I took a tissue from my pocket and wiped the disgusting semen off my face as we pulled away.

When we reached my building I got out and, as I was about to close the door, he thanked me and asked if he would see me again. I didn't reply and just left, knowing very well that the next time I called a cab, he would turn up.

– A. C., Lincolnshire, UK

The Invisible Woman

Nervous of my own daughter? Sure. But also excited. I'd not seen her for nearly two years. A long time for a mother not to see her oldest kid. You might think it but, before you do, no, we hadn't fallen out. She'd been in Australia, that's all. She went there straight after school, hardly took a breath, been badgering about it for years, couldn't wait to leave home. For heaven's sake, who can blame her? I'd have done the exact same thing at her age, been off to the sunshine like a bullet.

Her adoring uncle paid for it all, met her in Sydney and then up she flew to Cairns and the Great Barrier Reef. She was terrified of water when she was little. Now she's done the lot. Scuba diving, swimming with dolphins.

Hardly a foreign country, but still. The other side of the world. And the house was so silent when she was gone. I've still got her younger sisters. But Patsy's the noisy one. Actually it was a relief.

You may as well be invisible, the mother of a stunning daughter. A stunna, as they'd probably call her down under. Not a comfortable feeling, especially when you know you've let yourself go.

So I made a pledge as soon as she was gone. A pledge to myself.

We used to be mistaken for sisters. Maybe people were being polite, you know, taxi drivers, college lecturers, but she had the same ripe curvy jailbait body I had at that age. She was very precocious. Or is it promiscuous? Easy to get those two descriptions mixed up.

The photos say it all. There's me trying too hard to recapture myself, I can see that now, gripping at her shoulders, grinding my cheekbones against her matching face. Matching auburn hair. My lips fuller than hers. Her green eyes more slanted than mine. Patsy parting her red mouth to extend a curled wet tongue, practically giving the camera a blow job. Jutting her pert new breasts. Waiting to bolt.

By the time she went off to Australia we barely communicated. Not arguing, just never colliding. I was invisible. We no longer looked alike, but that was my fault. I found myself staring at my sex-bomb daughter, wondering, now she was grown, what the boys did to her cute body, whose dirty little hands and mouths and dicks groped and poked and licked at her, wondering if she enjoyed it half as much as I used to.

While I stared at her, everyone else stared through me.

At the airport when we waved her off she already *looked* Australian with her blonde hair in braids. Tiny khaki shorts creeping up her butt. A backpack and a bruising attitude.

And I looked – well, four stone heavier, for a start.

'You got the country wrong. It should be Austria,' Steve joked as we hovered at passport control. People glanced at her big strong legs, her Jessica Rabbit tits. I was invisible.

'Why?' She stuck her nose up, addressing him, as always. Never me.

66

Steve flicked at one plait. '*Fräulein.*'

We all knew he was joking because he was upset. She turned her back to whisper something to her little sisters. The envy in my stomach twisted harder. The admiring looks, the announcements, the tickets, the promise of somewhere more exciting to go. And my three daughters in a huddle. That was the day the little ones started to grow up.

Watching Patsy go, one of them said, 'She looks just like Lara Croft.'

On the way back from the airport I made that pledge.

Steve had been up since about six, cooking. Things had been marinating in olive oil and lime juice for days. Such a fuss! The girls were out the front, decorating the front door and the gate with balloons and banners which clattered and fluttered in the wind.

'She'll be freezing when she gets here,' they said, clumping into the house in their new high heels. 'She'll have forgotten how foul winter is.'

'You mean *they'll* be freezing,' Steve yelled from the kitchen. He was wearing a daft apron with a hairy he-man logo. He thought it would make Patsy feel at home. But it just made him look suddenly old and ridiculous. 'Don't forget this Mike fellow she's bringing.'

'Michel, he prefers apparently,' I said, lacing up my trainers. 'Who does he think he is?'

'Her boss. That's who. Up and coming young hot-shot chef.'

'Up and *coming*!' The girls giggled and nudged. 'Wonder if he's a *stud*!'

'Mum says Gordon Ramsay's a stud!'

Steve laughed. We all did. 'That's why we've got to get this meal just right.'

'I'd have given them shepherd's pie.'

'But then you wouldn't eat it, and what would Gordon think about that?' Steve slapped my rump with his wooden spoon. I tensed up, waiting for the flab to wobble, set a ripple in motion down my thigh. Old habit. He whacked at me again. 'Taut as a drum. She's not going to recognise you.'

'Oh, I doubt she'll notice.' I rubbed my sore buttock. The burning sensation felt good where my husband had slapped it. Often I made him do that when we were alone. Slap me, rather than fuck me. He liked the new masochist in his bed. It kept him away from screwing the other women. It turned him on to hear me squeal, watch me rub myself raw and wet on the sheets or against the sofa or on the carpet while he did it. At least it kept him happy, because I wasn't ready for fucking. I told him I was clutching onto the fat woman's inhibitions. But now I was starting to like it when others touched me. Strangers bumping me in the supermarket, shop assistants zipping me into tight dresses –

'Where are you going, Mum?'

'Just my usual run!'

'But Patsy will be here in half an hour.'

Nervous? Sure. As hell. But now, instead of stuffing my face with a packet of chocolate biscuits to kill the nerves, I wanted to be on the move. I left my warm house and my restless family and ran down the street, over the zebra crossing, off on my usual route. No rippling flesh now. No wobble. My thong was trapped between my tight butt cheeks. My breasts in the sports bra barely moved. But now that my nipples were back where they should be, pricking forwards instead of drooping somewhere near the floor, I could feel them, if I concentrated, shrinking in protest at the cold air.

Blood heating me up, speed making me breathe harder. Would Patsy notice? Did I care? This wasn't for her. It was my pledge, to myself. I reached the wine shop and reluctantly started the return journey. She had stopped all that diving and swimming and sporty stuff. She'd gone back to Sydney to work in a restaurant. Front of house, she called it. That's where she met the Frenchman, presumably. The stud.

I bit my lip, remembering my giggling girls, and jogged on the spot waiting to cross. Michel. What would he be like? Gallic and glowering? The thong wriggled up my damp crotch, string chafing at my pussy. The skin within, so fragile and tender, would be buzzing red-hot messages by the time I got home. My cheap thrill. Or would he be blond and chunky like a surfer? Would he and Patsy hold hands and make a coy announcement? Or would they kiss and fondle and make us all embarrassed, hands all over each other?

A low-slung car stopped at the zebra. I sprinted past. Slushy rain started spraying across the windscreen. The wipers slid once, lazily, to clear the glass and when I waved thanks the driver winked.

I pounded down the pavement towards my house. I felt as if I was flying through the rain. I was showing off. I wondered if he was watching. The car overtook. I shut my eyes, grunting with the effort of the home stretch. I sounded as if I was being rogered. I couldn't run like this two years ago. I couldn't even walk up the stairs without bursting a blood vessel.

I dodged through the side-gate and in the back door.

'Honey, they're early!'

I could smell the drink and the log fire in the sitting room and a fresh, nostril-pricking cologne.

'Mum?'

'Give me a minute –'

I wasn't ready. I bent over to catch my breath, sweat catching in my armpits. Still bothered by a small tyre of stomach I'd never shift. Well, it was never my intention to look sixteen from the back, sixty at the front. It'll always be there, unless I have it tucked. The swell of flesh round my middle reminding me. I'm a mature woman, after all. A mother with a daughter home from her travels. Introducing her rich boyfriend.

The new dress was laid out on my bed upstairs. The girls had chosen it, and the shoes. Fit or not, I couldn't face them yet. Would she notice?

I could hear Patsy and her sisters, already vying for who could screech the loudest. The booming approval of their dad.

'Steve said to bring the wine in here?'

A deep voice with the Ozzie question at the end of it. Michel was behind me. Between my knees I could see a pair of brown bare feet. What a sight. He must be staring straight up my bum. What would he call it? Up my Lycra jacksie. I straightened, unrolling my spine like they'd shown us in exercise class. Tits out, stomach in. The movement scraped the thong against my clit.

'Hey!' He was standing there, holding a crate. 'The jogger!'

Gallic, but not glowering. Grinning, actually. Dark stubble prickling around full lips which looked wet with kissing. Black hair, too long, and wet with the rain. He was so tall I had to continue my stretch like a ballerina.

'Hey!' I repeated. I was still out of breath. 'The driver!'

The moment elongated, because I couldn't speak. My sweatshirt clung round my ribs, right around my breasts. There was hubbub from across the hall, glasses chinking. I was level with his wet mouth. I saw a white flash of teeth.

'So you're the mum.'

My breasts juddered as I struggled to get my breath. I put my hands on my hips, trying to look casual, but I guess it only made me look brassy. My shirt pulled tighter, thrusting my breasts out. They looked bigger. His tongue ran across his lower lip. Sweat was cooling down, making my skin shiver. Hot and cold, I couldn't work out which. I watched him watching me. My nipples pricked harder again and my shoulders pulled back to show them to him. My breath got louder and he took a step closer.

'Hurry up, Michel, a girl could die of thirst!'

It was Patsy, crashing into the kitchen. With his back to her Michel went on looking at my breasts in the open, greedy way young men do, as if it's a gift barely wrapped, all new. I held my arms out stiffly to her, like a doll.

'Here you are, my prodigal daughter!'

A frown flickered under the fringe she'd had cut into her hair. It made her face look square. Her mouth dropped open exaggeratedly, like actors in American soaps do to register surprise. 'Mum, what on earth are you wearing? What happened to you?'

The others crowded in behind her.

'She looks great, doesn't she?' one of the girls prompted. 'All gorgeous and slim just like she used to?'

Patsy nodded, over and over, looking me up and down. Then she came into my arms. We were right in front of Michel. I looked over Patsy's shoulder, my eyes reaching as far as his neck, a point pulsing beneath his ear.

'It's like hugging myself. There's nothing to you,' Patsy said, letting me go. 'I can't believe you've lost all that weight!'

'Good, huh?' I said in a silly high voice. They were all staring at me. I started to go red. I flapped my arm. 'Now, then, this isn't how I planned your homecoming! I was meant to be all tarted up in your honour. Go on with you. Get some drinks. I'll be ready directly.'

'Amazing.' They shuffled back across the hall, Patsy still looking me up and down. She called to her boyfriend. 'Coming, babe?'

The girls tittered again.

'Sure, doll. Just sorting the wine.'

He put the crate down on the counter with a crash. His hands were free now and waiting by his sides. I stood still where Patsy had left me.

'Mother and daughter, eh?' There was a shaft of air between us. He came closer, crushing the air as he pressed up, pushing me against the counter. 'How horny is that?'

'You think we're alike?'

The edge jabbed into my back, forcing the words out in a kind of smiling gasp.

'Oh, yes.' He nodded. 'But different. You can take pain, for one thing. I wonder if you like it?'

I just ran my tongue across my dry mouth.

'A girl would have whined at me for bashing her. She'd have killed the moment.'

'Oh? What moment is that?'

Staring into my eyes, he dashed the tips of his fingers across my nipples. They went rigid, and I gasped again. I didn't think they could get any harder. His eyes were very dark brown, with gold flecks, watching my reaction. Inside I was sliding. I gritted my teeth and shoved my body, my breasts, hard into his hands, urging his fingers to fan out, grip round the soft flesh.

He looked down at what he was doing, as if it surprised him. We both looked down. All this in silence. His brown fingers caged my breasts, knuckles

72

flexing as he moulded them. My breath came out in a shudder. My breasts are my centre. He squeezed harder, until it began to hurt. How did he know? My head fell back, my knees giving way. I gripped the counter for balance and he pushed his knee between my legs, jabbed it into my crotch so that I was straddling his thigh. I rocked myself once against his leg, and there was the insistent thread of my bloody thong, rubbing me red raw inside.

The sitting room door opened.

'Stop this. We can't,' I whispered harshly, yet tipping desperately against his thigh bone for relief. 'I'm Patsy's –'

'I want the mother,' he whispered back, eyes so close I lost focus.

I pushed my finger onto his lips. The chatter flooded out into the hallway, and on his bare feet he was gone.

He was lifting my hand towards his mouth.

'Goodnight, Mum.'

Halfway up the stairs, Patsy snorted. 'How many times, Michel? She's Angela!'

He was unshaven like a rock star. Now I'd had all evening to study him I saw that, like all rock stars, underneath it all he was still very young.

His curved lips parted in a smile over my skin and I wanted him to lick me. I wanted to stuff my fingers between his teeth so that he had to eat them.

'It's late.' Steve was being the hearty father, locking up. 'Can't believe you've kept us up so late gassing, you two.'

Michel kissed the back of my hand. The tip of his tongue tickled my cold skin. He closed his eyes briefly, his nose still pressed against my knuckles, and that's when I knew it for sure, because it was real desire. No one else could see.

But I gave a silly, fluttering laugh and scrunched my shoulders like a child aping pleasure. I turned to my husband. '*You* kept us up with all that delicious food.'

'Too much of it, though.' Patsy patted her stomach. 'And Michel feeds me too much at work, don't you?'

Michel dropped my hand. We all looked up and saw how her body had thickened. The khaki shorts would never fit her now. A flowing turquoise garment covered her. It was exactly the precious gesture I used to use.

'Bed, my girl,' said Steve, following Patsy up. At the top he turned all the lights off. He kissed her cheek and they went their separate ways. I started up the stairs, too. My thighs brushed restlessly as I took each step, and then a hand was right up between them, curving round, snaking into my bush.

'I want to know what you look like naked.'

I stopped at the top, still with my back to him. The darkness was intoxicating. I lifted the silky skirt of the dress my girls had chosen, right up over my hips, and parted my legs. I wore stockings and no knickers for no other reason except that he was here, in my house, at my table, next to my daughter, opposite me and watching me all evening.

I opened my legs for him in the vague dark from the landing window and he came right up behind me, his fingers digging through the fur there, forcing open my throbbing sex to slide inside.

'I won't sleep,' he said, breath hot on my neck, cupping me so that one long finger was positioned to jab into me so roughly that I nearly cried out. 'I want to fuck the mother.'

My wetness drew on his finger. We could both hear the lap and suck of my cunt as he pushed further inside me, his other arm trapping me round my stomach. I staggered a little, spreading my legs further, and another finger, maybe his thumb, stroked my clitoris while he continued to finger fuck me.

'This is what teenagers do,' I whispered, lowering myself onto his finger.

'Not so long ago, then.'

'Oh, please –'

Laughter bubbled quietly in his throat, right next to my ear, and he speeded up the motion. I gasped and grappled about for him. I wanted to feel his dick. In my hand, if I couldn't have it inside me. I found his hips, his stomach, a buckle, his buttocks, but he had me pinned too close to the banisters, bending me over them, so I couldn't get to him.

The top step creaked as my cunt squeezed violently round his finger and I started to come in a short, violent burst. There was an answering creak of pacing footsteps from my room, maybe Steve coming to open the bedroom door to see what, or who, was keeping me.

'We can't,' I bleated, for the second time that day, staggering forwards. His fingers slid out of me, smearing juice. 'This is crazy, don't you see? We can't –'

'We already have. Oh, you're a pricktease, Mrs Patricks. I bet you were a tease when you were Patsy's age.' I didn't turn to look at him in the dark. I'd forgotten about her. 'And, as a punishment, I'll just have to go now and fuck your daughter.'

I pretended I had a headache. A hangover. Whatever they liked to call it. I lay there the next morning and let them peep round the door, let Patsy sit on the edge of my bed and tell me how she was going back to

Australia straight after Christmas. This wasn't really the grand homecoming. I didn't listen to any of it. I told them all to go to Grandma's as arranged. I wanted to tell them all, the lot of them, my loved ones, to fuck off.

I wanted to lie in my bed with my fingers probing and fidgeting between my legs. I wanted to raise my hips off the sheet and feel the frustration throb up me as my sex closed round them. I listened to them chattering downstairs, borrowing coats, sorting out car keys. I thought about the sleepless night.

Last night, just down the hall, Michel entered the guest room where my frisky Patsy was lying in readiness for him, her turquoise garments discarded, wriggling with glee because she was allowed to sleep in there with her boyfriend. Yesterday morning I made up the bed with the prissy sprigged linen kept for visitors and turned up the radiator and didn't think twice about it. Now, all I could think about was that mean little bed and Michel tensed on top of it, fucking her, and I was stiff with jealousy.

She would have waited for him, her arms and legs spread wide open. That's what youngsters are like, isn't it? The girls always have the hots. The boys permanent hard-ons. Any bed, anywhere, anyone, will do.

I lay there all night. They were deliberate about it, and brazen. Maybe that was his idea. Or maybe Patsy reckoned this was a grown-up rite of passage, to fuck openly and noisily in front of her parents, under their roof. Steve was already asleep, but I heard it. It was brief, and violent, but Michel was fucking her for my benefit. Don't care if that was big-headed of me. I knew it was true. His hard-on came from me, not her. It was only a moment after he'd shut the door that the spare bed started banging against the wall. Patsy yelped then let out a long sigh as if he was squeezing the life out of her.

You'd have thought I'd cringe and cover my ears. This was my adult daughter screwing, for God's sake. But she was invisible to me. I could only see Michel, what he was doing, his urgent movements in the cold spare room. Ripping at his jeans. I'd already loosened them. Crashing onto the bed, his knees knocking hers open. I bet he surprised her, taking out this great stiff cock, shoving it into her before she was really ready.

When the banging and grunting stopped I went to sleep. When I woke I thought for a moment it was all a dream, until I reached down and felt the stickiness on me and smelt my own fingers.

I had no headache. I had never felt so alive.

When they'd all gone I wanted to run. This is what they mean by letting off steam. I was going to explode. I lifted my jogging pants to my nose and smelt the tang of last evening's arousal. I wanted Michel. I pictured his young buttocks half out of his jeans, flexing and thrusting, making the spare bed creak. I tossed the pants aside, pulled on a baggier pair which kept slipping down my hips like pyjamas, and a cropped green sweater. I grabbed the toast Steve had brought me, gobbling wetly like a starving person, licking butter off my lips.

I was about to run down the stairs when a door banged. The house was full of draughts and open windows. I clicked my teeth, housewife again, and bustled along the landing. Perhaps the vase in the spare room had knocked off the windowsill, spilling lilies and water.

Spare rooms are always cold and prim and uninviting, aren't they? Anyone would think you wanted to get rid of your guests. The curtains were billowing, but the vase was still standing. I looked at the scattered clothes on the floor, all Patsy's, the open suitcases stacked neatly by the wall, and then I looked at the bed. Rumpled, of course, pillows halfway down the mattress. Had he dragged her down the bed when he came in last night, heaped the pillows under her to raise her fanny up to him, rammed his hard cock into her just a few feet away from where I was lying?

My knees buckled. I leaned on the bed. I wanted to straighten it. I wanted to launder away any signs of them together. I tugged the duvet right off. I threw the pillows back. I felt like a chambermaid. And this room was like a hotel room. Anonymous, cold, and wickedly sexy with it. I wouldn't feel like this making my own bed.

I leaned further to smooth and tuck the sheet and buried my nose into the place where it was most creased, sniffing like a dog, sniffing for his sharp cologne, sniffing also for the scent of his sperm.

I was on my hands and knees on the bed. I crawled backwards, feeling about for the sprigged duvet.

'Hey, Mummy.'

I nearly came just hearing that voice behind me. For God's sake!

'Just tidying up,' I said, aware of my bum sticking up awkwardly in the air. I twisted round to sit on my haunches on the sheet, and the baggy trousers slipped down.

'No need,' he said, stepping round the bed. He winked, as if he was back behind his steering wheel and I was miles away. 'We'll only mess it up again.'

I looked at his arm in its thick sweater sleeve, reaching for a camera case. 'Right. Of course. You and Patsy.' My face was burning hot. 'The lovebirds.'

He shrugged and turned away, slinging the camera onto his shoulder, ready to go. My hands were trapped between my thighs, fingernails digging into the skin. What a stupid, stupid bitch, I thought. What was I thinking of? Creaming myself over some young guy trying it on. Let's have a flirt with the old dear. My daughter's boyfriend, for Christ's sake. The stud. I shivered. A spasm went through my cunt, echoed right up inside me. He's probably forgotten all about that little grope on the stairs. Seeing the old bat in the cold light of day –

'They've gone to Grandma's.' He turned round. In the cold light of day he looked like a pirate, with the stubble even blacker this morning. But there were shadows under his eyes. 'What am I going to do? You're so much more beautiful.'

'Than Grandma?' I breathed weakly, feeling utterly beautiful. 'She lives the other side of town. They'll be all day.'

I raised myself on my knees, stretched one foot to stand up.

'I stayed behind, to take pictures of London. So we can be all day.'

He put the camera down and knelt on the bed. The mattress was soft, and it bounced with his weight, and I toppled backwards onto my elbows. Now he was the one like a dog, hanging over me on his hands and knees. I looked at his mouth, then straight down to his groin, his thighs on either side of me. There was a big bulge straining at his buttons. My legs twitched open at the sight of it, releasing a slick of dampness onto the worn fabric of my trousers.

Michel pushed me and I fell easily onto my back. Easy. The word flickered in my head. Loose. Whore.

'What about Patsy?' I croaked. He put his finger on my lips, like I did to him the previous night, except that I opened my mouth and sucked his finger in, turned on beyond belief to taste him.

'Yeah? What about Steve?'

He reached under my jumper and started to brush his warm fingers up and down my ribs as casually as if he'd just mentioned the weather. Daring me to stop him. There was guilt pinning me down on the bed now, mixed toxically with lust, but it didn't stop me. It drove me. I would face the evil slut in the mirror later.

'He thinks I'm invisible.'

He tweaked my jumper and the air rushed over me. I bucked against the cold, my bare breasts bouncing under his hands, the nipples rigid points. I fell back with a little moan of surrender.

'Warm you up, Mrs Patricks,' he murmured.

He pulled the jumper higher up and my breasts pushed at him like a feast. I was aching for him now, burning. It was maddeningly sexy that he was new, but not a stranger. Forbidden, but being invited, by me, to fuck me on my creaking little spare bed.

The promise of pleasure was crackling out of his fingertips as they inched towards my nipples. As he pinched them I jumped at him as if electrocuted, fastened my mouth onto his. I couldn't get enough of his lips. They were firm, like a man's should be, and yet they had a softness in them, and I was making them wet with kissing. I could taste coffee. Who had made it? Steve? Patsy? Or one of the girls?

The tip of his tongue, warm and slippery, sent shudders up and down my body, and I hooked my legs round his hips, crushing my groin into his, rubbing against him frantically, while a weight of desire filled me and plunged downwards. My pussy was warm and slippery, like his tongue, and I wanted him inside me. I was afraid the sensation would overtake me too soon, and I'd lose control, so I kissed him harder, sucked on his tongue and his teeth. It was feeling so good.

'How could a stunner like you be invisible?'

He laid me down again and pulled away. He was smiling, and his mouth was wet, but his eyes were deadly serious. He leaned over me, running my hair through his fingers. My hair the exact colour of Patsy's, though cut expensively as a reward for losing all that weight, and streaked at the front with pretend blonde and silver.

As he played with it, the tugging of the roots on my scalp turned me on. I felt like a cat being stroked. A stunner. Then he stopped and took his jumper off, tugging it from the back of his collar like a boy. Off with an old blue T-shirt, and there was his body, tanned by the Australian sun, brown in the cold winter light. I shivered again and scrabbled at the waist of his jeans, but he got to me first, easily hooked my jogging pants down, took my knickers with them. He pushed me down and, just as I'd sniffed around for his scent earlier, he dug his fingers into my bottom, hitched my pussy up to his face, breathed in, and started to lick me.

I wrapped my thighs round his head, pushed myself frantically into his nose and face and mouth. That wet mouth was sucking and licking at my hot cunt; I could hear him swallowing my juices, last evening's, last night's juices, this morning's juices – I'd been dripping wet for him since he walked into my house. The tremors of orgasm were starting, and I pulled his head away.

'Wait, wait –'

He sat back, and then he opened his jeans. He wore tight black boxers outlining his cock. He was a god to look at, and even more so naked. He peeled them off quickly and his cock slapped stiff and upright against his stomach. There was a stab in my own stomach as I thought about all the young girls, my daughter included, who had looked and would look

81

at and taste that gorgeous cock. All the years ahead of him of fucking.

'We shouldn't do this, darling –'

'This isn't a game. I'll die if I don't have you,' he said roughly, shocking me. I opened my mouth to say You kids, how you exaggerate, but the expression on his face stopped me. He was squeezing my breasts almost thoughtfully now, as if I was some prize and he'd forgotten his own arousal, but the delicious pressure was sending me wild. I was all animal now. He'd get over this. But I wouldn't. That's why it had to be a game.

'So have me,' I growled, reaching for his big warm cock. My legs were trembling, my cunt contracting with angry desire. And there was his hot, hard cock, pulsing in my hand. 'Now. Fuck me, big boy, before they get back from Grandma's.'

He grinned, white teeth biting his lip. It made him look so young. He was relieved, maybe, thinking that I was going to be so cool about this. He'd never know. He just knew he was back in charge again. He pushed me down, pinned both my arms above my head with one strong hand so I was powerless. I couldn't touch him any more. My thighs squeezed his cute buttocks, trying to pull him into me, angle his cock up me, but he kept his hips back.

'You'll have to wait for that, Mrs. I'm hungry to suck these big, mother's tits first.'

He licked his lips over the dirty words. I arched my back and offered them to him like a slut. Let him have a real woman's tits, then. Full and nurturing, yet bent on pain.

He coiled that gorgeous torso over me, gripping my wrists, then he bared his teeth, took one burning red nipple into his mouth and sucked it so hard that the pleasure burned straight down to my cunt and I

82

wanted to close my legs to stop myself coming there and then, except that I couldn't because I was split open and wrapped round him and every movement and rub and pressure urged my climax rocketing nearer.

He sucked and bit and again that torturing thought of all the other girls and women and breasts he would caress streaked across my mind. I wanted him to bite until the agony sheared through me and wiped out any thought. I wanted to be the one to show him how debauched an older woman could be.

He paused, then bit, and I screamed with the pleasure of it. His beautiful cock was lifting and banging against my thigh and I hitched myself without warning, tilted my pussy up so that he could feel the ready wetness of me smearing against his balls.

The wet sound was suddenly huge in that cold quiet room, and it was time.

He let go of my breasts and raised himself further up on his strong arms, so that he was hanging right over me like some kind of big warm hound. There was too much air and space between our bodies. Through that space I could see a feeble ray of winter sunshine arrowing briefly through the window. I wondered what the time was. How long before they all got back?

And then he was closing the gap. I could feel the warmth of his torso before it came to rest on me, his elbows shaking with the effort to be gentle, and I sank into the soft bed beneath him, raising my hips to meet his, feeling the tip of that beautiful cock introducing itself to me. He was cautious, edging the first couple of inches inside, stopping and starting too gently. I started to wonder how many times, how many girls and had they all needed it gentle, and the thought stopped being painful and started exciting me. I was going to be the best he'd ever had. Was ever going to have.

I pulled him hard and opened myself and my body swallowed his length easily, welcoming him, yes, in a motherly way because he was so fresh and new. I nearly screamed out loud with the naughtiness of it. I was making it easy for him to be the big man, to slide into me.

My body merged with his so that I couldn't tell where my stomach and pussy and legs ended and his stomach and cock and legs began. He rested on his forearms, leaned down and started kissing me again, nudging my mouth wide open so that his tongue could copy what his long hard cock was doing, reaching deep inside me, filling me completely and stopping my cries.

I wished I *had* been there for his first time.

As soon as his mouth slid sideways my cries started up, louder and higher, screeching round my empty house. The only other sound was the banging of the headboard against the wall. Normally I'd hate a distracting noise like that but the banging of the bed made me frantic with wicked lust. He thrust inside me and all the tiny muscles and surfaces of me gripped onto him, rubbed themselves against him to milk every last new exhilarating inch and sensation out of him, grinding on the wave of ecstasy. The wave started building and roaring. I looked at him. My knees flopped sideways. I was sluiced through with sheer gritty joy, and then there was the explosion I'd been waiting for ever since he walked into my house, and I was yelling out his name as his cock pumped in, out, in, his gorgeous young body pulling and pushing and straining to fuck and pleasure me and do it right. And then he caught up with me and shuddered and came and fell heavily on top of me.

* * *

His cock was in my mouth when they got home. The front door slammed, making the window and the bed rattle. I pulled his cock out, still rock hard, and kissed it. I pushed him down into the bed, arranged the sprigged duvet over him. Little boy. We snuffled with the motherliness of it. Our teacups and glasses rattled as I carried them to the door.

'He's asleep, guys,' I called. 'Think he's got some kind of food poisoning, like me.'

'Blame Dad's cooking!'

They stamped on through the hall, as if I was invisible.

'No worries,' called Steve in a hammy Australian accent.

The girls giggled. 'Patsy's decided to stay with Grandma.'

'What shall we do about Michel?'

I glanced behind me. He had pushed the duvet off. He was standing right there in the doorway of the spare room, the light from the landing outlining his stiff cock. It was glistening wet with my saliva.

'The stud,' spluttered the girls. 'Didn't you hear them humping last night?'

'So cool, these youngsters, nothing heavy, always on the move –' Steve took his coat off. If he'd looked up he'd have seen his dull, ordinary, much slimmer wife in her shabby joggers, holding the banister as if I was sick, juice catching in my pubes where Michel had licked me.

'What about Michel?' I asked, dancing with impatience. The spare room bed creaked. He was lying down again, waiting for me.

'We're all going to Oz to visit the rellies, and Michel has a job in London.' My husband tossed his coat on a hook, and headed for the kitchen. 'You don't mind, do you? Patsy wants you to stay here, and entertain him.'

– *Angela, Kent, UK*

Was It You?

I'm definitely remaining anonymous for this one because I know a lot of guys who'd be completely freaked out.

Maybe I'm just wicked, but I don't see it that way. It really pisses me off when men are into watching two girls together but they won't return the favour. Not that I mind snogging a friend, or even licking pussy if the mood is right, but, hey, if I'm going down on my mate, I want my boyfriend to go down on his. What's wrong with that? I'd love to watch my boyfriend go down on some big hunky man's cock and maybe take a load in his face so he knows how it feels.

They never will, and it's all bullshit. Hey, I'm not that into girls, but I'll go for it to turn our men on, because there's no harm in pussy licking. There's no harm in sucking cock either, but the way most of my boyfriends react when I suggest they try it, you'd think I wanted them to go base jumping without a parachute. It's only a cock, for fuck's sake. I say most of my boyfriends. Really it's all my boyfriends except one, which is where the confession bit comes in.

When I was a teenager I always followed my heart and went for whoever I found the most attractive. OK, so that generally means going for who everybody else finds attractive, but I was popular and didn't mind so much, at first anyway. The problem is that in almost any group of boys there will be one the girls single out as the best, which means he gets all the attention and inevitably gets big-headed about it and starts to cheat. It's probably the same for boys too, but it's a pain in the neck anyway and it's happened to me more times than I can count. Three, actually, but you get the point. They're also crap in bed, because they're too used to getting what they want, blow jobs mainly, and they're always pushing to go further and generally don't give a shit about safe sex. Most of them are too full of macho bullshit to go down on me, never mind another bloke.

Not that anything like that occurred to me until I was in my 20s, but things weren't that much different then. It always seems to be the macho shitheads who go for me. Not wanting to get too vain, but I know I'm a cutie and most of them are more interested in having me as a trophy than for my own sake. That means they're usually possessive as well. I got sick of all that after one seriously fucked-up relationship with a man who'd get into these stupid sulks even if I looked at a picture of another man in a magazine.

I did toy with the idea of going out with an older man, as I get asked out by them often enough, but that doesn't really do anything for me. What I wanted was someone with a nice body, but more fun. What I got was weird, but great. I'd just split up with the last macho man and was going through the stage when his mates come round and say how hurt he is and all of that. I just wanted out, and the best way was to be seen with a new man, so I suggested a date to a man at work who'd been mooning around me for months.

He was a pretty sorry specimen, shorter than me for one thing, and very lightly built, but he does have nice eyes, very big and pale, which makes him look like a lost puppy. He behaves a bit like one too, always following at my heels and ever eager to please. Normally that would just wind me up, but at the time I felt it was exactly what I needed. When I first suggested going out he thought I was trying to make fun of him, and I had to kiss him before he'd believe I was genuine.

The date was really strange, more like being taken out by a shy teenager than a grown man. He turned up in a suit, took me to a Chinese restaurant and insisted on paying the bill. All evening he was really nervous, fidgeting and tripping over his words, so much that I began to wonder if he was going to ask for something seriously kinky afterwards. He didn't. He didn't even try to kiss me or give me the old line about coming up for coffee.

That was really rather sweet, and I didn't feel ready for sex with him anyway, so when he wrote me a really nice thank-you note and suggested another date I accepted. Not that I was even particularly attracted to him, but he brought out completely different feelings in me, including not knowing whether to pat him or kick him sometimes. I'll call him Dog Boy, it fits.

There was a bit of a problem when Macho Man found out I was seeing Dog Boy, all the usual bullshit about how he was going to beat him up etc, but that only made me all the more determined. I didn't even tell Dog Boy because I thought he might be scared off. The second date had been much like the first, as the third would have been, only by that time I felt ready and invited him to come up.

I have never known a guy so diffident about sex. He was turned on, rock-hard from the moment I got him out, and he admitted he had been for most of the evening, but he simply would not and will not make the first move and has to be led through the whole performance. Whenever I'd had sex before I'd always felt that it was me being fucked, which seems natural, but with Dog Boy it's me doing the fucking, even if he is the one with the penis.

I had him on his back, straddled across him, and the look on his face as he watched my tits bounce was so funny it made it hard to concentrate on what I was doing. He came really fast too, despite being in a condom like a rubber sack, which I'd had to put on for him. Not that I minded too much, because I'd already figured out that he would do anything I said. I told him he was going to have to lick me and he went straight down on me, no complaints at all. I had to teach him how to do it properly, but he was eager and I found I was really getting off on telling him what to do and being obeyed.

That was the start of it. After a couple of months he'd picked up enough confidence to be a bit better in bed, quite good really, because he would always do exactly as he was told and never tried to push me where I didn't want to go. He'll lick for hours too, and not just my pussy, because he likes me to sit on his face so he can stick his dirty little tongue up my bum while I get myself there with a vibrator.

All my friends seemed to think I'd made a really bad choice and was pining for Macho Man, who most of them fancied as well. None of them fancied Dog Boy, and some of them didn't even want to associate with me while he was my boyfriend, which is pretty crap. I'm stubborn anyway, and won't let people push me out of the choices I've made, so I stuck to him and contented myself with all the great orgasms he gave me.

We'd been going out maybe six months before I discovered his secret. He'd invited me to dinner at his flat and left me in the house while he went out to get a bottle of wine. Being a nosy so-and-so I started to look around. I was also sure he had a huge stash of pornos and I wanted to embarrass him with them and make him grovel for me. I got more than I bargained for.

He had a stash all right, but they were not what I'd been expecting. It was in the chest of drawers next to his bed, the first one I opened. There were loads of them, and every single one devoted to cross-dressing. I knew about it, sort of, but I had no idea he was into it. It freaked me out a bit at first, though I couldn't help but look at some of the mags and I quickly realised there was no harm in it, just that it's a bit odd.

That wasn't all either. I started to put the mags back, not sure how to handle it if he realised I'd found them, and as I shoved the drawer in it got caught on a jumper. I had to pull open the next drawer up to sort it out, and when I did I caught a glimpse of pink among the clothes. I don't suppose I'd have even noticed if I hadn't just been staring at pictures of men dressed in everything from frilly undies to ball gowns, but, as it was, I couldn't help but stick my hand in. I pulled out a pair of pink knickers, which had me laughing, until I realised they were my own.

It's a bit weird realising your boyfriend is a complete and utter fucking pervert. It would have been bad enough if I'd thought he'd pinched them to toss off into but, after seeing his magazines, I knew he'd have been putting them on. I also remembered having to walk home commando one night because I couldn't find my knickers after sex. I wanted to kill him, and I took the knickers into the kitchen and put them on the table where he couldn't fail to see them as he came in, and sat down to wait. He came in five minutes later, but when he saw the knickers he looked so sorry for himself I really thought he was going to cry.

I suppose I must be soft underneath because, instead of having a go and storming off, I ended up telling him it was OK but that I would have liked him to ask. I got the whole story, about how his parents were divorced and his mum had always put him down, saying how worthless he was and how wonderful his sisters were so that he'd grown up thinking of men as basically a waste of space and women as the ideal in every way. He was in tears by the end, and I couldn't help but feel sorry for him, so I ended up giving him a hug and doing the cooking while he sat there feeling sorry for himself and asking over and over again if I really minded. I kept telling him it was OK, but he didn't seem to want to believe me. He wouldn't stop it, so I eventually told him to strip off and get into the pink panties to serve me dinner.

I've never seen a man move so fast. He was stark naked in about a second and had my knickers pulled up over a rock-hard erection in about two. I've always liked the sight of a man's cock inside a pair of pants, and the silky pink material made it even better: kinky as well as horny. I'd sat down again, and he brought me dinner like that, shaking with nerves so badly he nearly dropped a plate.

By the end of the meal I was really enjoying myself. He'd always been obedient, but now he was really grovelling, and looking at me as if he worshipped me. It's hard not to get off on that, for me anyway. He'd stayed hard all the time, and I really thought he was going to come in his pants, or my pants, but he'd brought out the bitch in me like never before.

I led him into the main room by his cock, holding it through his pants, then told him to fetch me a drink. He served it to me on his knees and stayed that way, kneeling at my feet and staring at me with a sort of dumb adoration. I was already quite drunk after most of the bottle of wine, and getting more and more horny over what I was doing to him. After a bit I took my bra off, down my sleeve so he wouldn't get a peep, and told him to put it on. He did it, shaking harder than ever.

With my bra on he looked so comic I made him put my shoes on too and walk around the flat like that, then my skirt, then everything else, so he was dressed up like I'd been at work. He really did look feminine, sort of, if not actually like a woman, and I had great fun making him go around the flat like that, just enjoying myself nicely while he was getting in a bigger and bigger state.

In the end I took pity on him, told him to lie on the floor and mounted him with his skirt turned up and his cock pulled out of my pink knickers to go in me. It felt weird, to be stark naked on top of him while he was dressed in my clothes, but it felt good too. Not that I get off on having a man in women's clothes, but to have all that power was a real kick. He stayed in my knickers and bra all night, and I have never had a man so grateful or so constantly turned on.

That night was the real start of my relationship with Dog Boy. I'm not claiming he's perfect, but it's the best I've ever had. We can talk, for one thing, because there are no barriers between us and if I'm not into cross-dressing in that it doesn't turn me on, then I do get off on the change of roles and having all the power in the relationship. Sex has always been about exchanging favours anyway, or a lot of it, so

I'm more than happy to indulge his fetish in return for having him as my plaything.

He loves me to boss him too, to do my housework and have me swat his bottom if he doesn't make a good job of it, or anything that makes him feel feminine. OK, so his idea of 'feminine' is straight out of the 50s and would make any modern feminist foam at the mouth, but what do I care? He's the one scrubbing the floor dressed in frilly knickers and a tarty mini-skirt.

It didn't take long for me to bring up my kink for watching men go together. He admitted he would do it, after a bit, but insisted, and still insists, that it's not because he's into other men, but because having me order him to do it is so humiliating. That night I made him masturbate while I told him how I'd like to watch him go down on a gay man and take a mouthful of spunk, which made Dog Boy come so hard it went in his face.

Just thinking about it kept us going for a while, but I wanted more and when he saw that it was what I wanted he made it very clear that he was willing. My first thought was to take him to a gay club and make him do it in the loos, but I wasn't sure how the gay men would react to a woman. We started to scan the web for possibilities and came up with several, but one was far and away the most satisfying. I didn't want him to suck off a gay man or even a bisexual man. I wanted him to suck off a 100 per cent straight, macho shithead of exactly the sort I'd been out with so many times, and I wanted the guy to think he was getting it from a girl.

Dog Boy was completely freaked out at first, but he had to admit it was possible. With his small size, slim build and years of practice pretending to be a woman he was pretty good at it, certainly good enough to pass as the real thing in a dim light.

We had great fun practising. First off we got some new outfits, because all the stuff he had for himself was frilly or pink and generally the sort of stuff no real woman would be seen dead in. It was great making him buy bras and panties in lingerie departments, and even better having him try on a skirt in a changing cubicle with me, which got him so hard I made him toss off in his knickers and wear them home all wet and sticky.

Training him to behave like a woman was even better, first taking him out at night and then in the car, always a long way from either of our areas. At first he got noticed quite a lot, with odd looks from both men and women, but nobody ever challenged him. He was better than me at make-up from the start. More practice, then once we'd got his hair right and he'd learnt to speak more softly, the odd looks became rarer and finally stopped altogether.

By then I knew exactly what I was going to do. While searching the net we'd found out about dogging carparks, and how you generally get loads of men for every couple, really. That was perfect: after dark, with a guaranteed supply of horny men and a quick getaway if things went wrong. I even thought of swapping roles completely and having me as the boyfriend getting off on making his girl suck strangers' cocks, but I couldn't swing it and decided to be a butch dyke with a bi girlfriend instead.

I went a bit over the top, maybe, because, let's face it, I haven't the least idea what the well-dressed butch dyke is wearing this year, but I was banking on the men in the car park not knowing either, or not caring. I felt good anyway, in men's work boots, ripped jeans, a black top without a bra, a leather jacket and my hair up underneath a cap.

Dog Boy wanted to call himself Letitia, but I was sure it would make them suspicious and made him go for Emma instead. I also had trouble getting him to leave the flouncy stuff and go for a short PVC skirt, stockings and heels, with a black top and a pink plastic jacket that was pretty hideous but had the big advantage of hiding the major defect: no tits. He, or she, looked a right tart, but that was the idea.

Our first outing was a failure. Nobody turned up, but before the second I'd read that the best thing to do was to advertise on the net in advance so plenty of men knew we'd be there, and the second time it worked a treat. We parked up carefully, facing the exit so that if there was any trouble we could make a quick getaway, and close to some thick bushes so Dog Boy's face wouldn't be too easy to see.

I flashed the lights as you're supposed to do to signal that you're up for fun and we waited. I was pretty nervous and he was shaking as badly as when I'd found my knickers in his room. We almost lost our nerve when a man stepped out of the shadows: a black guy, quite young and really furtive. I did the talking, and it was one of the weirdest conversations I've ever had as I explained that I was deliberately punishing my girlfriend by making her suck strangers off. He just loved that, the bastard, and out it came, a fat black cock, already half stiff, which he flopped out at the back window.

I could just about see Dog Boy's made-up face looking right at that big black penis, his mouth a bit open, knowing he wanted to suck it but unable to make himself move. I did it for him, taking him by the neck and shoving his face right against the man's cock. It felt wonderful, and if that makes me a sadistic bitch then I'm just going to have to accept it, but it wasn't half as wonderful as seeing Dog Boy's mouth come properly open and take in the man's cock.

I could have come right there, just from the expression on Dog Boy's face as he sucked on another man's penis, loving and hating it at the same time. The man was great too, well into it and never once suspecting it wasn't a real woman sucking him off. He even started to call Dog Boy a bitch, just before he came right down the poor bastard's throat. Dog Boy was nearly sick, but I've had enough men make me swallow not to be too sympathetic, while knowing he'd just swallowed spunk got me off almost as much as seeing him suck cock.

That was it, the first time. There were other men about, but Dog Boy bottled out. I didn't mind, because I badly needed sex but wasn't about to do myself in the car with a load of men in the bushes. Back at my flat I made him describe how it had felt to suck another man all the way, while I lay back on the bed with my vibrator. It was just the best orgasm.

Since then we've been out three times, and every single time Dog Boy has sucked at least one man, and always until they come. We always choose dark places, and never once has anyone been suspicious, even when Dog Boy's had to refuse to lift his top. On the best night he did four men, one after another. It was so dark we could hardly see anything, just the outlines of the bushes against the sky, and the men, one after another, coming forward to flop out their cocks, right into poor Dog Boy's mouth, to make him suck them until they spunked up, and never once suspecting he wasn't a girl.

One man gave him bukkake, pulling his cock out at the last moment and doing it in Dog Boy's face to leave his make-up running in the streaks of spunk. That was so good I just had to come, so we drove a little further, to be alone, where I could turn on the car light and bring myself off while I watched Dog

Boy wank with the man's spunk still trickling down his face and his mouth full of it. He was so high he looked like he was on drugs or something, and at the last moment he put his hand in the mess and smeared the other man's spunk all over his cock, adding his own as he came all over his hand.

That made me come so hard, and I was so turned on I didn't know what to think about – the state my boyfriend was in as he wanked in another man's spunk, watching him suck the men, or because they all thought they'd had blow jobs from a girl when really they'd been sucked off by a man.

Yes, I know it's wicked. I know I'm an evil bitch, but I don't care. I love it.

So were you one of them? Did you go out to a certain car park not so very long ago and get a blow job from a bi girl with her dyke partner? If you did, it was us, and you've let another man suck your cock. Now I'm going to go away and come over it.

– G. H., Warwickshire, UK

Angelo's

'I'm *so* excited! Thanks so much for giving me the time off! I'm going to Europe!' I gushed, while bouncing about with the vigour of a five year old.

'If you keep bouncing around like that, *I'm* going to get excited.' He snickered in a way that made me a little uncomfortable.

I had been working for Angelo for about a year. When I applied for the job at his family restaurant, it was only meant to be a temporary fix, but he and his family were so kind and accommodating that I had never had the heart to leave.

'I guess I'll finish setting these tables and then I'll get going,' I said, leaning across the table with a plate.

'That's fine. I better get something nice for letting you go on vacation with such short notice,' he said in his thick Italian accent, his face a bit more serious than I had expected.

'I'll bring you a bottle of the best wine ever!' I smiled, grateful to be leaving for my holiday.

'There are things that are a lot better than wine . . . maybe something else?' His tone once again was making me uneasy.

'Ha ha,' I joked sarcastically, knowing full well what he was implying and afraid of giving him anything else to go on.

I wasn't sure what had gotten into him. I knew he was a bit of a womaniser and had been involved with women outside of his marriage in the past, but he had never spoken to me that way. We always had more of a father-daughter type relationship, or so I thought.

He was in his mid-50s, and certainly not much to look at, especially in the eyes of a 20 year old. Angelo dressed very much the part of the wannabe suave European male. He wore overpriced colourful sweaters, and dress slacks, and way too much cologne. He was not very tall – I'd guess only a couple of inches taller than me – his hair was thinning and almost non-existent, but he managed to grow what little he had long enough to pull it into a tiny little ponytail at the nape of his neck. And then there was the goatee; it seemed he had more hair on his face than on his head.

'Are you gonna give me a hug?' he asked, opening his arms for me as I got ready to walk out the door.

'I'm only going for a week.' I tried to avoid the looming embrace.

'Come here.' His eyes opened wide as he wrapped his arms around me, holding me uncomfortably tight.

'You have a good time,' he snarled into my ear, his hands rubbing my back and inching their way lower.

'Thanks. I will. Bye!' I called out, pulling away and booting it towards the door, hoping that his newly found interest would pass before I got back.

My week in Europe was great and I quickly forgot about Angelo's odd behaviour. I was back at work the night after I returned from my trip. Tired and jet-lagged and very glad to have returned on a slow night, I managed to sit for a few minutes and enjoy a cup of coffee with Rosanna, my boss's wife. She was a heavy-set woman with a warm smile who loved to chat and bake. 'Take a cookie, they're fresh.' She smiled, practically shoving the cookie down my throat. 'So, your trip was nice?' she asked.

'So good! I really needed it,' I said, collapsing back into my chair.

'Really needed it, eh?' I heard Angelo's voice. He had just walked in to take over for Rosanna, who clearly didn't catch what he meant.

'Hi, sweetie, it's nice to have you back.' His tone changed to one that was more appropriate.

'Thanks. Oh, those customers look like they're ready to go, I'll be back,' I said, dashing off. When I went around the back of the bar again, Angelo was just standing there with a grin on his face.

'Where's Rosanna? Did she go home already?' I asked as I pottered around the bar looking for a corkscrew.

'No, she's in the back getting changed.' I heard his voice getting closer behind me.

As I went to turn around, I felt his hands press against my hips, holding me there, unable to move. Before I could say anything, I felt his body press against me and a hand run along the back of my thigh, just under my skirt.

'Mmm ... You feel so soft,' he whispered in my ear, as his hand slid between my thighs and lingered over the crotch of my panties.

'What are you doing?' I asked, trying to be discreet, very aware of the customers seated just a few feet away.

'I couldn't help myself. You're so young and beautiful. And I know you like it. You're wet, I can feel it.' His words almost slurred.

I was in shock and didn't know what to do. I was appalled that he would do this, but I didn't pull away. I don't know if it was the fear of having to face him, or that maybe he was right and that I was indeed enjoying it, feeling his body pressed behind me and his hand in the warmth between my legs.

His hand eventually slid out and he said, 'There it is; now get over there and serve those people.'

I realised that someone had walked in. It was Rosanna, just popping her head in to say goodnight, and he must have covered up well because she didn't seem to notice.

My hands trembled as I served the few clients that I had that night. I couldn't believe what had happened and wasn't sure I could look him in the eye. I was dreading having the last customer leave for the night because that would leave only the two of us.

'Thank you for coming,' he called out from behind the bar as the final customer left.

I was a wreck as I locked the door behind them, certain that he would make another advance; only he didn't. It was business as usual, and he acted as though nothing had happened. Even stranger was that I wasn't relieved, but almost disappointed. What was wrong with me? He was old, and unattractive, and just – greasy!

The next night we were quite busy at work, and needed to enlist the help of the entire family. I was serving, Rosanna was cooking and Angelo manned the bar, while his daughter Lia, who was just a bit older than me, helped all of us out.

Though it was hectic and I barely had time to breathe, I couldn't get what had happened out of my mind, replaying it over and over.

Angelo sent his wife out to get something which left Lia to take over the kitchen duties. 'Can you come help me with these?' he asked, motioning to the clean glasses that needed to be put away.

I stepped behind the bar and began to make space for the glasses, when I felt him inch closer, once again standing behind me. 'Shhhh. Don't let Lia hear you,' he whispered when he realised that I was about to speak.

I didn't say a word. He put his hands on my bare legs and ran them up under my skirt, slipping them between my panties and skin, kneading my ass cheeks. I could feel his fingers pulling them apart; his grip was hard and almost hurt.

Keeping his grasp on one side, he used the other hand to slide his fingers back and forth in my crack, just grazing my cunt. I could feel myself getting wet and could hear his breath behind me.

My heart raced, and I was horrified at the idea that someone might see, but I didn't dare move. His fingers were moist from my pussy, and I could feel them leaving a trail of my juices along my skin. He pulled my panties to one side, and called out in a fake tone, 'Oh, you dropped that – let me get it.'

Keeping my panties pulled to the side, he squatted down behind me and, within seconds, my skin was tingling at the feel of his warm breath on my ass. With his head under my already short skirt and his hands holding my panties away from my skin, he stuck his tongue between my cheeks. It was hot and so wet and felt so good – unlike anything I had ever done before. He pushed a finger into my cunt while his tongue darted in and out of my ass. I struggled to stay on my feet and kept looking out into the full restaurant to make sure that no one was noticing what was going on. His saliva began to run down my leg and in spite of the clanging of glasses and voices of the patrons, I could hear only his tongue lapping away at my asshole. With my insides starting to quiver, I knew I was close to coming. Just then, Lia called out from the kitchen, 'Dad, come here for a sec.' And, with that, he quickly stood up and walked away, wiping his face with one hand and adjusting his obvious erection with the other, leaving me there on the brink of a climax.

In the days that followed, it seemed to be back to work as usual. Angelo refrained from any inappropriate behaviour – there was no touching, no dirty little glances, and not one mention of our previous encounter. I began to wonder if he was suffering from some type of multiple personality disorder, or if maybe he was very much aware of what he was doing and the effect that it was having on me. This man repulsed me. He was a greasy middle-aged Godfather wannabe with a wife of at least thirty years and a daughter about my age who believed him to be wonderful. And yet here he was touching me, practically against my will, doing things to me so improper that I felt dirty afterwards, but yet craved in a way that I could not comprehend. I could not stop my mind from replaying the last incident, the way his small, rough hands slipped about sloppily between my thighs, and the way his breath felt hot and dirty behind me, and the knot in my stomach that I could only compare to the guilt of doing something bad – how that ill feeling took over every inch of me, sending chills to my very core, while making me feel more aroused than I ever had before.

At least a couple of weeks passed, and my craving began to dissipate. I guess I had accepted to the possibility that maybe he had realised that what he was doing was wrong and just wanted to let it go.

'Can you stay to close? I have Domenic, one of my old partners, coming by later and we have some things we need to discuss, so I really need the help – if you don't mind?' he asked, barely even glancing at me.

'I guess so,' I replied, disappointed at having to stick around so late.

I was in the middle of chatting to a couple of old ladies I was serving when Domenic walked in. 'That's gotta be him,' I giggled to myself, noting that he too looked as if he had wandered in off the set of *The Sopranos*.

He was tall, and in his late 50s at least, sporting the fullest head of dyed black hair I had ever seen, with a handlebar moustache to boot. His ensemble of a lilac shirt and shiny dress pants were bad enough without the thick gold chains that adorned his neck and wrists. He made his way behind the bar to greet Angelo and I wondered if he would drop and kiss his pinky ring. Angelo spotted me watching and called out, 'This is Domenic,' as if I cared.

I was a walking zombie by the time the last customer left. It had been a busy night, and I had been serving pretty much alone as Angelo was busy entertaining his friend. I was standing behind the bar, wiping off the glasses as quickly as I could, in the hope of being home at a decent hour.

My mind was distracted when I felt the familiar presence of Angelo behind me.

'We're finally alone now,' he whispered, running his tongue lightly along my ear.

As before, I said nothing and just stood still, allowing him to take over. His hands moved quickly to my skirt, and he raised it as high as he could. The draft from the air conditiong above felt good against my skin as he lowered my panties to the floor. 'Beautiful,' he said as he caressed my ass.

He reached around me and began to unbutton my blouse. The thin white cotton fell to the sides and I glanced down to see him pulling my tits out of my bra. He left them just hanging there and proceeded to squeeze my nipples. I could feel his erection through his pants, pressing up behind me. 'You're getting wet, aren't you? I know, I know. You love this.' His voice snarled against my ear. 'Bend over for me,' he instructed, while gently pushing me forwards from behind.

As I leaned forwards, resting against the lower part of the bar, my ass cheeks naturally spread apart. My cunt lips also parted slightly making just enough space to allow me to drip a little. He slid a finger in and out of my slippery cunt and brought it up to my asshole, tracing the opening with my own juices, and then he began to slowly push the lubed finger into my ass. I tensed up and felt a tinge of pain, but he continued to slide it into me until I could feel his knuckle against my skin.

Holding his finger inside, I felt his body shift off to the side, and was startled to hear him say, 'Hey, Domenic, look at how tight this is. It's beautiful!'

I glanced behind me to see Domenic, sitting in a chair just staring. His gaze was sharp, but the rest of his face was almost somber. I could see one of his hands moving about in his pants as he looked at me, and this brought on a feeling of disgust so intense it made me nauseous. How long had he been watching?

'Relax,' Angelo growled, moving the finger in and out of me slowly in what I believe was an attempt to calm me down. It worked. The pleasure of having something in my asshole for the first time consumed me, and soon the idea of this perfect stranger watching this intimate moment excited me beyond comprehension. I pushed my ass towards Angelo, wanting his finger as deep inside me as possible and glanced back every now and again to see the expression on my audience's face. The only sound in the restaurant was our heavy breathing and my soft moans. I could feel my cunt dripping and the warmth of my sex running down my thigh as the rest of my body began to tingle and crave something more. 'Fuck me!' I cried out, while pulling away from Angelo's slippery finger.

I turned to face the two of them, pulling myself up onto the counter and leaning back, spreading my legs as far apart as I could. It excited me to feel my cunt spread open to the eyes of these two disgusting men.

Angelo quickly undid his pants, exposing his hard cock that was not as I had expected an older man's to be. He gripped the shaft of his cock so hard that a tiny drop of jis appeared from the swollen head. I braced myself, holding the edge of the counter to keep my balance, and he pushed his cock into me. It slipped in with ease and I could hear just how wet I had become. He grunted as he pushed in and out of my cunt, not making eye contact with me at all. I focused my gaze on Domenic and his now exposed cock, as my cunt got fucked hard. Sweat was building on his brow and his lips were parted beneath his moustache as he watched his friend fuck me. His hand moved fervently along his dick, causing him to grunt now and again. My clit ached as I got fucked, as if it were wanting even more. I pushed my hips back and forth, fucking him like a champ. I don't know what had come over me. How could these horrid men have such an effect on me?

I arched my back, pussy pressed hard against him and my insides began to shudder. I wanted to come. My eyes were closed but it was as if I were seeing stars as every inch of me was overcome with sensations like never before.

'My turn.' I heard Domenic's voice right in front of me, causing me to open my eyes.

Angelo quickly obliged and pulled his cock out of me, a string of come following. I didn't even have a chance to object before Domenic pushed his even larger cock inside my already swollen hole. He was rough and pumped hard in and out of me. I felt dirtier than ever as I felt his cock pushing around in the mixture of my and Angelo's jis. He didn't care that his friend's cock had just been deep inside the same hole. He didn't even know my name.

He looked down as he fucked me, watching his dick slide in and out of me. Every now and then he would pull out all the way and then slip it slowly back in, enjoying the look of his purple head against my stretched-out pink lips.

They were using me, and I was loving it. It took everything in me to keep from coming. My body trembled and my knees shook as the urge to climax built up inside me, but I held on. I had to, because they weren't finished with me yet.

Domenic must have fucked me for almost twenty minutes before I felt his cock quiver. He reached down to pull out, but I gripped my cunt around him tightly and pulled him to me, causing him to blow his load deep inside me. A final grunt and he practically collapsed against me, breathing so heavily that he was almost left gasping for air.

I reached my finger down to my hard clit as soon as he moved away and began rubbing it as hard as I could. I wanted to come and couldn't wait any longer.

As I clenched my pussy lips tight and pushed my finger hard against my clit, I felt Domenic's warm come oozing out of me. I became aware of Angelo moving towards me and, before I could finish climaxing, he was pushing his cock into my hole, still filled with Domenic's jis. I continued to rub my clit with one hand as the other held me from falling off the bar. A hot rush came over me and my insides convulsed violently as I came. My pussy contracted frantically and before long brought Angelo to the brink. As his cock pulsed within me, I gripped him hard and took in his entire load as well, revelling in the knowledge that both men had filled me with their milk.

We dressed and went on about our lives. I didn't work for Angelo for much longer after that, having decided to go back to college instead. And though a couple of years have passed, I still meet up with him every now and again for a free meal and a fuck.

– *Sarah, Illinois, USA*

Linda's Misdemeanours

I started in my new office with all the best intentions. A clean slate, you know? A new haircut (putting my blonde hair into bushy ringlets the week before), new clothes (smart, sexy office wear, dress suits, a selection of heels and so on), and I even bought a pair of those spectacles with the flat lenses (a fashion accessory, for the intelligent look). The aim was to change myself, outside and in, and leave my naughty past behind me, to get to know a new group of people who wouldn't judge me on rumours and locker-room talk.

I have had my wild days, and I decided on the day I received the new job offer that they were behind me. No more one-nighters with colleagues, I said to myself. This is a chance to change your ways, Linda, I said, in an environment where your past won't catch up with you. And I meant it.

In my previous office, where I worked for the council, I'm afraid I enjoyed myself a little too much for my own good. It all started pretty harmlessly, snogging the office hunk one night, then shagging him the following week. But then I moved onto another, and another, then found myself going back to the first again to try something a bit more daring. You can imagine the cycle I'm sure. Eventually, the boys in the old office started to take me for granted (one of the things I really wanted to avoid this time around).

Things really started to go downhill at the council, I think, when I got drunk one Friday night and confessed to one trusted male soul that I liked it up the arse. He was a little older, very pleasant, and very conservative. Poor chap didn't know where to look. But I bet he was still thinking about doing me despite his strait-laced image, especially (and I blush to even think about it) when I explained to him that I liked it slow and with short thrusts at first, then slow long thrusts, then a really deep humping up there with my hair pulled a little at the end. God, I was so drunk that night; what was I thinking? Anyway, he was all very discreet and gentlemanly on the night and toddled off to his wife after he had seen me safely into a taxi and, although I cringed with horror during the morning-after recall, I thought the chances were fair to middling that he would keep it quiet.

Anyway, as you can probably imagine, word got round. Faithful old darling to his wife that he was, and pleasant as anything to me in the workplace and social arena, I'm afraid he just couldn't sit on the details of my lubricated confession and confided the content of our chat to a fellow male worker. Can I really blame him? Before I knew it, the same group of four or five guys I had let taste the strawberry before were queuing up to try the chocolate. It can tend to make you feel a little taken for granted, like I say, when guys expect to get a shot of your arse just for asking. Especially as they had all seemed to work out somewhere along the line that I simply can't say no.

So that was the plan then: no snogging and shagging in this new office, and no drunken confessions to co-workers. No more letting horny guys take advantage of me. I had put my past behind me.

It started well. I settled in, got to like the job, made a few new girlfriends, had some laughs. Obviously, I still wanted to look attractive. Who doesn't? But I kept it respectable, a kind of business-sexy as opposed to business-tarty. I was still out there; a girl's 'gotta eat', after all; but I resolved only to go out with guys who tried to romance me a little and showed how keen they were. That was an attitude that would keep me away from casual affairs and preserve my reputation, I felt.

It went really well for at least three months. In fact my new attitude kept me completely celibate for the entire period. That was unexpected – not necessarily part of the plan, but I was kind of proud of myself. I had proved that I could do it, and I began to wonder if my life had changed for the better.

I tried to ignore the fact that my pussy was biting my leg off. That was no more than an incidental complication.

One fellow in the office came closest to my hungry pussy. For some reason I haven't got my head round yet, his parents had called him Troy. I think they were either hippies, or they liked to be different, or they conceived him in Turkey. One of the three anyway. I knew he was interested in me – he couldn't keep his eyes on his computer screen whenever I was in the area and I would always note his tendency to watch my legs if I was in a skirt and my feet if I was in heels.

He was an affable chap and seemed to know everyone, so it was only natural that we would be introduced at some point. As things got more familiar, he got confident enough around me to pay me compliments on my, yes, you guessed it, skirts and shoes. I began to suspect he might be building himself up to ask me out.

The old Linda, the council worker Linda, would have helped him out by flirting back and letting things escalate until, inexorably, she found herself bending over the arm of a sofa with a twitching cock pushing into her soft wet pussy and having her ear bitten, or hair pulled back, or both. But not the new Linda; she – that is, I – played it differently. 'Hard to get' I think they call it (I don't really know because I haven't played it that way before).

I told myself not to encourage him and see if he took it any further. If he did, then I would go for it; if he didn't, then he wasn't for me. It was a radical new concept. Anyway, he made a few more hints about 'going for drinks' but it wasn't quite an official proposal so, despite the temptation, I let him slip away. Silly boy, he doesn't know how close he was.

So that was the sum sexual catalogue of the first three months at the new office; it was a crunching gear change from weekly anal sex with, erm, whoever. I think I could have kept it going for at least another three months too, if it weren't for the announcement.

The Customer Service Manager (to give him his full title) Douglas Kennedy sent a brief and innocuous email to us all telling us that from now on, payday would be a dress-down day – wear what you like, in other words, no need for smart office attire.

Now most people would immediately think jeans, or sportswear. But my mind works a little differently, and, whether my forgotten pussy was thinking for me, or whether its because I think on a whole different level to everyone else, I thought of it as a licence to dress provocatively.

I wore a tight low-cut top, dark purple in colour, with a neckline that allowed my cleavage to peek out. I liked it because the contours of my nipples could be seen through it, perfect for impressing an audience. I matched it with an extremely short black skirt that showed the lower half of my thighs, and shiny black high-heeled shoes with a fully covered toe and a T-bar ankle strap. I got up early to give me enough time to apply some rich milky moisturiser to my legs, which made my skin glisten as it sank into my smooth flesh. I was intending to go bare-legged, knowing well that the contrast between the black clothing and my creamy flesh would catch eyes, especially the way the essential oils brought out the vein on top of my foot, the cut of my calf muscles, and the turn of my ankle.

Boy, was I out of place in comparison with the casual clothing my colleagues wore that day. I was drawing looks from everyone, male and female alike: a mixture of jealousy, admiration, lust, disgust and awe, I imagine.

It was great to break the rules of engagement. I felt totally wicked inflicting all this frustration on the boys in the office, and equally wicked at having thrown all the other females into the shade.

Word must have got round, probably during tea breaks and lunch hours, in the form of nudges and winks indicating that it might be worth swinging by my desk to take a look, because, at around half past two, Douglas Kennedy, in his casual slacks (of a drab stone colour), open shirt (not a good style for a man of his age), and rather outdated slip-on shoes (trying too hard to be casual I think) came by and started loitering around talking to nearby staff members and trying to steal glances at me. I smirked to myself at first, but, after a while, it got to be a little too much like being leered at. Finally, he decided he wanted a closer look and walked right past me for a closer inspection.

'Naughty girl, Linda,' he said with a raised eyebrow and half-smile.

Not what I expected. And it was pretty ambiguous. Did he mean to give me an official warning about inappropriate clothing? Was he just making a joke? Or was this a deliberately sexual suggestive comment? Perhaps a bit of all three, I thought.

My friends tell me I was the talk of the office over the next few days, which rather pleased me, even if some of the talk was derisive. I didn't care; it was great to get back to the super-sexy-charged me for a day. But I did not want to undo all the good work I had done behaving myself in the past three months, so it was a return to the respectable retiring self again the very next day.

It came to the day before payday again, and a similar email was sent round the office from Douglas to remind us of the relaxation in the dress code. A few comments were made to me in jest, including one from that Troy character who said he was looking forward to seeing me tomorrow. I just tutted and ignored him.

However, it was harder to ignore the email I received about five minutes later, which came to me personally, direct from Douglas Kennedy: *'I hope I won't have to discipline you over your dress tomorrow. Douglas.'*

I fought back a blush and looked around nervously to see if anyone else had read it over my shoulder (no one had, thank goodness). Now I may have given his previous comment the benefit of the doubt, but this one *was* dodgy, distinctly dodgy. To be frank, I felt harassed. I was not in the least bit interested in an older man with no sense of modern style.

You see, I prefer them in their prime, between 25 and 35, and with a bit of energy and masculinity about them. It helps the performance if they've got that get-up-and-go, especially considering that I like it a bit rougher than most. I like being grabbed, manhandled, bitten, having my hair pulled. Nothing I had experienced up to then had turned me on more than giving one of those 'rag-doll' performances for a guy while he swings me around humping my pussy from whatever position he feels like posing me and holding me in next. Douglas just did not look like he had that in him.

I suppose the wise thing to do would have been to tone things down and avoid encouraging the little pervert. Perhaps I should have turned up the next day in a sweatshirt and a pair of baggy jogging bottoms.

Unfortunately, I'm not the sort to be intimidated or deterred, and so I rebelled. Next day, I chose an outfit in direct defiance of my lecherous boss: a short red tartan skirt even higher than the skirt I had worn before, some Oxford pumps, and a white low-cut top with no bra.

The reception as I walked in was unique, and very hard to describe. There was a kind of buzz about the place, even though nobody was saying anything. Is that possible? I don't know, it's the best I can do. Once again I felt delightfully wicked, very naughty and horribly self-serving. Strutting around the place gave me a lovely moist feeling in my white knickers and I found myself seriously thinking about breaking my sexual fast (it would have been easy to lure someone in for a quickie after work, the way some of the office talent were feasting their eyes on me).

Soon enough, though, Douglas came sharking around the place. This time he perched himself on my desk while I was working. I glanced at him, and then back at my screen.

'Hello, Linda,' he said.

'Hi there,' I replied.

I noticed him glancing down at my legs. They were hardly going to be missed; even tucked under the desk the sight of bare flesh would have caught and drawn the eye.

'Nice to see you making the effort on our dress-down days, Linda, you look very smart,' he commented, and then stood up and continued his rounds.

I thought it very strange, I must say, and totally at odds with the tenor of his email the previous day; the safe language, the lack of suggestion, the briefness of the encounter, were all most unexpected.

Ten minutes later, I was snapped back like a rubber band when I received another email. It came from Douglas, and was obviously written the moment he had wended his way back to his desk. It read: '*You really are a most disobedient girl, and this is your last official warning. If you dress inappropriately again I will take disciplinary measures. Douglas.*'

What a psycho. One minute he comes round all sweetness and light, the next he starts harassing me and talking to me like a schoolgirl. I really didn't know what to make of it and I spent much of the afternoon scouring the personnel manual for details of the disciplinary procedure. There wasn't an awful lot about dress code, but what there was seemed to indicate that a casual warning was considered sufficient and that official procedures should only be invoked in extreme, long-term cases. I printed the relevant page for possible future reference, but was rather puzzled that he would not know that. Did he perhaps have some other meaning? Pervert.

I had rebelled once and Douglas's attitude had left me wanting to rebel again. I get this way when people start on me; I deliberately press their buttons to show them I'm not scared. If he was leering at me and making lewd comments at me I felt the best way forward was to make him jealous.

That's when Troy's luck changed.

He chose that moment to come by my desk on some work-related pretence, and spent the whole time waving a bit of paper and yapping about some customer's direct debit payment, and all the while he was just looking at my legs under the table and glancing at my cleavage. Never once did he look me in the eye.

Like I say, he got lucky. I would not normally have been in the mood to tolerate that level of ogling but, on this occasion, I let it pass; I had uses for him.

'I need your help, Troy. You want to go for a drink after work?' I asked.

He looked a little stunned.

'Erm, yeah, sure,' he agreed nervously.

I smiled and then leaned in towards him to whisper more quietly so that no colleague would hear. 'I'll be honest, I need your help to make someone jealous . . . but I'll make it worth your while.'

I winked at him and, rather surprisingly, he beamed like he had just won the Lottery. Troy was clearly so pleased to get some time with a sexy girl, he didn't care about the motive.

'See you at five,' I said as he drifted, trancelike, back to his desk. Poor lad must've had a semi for the rest of the afternoon.

The plan, to put you in the picture, was based on the knowledge that, as the senior manager, Douglas would be working a little later; he would therefore be leaving the office at around dusk while the streets were a little quieter, and certainly while none of our co-workers were about. The idea was, accidentally-on-purpose (as they say), to let Douglas see me snogging the face off Troy in the alleyway down the side of our building, thereby cocking a snook (or whatever the phrase is) at Douglas for his lecherous behaviour. The pathway is fenced off, has bushes along one side, a wall on the other, and runs parallel to the driveway into and out of the car park, and then around the back edge of the lot.

I met Troy at the door, to some raised eyebrows from colleagues, especially those still with bulges in their trousers from looking at me and wishing all day. We made our way to a nearby pub and I explained my intentions to Troy. I was afraid he might not like the idea of being my pawn, but as it happens he seemed to like the idea of kissing me so much that he didn't even question my weird behaviour.

I took a drink with him, and listened dutifully as he made his pitch to me (he obviously saw this as an opportunity to win me over), telling me how I was his sexual ideal, how I dressed with class and held myself with a respectable but sexual poise and that he could not keep his mind off me, etcetera, etcetera. I thanked him for his compliments and put an accepting hand on his forearm for comfort (it's not easy to confess your undying lust for a girl), but was careful not to offer him any hope beyond this evening's antics.

It was about time for Douglas to leave the office and I made Troy drain his beer before taking him by the hand down the alley. He followed, his eyes fixed on my tartan skirt and toned bare legs.

Peering through the wire fence and the patchy bushes, I could see Douglas's big silver car, so I knew we were on time. We stopped where a gap in the bushes provided a little alcove of privacy from the footpath, but which allowed full view of us, through the diamond mesh, from the car park. There was no sign of Douglas yet. There was no harm in getting started, so I put my arms around Troy's neck and kissed him.

His kiss was nervous at first, and his hands shaky, but soon he became warmer and more passionate. He drew me nearer to him, squeezing me into the bulge in his trousers. I glanced over Troy's shoulder as we kissed, hoping for a sign of the boss.

I had tried to tell myself this was simply a professional kiss, but my desperately hungry fanny had other ideas: she was juicing like a water melon. I don't think, given her four-month run of complete emptiness, that she had quite got the message about me not really fancying Troy. She can be like that sometimes. Often I've had to wait patiently while she fucks the cock of a guy who I didn't really fancy. The pity is that I'm attached to her and, when she gets an idea, sometimes I just have to follow.

My skimpy white panties were now drenched through and probably completely see-through. Perhaps Troy sensed the pheromones on the air, wafting up from my moisture-heavy underwear, but his hands began to wander – now his fingers were caressing the backs of my thighs just under the hem of my skirt.

I glanced over again, but no sign of Douglas. I should have pulled back with Troy at this point; it was only supposed to be nipping him, not giving him a feel, but my pussy pulled me forwards to rub herself, and her clitoris, on his thigh and by then I kind of forgot myself. We kissed and writhed like this for a little while. Troy was far too polite to go any further without prompting (he clearly wasn't the sort to just take me like I wanted), so rolling my eyes I reached back and guided his hands up onto the succulent flesh of my buttocks. I glanced over his shoulder again but there was no sign of Douglas.

I wiggled my arse against Troy's hands and continued to rub myself on his leg, but he still needed encouragement. I reached back again and directed his fingers to hook under the back of my knickers.

He took the hint, pulling them to one side and tickling my sensitive anus with his middle finger. I arched my back to give access to my sopping pussy lips and thankfully he followed his cue, dipping his finger in the moistness and pressing into my hole with increasing circles until my entrance was opened.

'Ah, yes,' I whispered, as I reached down to his belt and fly. By now I had forgotten Douglas and even the possibility of being seen by passers-by.

His well-proportioned, circumcised penis was tenting his underpants and I reached in to liberate it, wanking it slowly. He nearly bent double from the sudden wave of pleasure.

I bent myself over, clawing the mesh of the fence for support and pointing my arse into the air. To my pleasure he took the hint this time, throwing my skirt up and pushing his cock-head against the soft wet entrance, knocking at the door. At last, some initiative from the far-too-gentlemanly Troy. He pressed his cock a couple of times to the slick inside part of my labia, until the well-defined, circumcised head popped inside. Finally, after four months, I was being fucked again, and my pussy gave a ripple of approbation to the concept, making my fingers tremble as they held onto the fence.

Troy lengthened his strokes and it felt good again to receive a penis where God intended. The danger of it all was adding to our excitement and Troy was going at it as fast as his reserved nature would allow him. My first complaint was that he was still politely holding my hips in his hands rather than slapping me or pulling my hair and that he was repeatedly telling me how beautiful I was, instead of telling me how much of a bitch I was for liking cocks up me. I could've asked him, I suppose, but if you have to ask it ruins the fantasy.

Still, despite the etiquette, I was getting it and getting it good and feeling better and better by the second, reaching a wonderful little plateau of delight as I felt the pumping and twitching of an ejaculation followed by the warmth of his spunk. He was one of those squeaky comers who gasp and whine rather than cry out. It was good, very good. It might even be good enough to get me through the next four months of celibacy, I thought.

I reached down as Troy withdrew, muttering to me how he'd never forget this, the best day of his life and all that usual needy stuff. I reached down to adjust my knickers again, and as I did so, I heard a car door shut and an engine start. I looked up.

Douglas was pulling away in his car some thirty yards away. I nearly swooned. He must have seen. I shrugged. So what if I had got a wee bit carried away and given slightly more of a demonstration than I had intended? The message to Douglas was the same, just louder.

'Thanks, Troy, you can go now,' I said to Troy's stunned face as I walked away. 'You can put that in your diary,' I added cruelly.

There were two emails waiting for me the next day: one from Troy professing undying love, which I deleted without fully reading; another, more distasteful, from Douglas: '*Last night's behaviour was sufficient grounds for dismissal, young lass. If there are any further misdemeanours I will take corrective action. Douglas.*'

I just did not know where the old fart was coming from here. If he was wanting to discipline me why not sack me? What's all this corrective action nonsense? I deleted the message with every intention of pushing his buttons again on the next payday, regardless of his threats.

As it happened, I did not have to wait that long. I had forgotten that not two weeks away was the mother of all dress-down days: 31 October. Sure enough, we all received a notice through our inboxes to say that costumed attire was encouraged and there would be prizes for the best outfits.

Hallowe'en. A licence to wear just about anything you wanted really, especially since the mentality that has recently been seeping across the Atlantic suggests that the ghosts and ghoulies theme was purely optional. I knew exactly the best way to defy Douglas and turn some heads once again.

The night before, I picked out a little white blouse I had, which was cropped at the tummy to display the navel. I rummaged around in the box in the loft containing my old clothes for my hockey skirt from school – it was navy blue with pleats that flared out, which makes it bounce as you walk, but its most important feature was that it was way too short for me. I also found my old school tie and squeaked with delight as I fished it from the corner of the box.

I then moved on to my older sister's old clothes hamper – she had kept all sorts of stuff from younger days claiming it would all come back in one day. I was looking for one item in particular – a pair of the knee stockings that had been so popular back in the mid-90s and with which she had made me insanely jealous every time she went out on the pull in them. I found a black pair (underneath an awful pair of trousers that had a matching skirt attached to them, yuk! Did we really wear these awful things?), and eagerly unrolled them to see if they had retained their shape and elasticity. Thankfully, they had. I came back down the extendable ladder and set about picking a pair of shoes to match the outfit, settling on a pair of very shiny high-heeled courts.

Before I went to bed I gave the ensemble a dry run and, putting my curly blonde hair into bunches and applying an unsubtle blue eyeshadow and red lipstick, I posed in front of the mirror. I looked a knockout. I had not bothered with knickers so far and enjoyed myself so much flashing my cute bum at the mirror that I decided not to employ any (it would be my little secret joke on Douglas; after all, knickers are not mentioned in the stupid personnel dress code). The teasing band of white flesh between the knee stockings and the skirt hem was the most tantalising piece of seduction ever designed and I could not wait to try it out.

Once again, heart racing and pussy trickling, I strutted into the office as the slutty schoolgirl, drawing the attention away from some very jealous ghosts, werewolves and vampyra who were clearly not best pleased that I had not bothered with the Hallowe'en theme at all. I did not care, I just relished being the belle of the ball again and set about making unnecessary journeys to the printer or the photocopier to tease as many guys as possible.

Again I was the talk of the corridors and staff areas and Douglas took no time to react to the rumours. There was no email or pretence of being on other business this time, he just strode out of his office, looking serious, and approached my desk.

'Linda, could I have a word with you in my office, please?' he said.

I looked at my friend at the desk across from me and she gave me one of those smirks. I responded with a suppressed smile.

I stood up and, curiously, Douglas gestured for me to lead (perhaps he wanted to ogle me as he followed). I wiggled and strutted defiantly to his office.

He closed the door behind us and I turned to face him.

'I am sorry but I find this mode of dress unacceptable,' he stated, walking around me towards his desk.

'Its just a bit of fun for Hallowe'en,' I answered, turning to follow him as he paced.

'What it is is the action of a little fucking tart,' he snapped, walking around me again and passing behind me.

I was shocked into silence. I was pretty sure that the personnel manual did not allow staff members to be verbally abused and my mouth gaped with astonishment.

'Yes, you heard me, you little fucking tart,' he repeated calmly.

I turned to confront him and saw his eyes looking down on me like I was a pet or a piece of furniture, emotionless, cold. I felt a shiver of pleasure in my tummy and nipples that I fought to ignore.

'Face the front,' he said sternly. His voice gave no room for negotiation and my face reddened with passion. I had a mind to scream and bawl at him and demand he speak to me in a civil fashion, and threaten to report him to his superiors. But my pussy trickled with the thought of actually obeying him. I even wondered if he would grab me and shag me the way I love so much. Barely believing I was doing it, I turned to the front.

'Good. Good little bitch. Now I cannot allow you to continue to work today dressed like that and I have arranged for you to be taken home.'

I listened to the words spoken behind me and I wondered how many other girls he had harassed and exploited in this way. I felt all sorts of distaste and pity for the dirty old man, but my pussy seeped with four months' worth of desire for a proper, rough poling and, do you know, I did not care in the least if it was this horrible drooling little pervert that gave it to me. In fact the idea of it being him was turning me on.

'Go and switch off your computer and then take your cheap little arse down to the car park,' he told me.

Without a thought I obeyed him again, shuffling red-faced back to my desk to log off my PC. I fended off whispered questions from my friends about what had happened, telling them I was being sent home to get changed. The rebel in me was loving the moment: the defiant walk-out. But my mind was really on what was to come. I made my way downstairs.

My sex felt wet and gooey, and my nerves buzzed with expectancy. I speculated wildly about what Douglas had planned for me. He was waiting by the rear entrance, looking every inch the sleazy middle-aged man I had him down for, in his open-necked shirt and slacks with slip-ons. He gestured me in the direction of his car. Like a harlot I deliberately wiggled for him, showing my compliance – whatever I thought about him, the chance that he might give me my kink overrode it.

Even the little things turned me on now – my legs quivered when he didn't bother to open the car door for me, instead climbing in his side without a word. I opened the door on my side to get in.

Douglas reached across the seat and grabbed my bushy pig-tails, gathering them into one hand, pulling my hair taut. I gasped with pleasure.

'Lift your skirt up before you sit down, bitch.'

I did it, gasping with pleasure as I felt the cold leather of the seat against my buttocks and pussy. I became very conscious of the wet patch I was leaving there. We drove away.

'Don't speak, and look straight ahead,' he ordered.

I loved being spoken to in this way, and I fought in vain to quell the urge to reply in the way that I did; it felt silly, but on saying it my stomach and loins buzzed with excitement: 'Yes, sir,' I said.

He drove me as I sat quietly juicing the seat. The excitement increased when, without a word, Douglas turned off the main road and the surroundings became more rural. It was only then I really believed he was going to fuck my hole, possibly even my holes, for me. The waiting was too much to bear.

Finally we pulled into a deserted gravel lay-by in a nature reserve and he stopped the car. I wondered how many other little tarts had had their hungry little pussies pummelled by Douglas here.

'Get out of the car, whore, and walk around to my side,' he said, without even looking at me.

'Yes, sir,' I answered.

By the time I had walked around, Douglas had opened his own door and was sitting with his legs out to the side, his feet now flat on the gravel. I stood by him, looking straight ahead.

He grabbed my hair again, just like before, and pulled my head down to his side until I lay face down over his knee. Again I gasped with pleasure as he lifted my hockey skirt to bare my knickerless arse to the fresh October air. I felt the skin goose on my buttocks. Douglas waited, probably admiring the sight of my legs in those kinky knee-stockings and that quivering bottom staring up at him.

I felt his rough manly hand caressing both cheeks before the spanking began. He knew what he was doing, sensitising my cheeks with soft touches before applying the force. I cried out in absolute ecstasy as the barrage of seven spanks fell on me and then once again I felt the soft caresses of his palm on my buttocks.

'Dirty little bitches must accept their punishments,' he whispered, barely audible over the autumn breeze.

'Yes, sir,' I said.

Another barrage fell upon me and the tremors ran through my pussy. I did not want them to die away.

'Please, more, sir,' I said.

He continued, goading me for liking it and spanking me, it seemed, endlessly as my genitals became more and more excited. The pleasure grew until it began to match the intensity felt during a fucking. I wondered if it were possible to come from being spanked like a dirty whore. I hoped so.

'Please, sir, more,' I begged.

He obliged. Telling me I was only good for cocks and spunk and that I had no other value to the world. It was exactly what I wanted to hear; I swear I could feel those imagined cocks and their spunk going into me as he leathered me and squeezed harder on my hair. Shamefully, but incredibly intensely, I came, screaming 'Please no, please no, please no' as the orgasm swept through me. I don't know why those words came to me. I continued to sob as he again caressed my buttocks and spanked me intermittently. I tried my best to use the lull to catch my breath.

Soon, I heard the electric window on the open door being operated and followed compliantly as I was lifted by my hair through the window. My feet fought desperately to find their footing on the gravel; I am not very tall. I stole a glance back to look at my arse which was a strawberry red, with some discernible finger marks on it. He spanked me for turning around.

I lay there, draped through the car door, waiting to be entered.

'Like you own me, like I'm worthless,' I said, not daring this time to turn around.

My soaking wet pussy offered no resistance to his first thrust, which ran me through, ball-deep, making it clear to me that no corner of my pussy was to remain unfucked.

'Take my cock, you little tart,' he said calmly and coldly, again gathering my hair in his fist. I groaned with pleasure.

His fucking was frantic, despite the calmness of his voice, and, before long, the choppy thrusts became longer and more forceful and were punctuated with spanks on my right buttock. I squeaked with pleasure at each one.

'Are you ready for my spunk, bitch?' he asked at last.

'Yes, sir,' I answered.

He asked me again

'Yes, sir, I need it,' I replied.

'Yes you do, yes you do,' he replied, before pumping me full with cream. I savoured the throbbing and the warm wash of semen up inside me. It is a wondrous sensation and I live for it.

I heard him zip up almost immediately.

'Get back in the car, bitch,' he said.

That was the phrase that excited me the most: even post-coital, he was still treating me like dirt. It gave a realness to the fantasy that thrilled me to the core.

I did not have to be told to lift my skirt up before sitting down, I did it without thinking. As we drove away, I felt his spunk trickling down to mingle with the wet patch I had left earlier.

– *Linda, Renfrewshire, Scotland*

Playing with the Computer

'What do you think, Kate?' Robert asked me. It was a picture of my backside, bent over and showing the tight ring of my anus and the long split of my sex lips. The cheeks of my bum were smooth and lightly tanned. The anus was a crinkled hole – but open slightly as though a finger had just been inside. The cluster of hairs was darker nearer the lips, as though they were wet. Because Robert had just installed a new TFT monitor for his PC the image filled all twenty inches of the screen and looked huge and excessive. The sight made me desperate to feel him inside me.

'It's impressive,' I said. I was talking about the picture and not arrogantly boasting about how good my bottom looked. Robert's new digital camera, and all the other computer equipment he used, always made me feel a little wondrous. I grew up in a time when photographs were taken on rolls of film over a few weeks. They were then sent away for developing and returned two months or more after the event. Nowadays, within moments of Robert pressing the shutter release on his camera, any photograph could be displayed on his PC. He could also print out a hard copy on glossy paper if he wanted, although that would take a few minutes longer. It really was impressive. And the picture on the screen really did make me desperate for some action. I rubbed my bare thighs together and implored him with my gaze. 'It's very impressive,' I repeated.

'I wonder if everyone else will be equally impressed?' Robert asked.

I stared at him in horror. I had consented to have the private picture taken on the condition that no one else – *absolutely no one else* – would see it. 'Don't you dare,' I told him. 'Don't you dare send that out to anyone.'

'Too late,' he chuckled. 'It's already been sent.'

My stomach plummeted. I felt sick, embarrassed and shamefully excited. The arousal that already held my body went into a momentary overdrive. I had to hold my breath for fear of suffering an orgasm on the spot. When we had discussed my mild interest in exhibitionism, Robert had suggested the digital camera could be the answer to the most depraved of my fantasies. I had thought he was just looking for an excuse to buy the latest boy-toy, but his arguments about anonymity and convenience had caught my interest. Ultimately my sexual fantasy was to be with another couple, experiencing another man and watching another woman having sex with Robert. But, to build up to that, I wanted to boost my confidence and assure myself I would be desired if I made myself available. Robert's suggestion offered me the chance to secretly flash myself to selected members of our social circle. Whenever we discussed that fantasy the muscles inside my cunt twitched hungrily. However, I had never thought he would do something so bold without my permission.

I calmed down a little after Robert told me about the security measures he had taken to maintain our anonymity. He'd sent the picture from a 'disposable email address' that could never be linked to either of us. The photograph included no personal information or identifying marks. Assuaging my fears, he explained that a selection of our friends would simply receive an unexpected picture of an unidentified backside. 'Some might respond,' he laughed. 'Most will ignore it. But, unless one of them recognises you from that particular view, your secret is safe.'

'Who did you send it to?' I asked.

'Derek, Tony, Tom, Colin, Rupert, Nelson, Blakey . . .'

He continued to list names while I came close to weeping with excitement and horror. Some of them were little more than acquaintances, names from the Christmas card list who we saw maybe once or twice a year. Others were the male halves of couples whom we met with more frequently. These were mates from the pub, closer friends that we'd kept over the years, and the names of some people who lived on our street. A few of those that he mentioned were Robert's closest work colleagues. Most distressingly, three of them were people from the office where I worked.

'Robert!' I gasped. 'Why did you do it?'

He pulled me close and placed his hand between my legs. I was still naked after the impromptu photo shoot. His fingers fell against the wetness of my cunt and easily slid inside. I was stunned by the coolness of his hand, and then realised it only felt cold against the heat inside me. He pushed the fingers deeper and I gasped again. 'That's why I did it,' he admitted. 'I knew this would get you horny. But I knew you would chicken out if I allowed you the chance to back down.'

I started to protest but he stopped me with a kiss. His fingers continued to slide in and out. He had sparked my arousal so deeply I struggled to unzip him and guide his swollen cock towards my cunt. My desperate need to be filled was like a fever.

'No,' he said, arrogantly pushing me away.

Bewildered, I stared at him.

'You've got to thank me the right way,' he grinned. 'And I'm sure you know how to do that.' He spun his chair a little and pointed to the floor. As soon as I understood what he wanted I knelt over his lap and took his erection in my mouth.

The flavour heightened my arousal. I sucked on him, taking him between my lips and stroking his throbbing length with my tongue. I don't normally find a lot of excitement in blowing my husband but, that evening, the act was exceptionally arousing. My fingers found my clitty while I sucked on him and I thought there was a chance we could come at the same time. I didn't think it would matter that much. Robert's arousal was as intense as mine and I was grudgingly enjoying the way he dominated the situation. Once he'd come I expected he would demand that I suck him hard again so he could come a second time inside my cunt, or somewhere else. That thought, and the pressure of my middle finger on my clitty, was enough to take me nearly to the point of climax. My need to be filled was close to being an obsession.

'Hold that pose,' Robert instructed.

I glanced up in time to be blinded by the flash from the camera. My shock hadn't completely disappeared and my eyes hadn't adjusted from the glare by the time I saw the image appear on his new TFT screen. My face was clearly visible. Robert's cock filled my mouth. My lips were silvered with smears of his pre-come. I stared at the image aghast, and prepared to tell him it was too revealing to be sent to anyone.

'*You've got mail.*'

The sound of his computer advising him about the email made us both glance at the screen. Robert clicked the button on his mouse twice and I watched his eyes open wide with surprise. It was good to be sharing the computer with him. We had spent too many nights apart with him sitting in solitude in front of his boy-toy while I kept myself amused in a nearby room with only the TV set or a book for companionship. This adventure in exploring our fantasies was truly exciting and I felt sure Robert would satisfy my needs before the night was over.

'Someone was fast to respond,' he muttered.

I glanced at the screen and saw a huge picture of a gaping vagina. There was so much pink and purple skin on show that it took me a moment to work out what I was seeing. The lips were glossy and smothered with a lather of white semen. The liquid dripped from the dark centre of the picture and I understood I was looking at a freshly used cunt. I trembled. 'Who the hell is that from?' I muttered.

Robert shook his head. 'Someone else using a disposable email address,' he said. There was a nuance of frustration in his voice. 'Damn! We have some sneaky friends.'

I could have pointed out that he was the sneaky one who had started using disposable and untraceable email addresses, but I knew this wasn't the right time to antagonise Robert. He was having fun at the expense of my shame and humiliation but I always worried he might one day cross the line beyond what was acceptable. I hadn't been wholly sure it was wise for him to send my picture out to our friends and neighbours, yet he had done it anyway. There was always the danger that, in his endeavours to show his full understanding of the technology, he would do something that transgressed my limits. I pointed at the screen and asked, 'Why has someone sent you that picture?'

'One of our friends is playing the game with us,' he chuckled. He was enjoying himself but I think he was frustrated he hadn't seen this coming. Pointing at the screen, Robert said, 'You're currently looking at the come-filled pussy of one of our friends or neighbours.'

I put a hand over my mouth to conceal my surprise. I was shocked and aroused. I immediately understood this response was similar to what our circle of friends would be experiencing when they saw the picture of my bare bottom. Whoever the woman was, there was no chance of guessing her identity. She had no hairs on her sex and I didn't know any of our friends so well as to identify them from a photo like that one. If there had been blonde, brunette or auburn curls down there, it would have narrowed the options and I might have had a chance of guessing her identity. As it was, I knew I would spend the rest of my week staring at our mutual friends, while wondering if I had seen a picture of their come-filled pussy. The thought made me shiver.

'They've added a message,' Robert mumbled. Reading from the screen, he said, 'Nice arse. Great-looking pussy. Thank you for sharing. Here's a cream pie as my way of saying thanks.'

I was blushing and trembling.

Robert grinned like an idiot.

Someone had seen my most intimate parts and written back with an endorsement of approval. I realise it's probably shallow to get satisfaction from such praise but I couldn't help feeling boosted by the coarse compliment. 'What's a cream pie?' I asked.

Robert touched the centre of the screen, his fingers sliding over the lips of the woman's cunt and

136

indicating the semen that dripped out of her. I swallowed, sick with excitement when I thought that was how his finger would look if it was genuinely touching another woman.

'It's a slang term for a pussy dripping with come.'

I wrinkled my nose. The phrase was vulgar and disgusting. But it heightened my arousal. My need to have his length was suddenly insatiable. I desperately wanted to feel him inside me and end the evening with a passionate bout of lovemaking.

But I could see Robert was having more fun with the computer. He was clearly anxious to take the game to the next level. I didn't know if he wanted to fuck me, photograph me, or do both so that we had a picture of our own cream pie. But I did know his enjoyment had little in common with my immediate needs.

I opened my mouth to tell him what I wanted.

'*You've got mail.*'

'Another of your adoring fans,' Robert mused as he studied the message and attachment. He laughed dryly and said, 'This is from Tom. You've certainly made an impression on him.'

I glanced at the picture on the screen. It showed a huge and swollen erection. The long length was held in a tight fist that had made the mushroom-shaped end dark purple.

'This is what your picture did to me,' Robert read.

I shivered. 'How do you know that's from Tom?'

'Silly bugger used his own email address. Not very discreet, was it?'

My stomach churned. I would never be able to look at Robert's friend again without thinking about the picture of the huge erection and knowing that the sight of my bum had caused him so much excitement. I felt sure, the next time we met, I would blush so severely he would know it was my photograph he had seen. The thought stirred the muscles inside my cunt. My fingers strayed back to my clitty. It wasn't the full penetration I needed, but the gentle caress of my hand against my lips did promise more satisfaction than my husband offered.

'Should I send this photograph to our respondents?' Robert asked. His earlier picture filled the screen. This was the one that showed my face as I devoured Robert's cock.

'You can't send that!' I shrieked. 'They'd know who I am.'

'I can edit it a little. Blur the focus on your eyes and . . .'

'No!'

His mischievous grin grew wider. I could see him doing something with the mouse. Before he had a chance to send anything against my wishes the computer interrupted him.

'*You've got mail.*'

Robert clicked three buttons and then whistled his approval. 'Now that's raised the ante,' he mumbled.

I put a hand over my mouth in surprise. This was a picture of a woman's large bare breasts. They were round and fat and swollen. Coffee-coloured areolae defined the centre of each breast and hard nipples punched out at the camera. But it wasn't the breasts that made me gasp, it was the fact that the breasts were being touched by *two* cocks. 'Who the hell is that from?'

Robert's grin faltered. 'It's from someone who knows how to set up a disposable email address. Sneaky bastards.'

I stared at the picture, shocked that someone within our social circle had done something so daring. My arousal was momentarily tempered by jealousy. This woman had two cocks at her disposal and I only had Robert and his overriding interest in the computer. The injustice was sharp enough to hurt and I was desperate to know who she was. Studying the picture, looking for clues from the glimpse of background behind the woman, I racked my brains to put a face above the top of the photograph. Something in the image suggested that if I only concentrated a little harder, I would be able work out who she was.

'It gets worse,' Robert frowned. I glanced at him uneasily. His tone was ominous and I detected the suggestion of an apology in his voice. Glancing down at his groin I could see his erection had dwindled to a sliver of its former size. 'This picture is from someone who's guessed who we are.'

I felt physically sick. I glanced at the email that had accompanied the picture and read the message. '*Katy? I'd no idea you did this too.*'

'Damn,' Robert mumbled. The picture disappeared as he clicked on various elements of the email message searching for properties, protocols and other computer-related clues that might reveal the identity of the sender. I watched his interest in me evaporate and realised there would be no chance of satisfying myself with Robert that evening. I took a final glance at the remnants of the picture on the screen, picked up my clothes from the floor, and told him I was going to call a friend.

'Karen?' I said, two minutes later, whispering into my mobile phone. 'I loved your picture.'

'Likewise, Katy,' she giggled. Karen is the only person who ever calls me Katy. 'Colin and Tony both got a lot from seeing yours, although I expect you could see that much.'

My stomach churned. I'd seen Colin and Tony's erections. Colin was Karen's husband. Tony was a workmate who shared an office with Robert and Colin. I had no idea that Tony and Karen and Colin did the things that were suggested in that picture. But I was delighted to think their erections had been hardened by the sight of my bare backside. My heart trembled and the muscles inside my cunt went into a liquid convulsion. 'Are they both with you now?'

She sounded excited. 'Of course. That's how we were able to take the picture. Are you two thinking of coming over here?'

I lowered my voice to a whisper and glanced towards the closed door of Robert's computer room. 'I'll come over,' I decided quickly. 'But Robert won't be able to make it. He's busy playing with the computer.'

– Kate, Yorkshire, UK

Out of the Closet

Aunt Emma is shopping in the city and won't be back for at least three hours. It is just after 2 p.m. and I stand before her bedroom door, my heart pounding, my mouth dry, my cock so hard it hurts.

It's Saturday afternoon. I've been in my Aunt's house for less than twenty-four hours and already I am overwhelmed by the desire that has come to dominate my life so absolutely over the last two years. Tomorrow is my eighteenth birthday and I have decided to celebrate early.

My mother is due to arrive later tonight, returning from a business trip. Tomorrow, my sister will return from university. It will be a simple family occasion: my divorced mother, my widowed Aunt, my older sister and me, the only son, nephew and brother.

I think of my father briefly. I haven't seen him for nearly three years. I feel a familiar shame as I ponder what he would make of the son he left behind, the son he had always seen as disappointingly effeminate. The son who is now trapped inside a powerful, utterly irresistible and deeply sexual attraction to the various intricate and delicate trappings of femininity and to what I have come to understand as a very real and powerfully erotic thing called the Feminine.

My father had recognised the early signs of what, in moments of true despair, he would refer to as my 'strangeness': my dislike of boys' games and activities, the rough and tumble of 'a boy's life'. Then there had been my lack of male friends and my always rather effeminate demeanour, a fact made more disturbingly real by my slight physical build and my soft, girlish features. Then he had left, without announcement or plan. He had gone to work one morning and never come back. And, ever since, my obsession has grown steadily into one single and very fundamental desire: the desire to dress in female clothing.

This desire has never been fully realised. However, I have spent many secret hours during my mother's frequent business trips investigating the silken scented secrets of her bedroom, educating myself in the astonishing variety of fabrics and designs that inhabit the soft, sensual and always so welcoming world of the Feminine.

I remember being alone in the holy space that is my mother's room, the temple where I first worshipped the Feminine. Here I have experienced a fierce and utterly unforgiving sexual pleasure, a pleasure so powerful that even the thought of its suppression is impossible. As my hands have passed nervously and hungrily over her most intimate satins and silks, it has felt as if my heart were about to explode. On sex-charged afternoons and evenings, I have slipped open her underwear drawers with a sense of terrible guilt, a dreadful fear of discovery and an all-pervasive, utterly inescapable elation. The sight of her carefully ironed and neatly stacked panties is enough to induce a moan of terrible aching pleasure and an erection like a burning metal torch. I have held a pair of lace-frilled white silk panties to my face, inhaled their strangely suggestive perfume and felt a new world of sensual possibilities open up before me.

Then there have been the even more intense delights of her pantyhose. Kept in the lower drawers are piles of tights and stockings, mostly tan- and grey-coloured, but also black and white, and even more exotic colours – red, blue, pink. Here I have experienced a profound ecstasy and discovered the strongest and most unforgiving of my sex-fuelled fascinations. Nothing has ever aroused me more than the feel of soft sheer nylon. Indeed, since my hands first touched the soft second skin of my mother's tights and stockings, I have seen the world through a fetishistic film of semi-transparent nylon. I have plunged hot shaking hands into a sea of soft nylon and entered a word of indescribable physical pleasure that has often resulted in an automatic and devastating orgasm, a giant coming stimulated only by the sight of this most potent and beautiful symbol of the Feminine.

My explorations have included many other aspects of my mother's gorgeous, elegant attire: her erotically varied selection of foundation wear, including panty girdles and a number of panty corselettes, elastane-walled prisons for a beautifully generous figure; her many elegant brassières, each designed to contain in a soft yet firm embrace a truly impressive and beautifully shaped bosom; a variety of silk slips and petticoats; a vast array of stylish dresses designed for the mature yet highly contemporary figure; a carefully chosen and maintained collection of shoes, all heeled and designed to accentuate long, statuesque, perfectly shaped legs sheathed in sheer nylon to maximum giddying effect.

Yet never, in all of my erotic expeditions, have I actually tried any of these garments on. Fear of discovery and the shame such exposure could inspire are far too strong for me to take any risk greater than idle caresses and worshipful kisses; an ecstatic but also relatively safe burial in the secret world of my mother's glorious and proudly displayed femininity.

But then there is my Aunt. My mother's junior by five years, a woman in her late 40s. Like my mother, a striking red-lipped brunette with large, soul-melting, honey-brown eyes. Slightly slimmer, but still pleasantly plump, Aunt Emma shares my mother's commitment to classic femininity in all its forms and, as I have entered my late-teenage years, her visits have become a source of significant sexual excitement, a fact she is clearly aware of, and which she has sought to exploit in a rather obvious manner my mother could not fail to notice, but which she has never openly acknowledged.

For her visits to our house, Aunt Emma always ensures that she is 'appropriately attired', dressed in a way guaranteed to tease my puberty-addled mind and – more importantly – body. She sits across from me in the living room, following a tight and disturbingly intimate welcoming embrace that always finds my face buried deep in her large scented bosom. Typically, she is dressed in a knee-length black or check skirt, virtually always black tights, always heeled shoes and normally a tight black or white nylon sweater with a jacket that in some careful way matches the skirt. Yes, she looks stunning, with her thick black hair bound in a tight bun by a diamond clasp, her lips blood-red, her eyes filled with a darkly erotic fire. And I am helpless before her, my eyes fighting to avoid hungry glances at her perfect ample form, my mouth struggling not to drop idiotically open in sex-fuelled awe.

Then, slowly, while talking to my mother, she crosses her legs. A casual gesture, done almost unconsciously, but driven by a teasing intent: to arouse and, in some way, to shame me into the confession of a helpless and furious desire. As her sheer black nylon-wrapped legs cross and rub together a strange, static electric whisper always echoes across the room and I fight a gasp of perverse delight. Inevitably, the skirt rides up over her knees to reveal a torturing hint of firm muscular thigh sealed tightly in dark hose and the toes of her stiletto-heeled black patent leather court shoes point down towards the ground as if identifying the place I should be – at her feet, worshipping, begging to be forever enslaved. And maybe, just for a second, her knowing, slightly contemptuous gaze meets mine and I see she knows everything there is to know about me and my secret kinky desires.

And now, as I walk into my Aunt's bedroom, it is as if her eyes are still upon me, seeing every move. For a moment, I wonder if there is a camera in the room, a camera through which all my subsequent actions will be recorded and revealed. An absurd thought, but one which sends a quiver of almost delicious fear down my spine.

The room is slightly smaller than my mother's and is dominated by a large double bed, an island of erotic promise covered in cream silk sheets. Surprisingly there is little other furniture, just a simple white bedside table and, by a far wall, a long, very beautiful dressing table dominated by a large oval mirror. The dressing table is made from a sparkling white wood and the mirror frame is gold. Along the long flat surface of the table are a vast array of items of female make-up and preparations and I stare at them with curious and hungry eyes. Yet it is the large double doors built into the wall just beyond the dressing table that ultimately draws my gaze away. This, I know, is the large walk-in closet that contains all my

Aunt's clothes. This is the cave of delights I have come in search of.

Each step now is a nervous challenge. I walk to the bed and place the black plastic bag I am carrying upon it. Then I turn back to the closet. As I walk towards the closet doors, I feel my heart speed up and a thick film of sticky sweat seep through the always disturbingly soft and pale skin of my face. I rub the hot damp palms of my hands against my thighs and feel an embarrassing fear grip my heart. My erection suddenly dies and I feel my balls shrivel to nothing inside my underpants. For a few seconds, I am aware of the terrible risk I am taking. For a few seconds I imagine being fully dressed, for the first time ever, intricately and carefully feminised. Then I imagine exposure: before my Aunt, my mother, my sister. The simple horror on their faces. The contempt and disgust. Then, once again, there is the face of my father, a face filled not with anger, but with a strangely resigned satisfaction, as if he were saying 'I always knew this was what you were'. Then, with an equal suddeness, fear turns to anger. I feel something like rage wash over me and then, defiantly, I step forwards. Yes, he always knew. And I have always known: not just what I am, but that there will never be any escape from this dark, unforgiving and so desperately pleasing essence.

I turn the elegant gold-coloured handles of the closet doors and pull them open. Momentarily, I am facing a teasing blackness, an unseen potential. Then an electric light flickers desperately, rapidly. For a few seconds it seems the light is broken and a strange clicking sound, like a fly buzzing deep in the electrical element, fills the darkness. But then, miraculously, there is an explosion of light and the secrets of my beautiful Aunt Emma are finally revealed.

I am looking down a corridor between two rows of clothing. Beneath each row are metal racks filled with shoes. And at the end of the corridor there appears to be two more closet doors – a closet within a closet!

I step nervously into the corridor. The sweet, erotic scent of roses fills the cool air. The right row is made up almost entirely of blouses and, after maybe twenty or so, a further collection of skirts. The left row is exclusively dresses, a striking collection of intensely feminine and very stylish female attire, each betraying the beautiful, intelligent and highly sexual personality of my amazing Aunt.

I draw to a halt in the middle of the corridor. I run my hands across the gloriously erotic fabrics of the blouses, the feel of silk and satin and expensive, electric Indian cotton. I gasp with a familiar soul-imprisoning pleasure. All fear and trepidation is lost in the immediacy of a furious arousal. Suddenly my balls are bulging and my cock is rock hard, pressing with a savage male strength against the harsh, ugly fabric of my jeans, almost demanding to be encased in these wondrous feminine fabrics.

One blouse takes my kinky fancy: an exquisitely cut white silk number with a high wide lace-frilled collar. I lift its silver hanger from the long thick pole that is the spine of the right rack and then hold it before me, my eyes drinking in every fascinating, elegant, intricate detail of its gorgeous design. I remember this one from my Aunt's visits. I remember her slowly, gracefully slipping out of a tweed jacket and turning to face me on a warm July afternoon a year ago.

'You should visit me, Chris. Give Lucy some time to herself. You're always welcome.'

I had nodded weakly, struck dumb by her beauty and by the thought of being alone with her, in her home, in the heart of her spectacular, erotic universe.

I hold the blouse before me and remember the way it had seemed to hold her large, perfectly formed breasts in a gentle embrace of expensive Italian silk, to tease and torment her body as much as it had (and is) teasing and tormenting mine. I feel sick with need. I must have this wonderful piece of female clothing next to my body.

I hang the blouse so that it is draped across the edges of a number of the other still-hanging blouses, then I go in search of the rest of my outfit for this first changing.

As I walk the narrow corridor between the rows, my eyes now bathing in the erotic perfection of my Aunt's collection of dresses and skirts, I feel a powerful sense of contentment. The fear and nerves pass as the reality of dressing sets in. Being surrounded by the objects of my most intense and prolonged desire has an immediately calming effect. I feel like an actor finally assuming a role after waiting nervously at the stage's shadowed edge.

I run my hands along the wall of soft feminine fabrics created by the row of dresses. Like the blouse, I find myself remembering my Aunt in a number of them. They still seem to contain her intimate warmth. The trace of her scent, the unique blend of expensive perfume and the muskier, more exotic odours of her body, is more real, and still lingers on some of the dresses. I press my face into them and breathe deeply. My cock presses harder into my jeans. I moan loudly and freely, my desire frustrated, angry and desperate.

I reach the skirts and pause. A more careful eye is turned upon them. Just as the dresses and the blouses reveal my Aunt's deliberate taste for the aggressively feminine, so the skirts reveal her taste for the subtly provocative. She is 46, yet still very beautiful. Her body, amply formed, even plump, is an object of always helpless erotic interest for any male who comes into contact with or sight of her. And often the first things they cannot help but notice, the things that attach the hook of need deep into the sexual consciousness, are her long, so long, statuesque legs. Legs always carefully sealed in the sheerest nylon hose and brought to a perfect sado-erotic conclusion by high heels. Legs that demand display and the helpless adoration of male eyes. Legs revealed by carefully designed and chosen skirts, whose shape and length betray confidence and style in equal measure.

Most are above knee height, one or two slightly more modest. But it is one of the shortest that draws my fetishist's helpless gaze. A black-and-white check mini-skirt, a skirt I have never seen her in, but imagine her filling with a gasp of dark sexual craving.

I take it from the rack and hold it against my body. Suddenly, for a mind-bending moment, I can hardly breathe. My heart pounds louder and harder than ever; my knees weaken and threaten to collapse beneath the weight of my feverish desire. I run my hands over the soft, yet also slightly rough material of the skirt, a strange sensual paradise that in some way symbolises this first, much anticipated dressing, this breaking into reality of an intense and extended sexual fantasy fuelled by inescapable inclination and the secret journeys into my mother's far less exotic and extensive wardrobe.

I place the skirt by the blouse and ponder their aesthetically correct relationship. Yes, they will look good together, on me.

After the skirt, I consider the rows of beautiful, elegant and always very sensual footwear. Soon I am on my knees considering the vast array with wide sex-stained eyes, my cock digging into my lower stomach like a metal pole.

My Aunt's attraction to heels is obvious and, given her beautiful legs, logical. Before me is a gorgeous, gleaming army of mostly stiletto-heeled mules, court shoes and sandals. Some I recall from her visits, others are new to my tormented gaze, and some inspire genuine gasps of surprise and admiration. For it seems my Aunt is not beyond genuinely outrageous foot-wear when the mood takes her. One pair of black patent leather court shoes with stunning five-inch heels particularly takes my fancy, and I find myself lifting them from the angled metal rests with shaking hands and the slightest sense of disappointment for I know this is the one item of hers that I cannot feel against my own body. No matter how much I desire to be consumed by femininity and thus to become truly feminine, there is no denying the fact of my male physique. While I am, by male standards, slight in my overall build, I have the usual problems faced by most transvestites: big feet and hands. Although these two inescapable physical realities can be disguised, they cannot be overcome; my feet will just not fit into these gorgeous shoes, they will not fit into any of my Aunt's incredible shoes. But I have come prepared. In the plastic bag on the bed there is a shoe box and in the box are a pair of specially ordered black patent leather court shoes. Shoes ordered via an internet site using a tortuous cash transaction agreed after lengthy email correspondence. Shoes that I had pretended to my mother were new training shoes bought with money from my part-time job in a local book store, training shoes that were actually bought a few days before the elegantly wrapped, suspicious looking parcel had arrived! Yes, having had two months' notice of my visit, I have been able to prepare properly.

Lost in the grip of fetish sex heat, I worship my Aunt's shoes with a helpless intensity. I press my lips to the gleaming tips of each of the toes; I press the inside soles, made from curving, tan-coloured and no doubt very expensive Italian leather, to my nose and breathe in the intimate aroma of soft warm leather and a hint of female sweat. This dark animal odour inspires immediate visions of my splendid, gorgeous Aunt walking through our house, each heeled step part of an erotic ballet of feminine perfection that had often forced me to run to my bedroom and masturbate furiously, crying out her name into the eternal black void of earth-shuddering orgasm, hot, thick come, my secret offering to her, shooting in spasmodic eruptions high into the air and then splashing against my stomach and chest. I remember the precise wiggle of her hips and the gentle swaying of her large curvaceous backside stretched tight against a suitably sexy skirt, a swaying demanded and created by the sensual counterbalance at the heart of walking in heels.

I gasp with an angry, bottomless frustration and place the shoes back on the rack. With tense, shaking hands, I lower my metal fly zipper and tease my long, hard, boiling cock from my underpants. It rises through the gap of my fly and demands immediate release. I imagine the spunk splashing against these beautiful, perfect shoes. I begin to masturbate, tears of need filling my eyes. I must come! But also, more importantly, I must dress! A terrible wave of anger and frustration crashes over me as I manage to restrain this appallingly urgent need and replace my tortured sex.

I climb to my feet, my knees weak, a thick sweat of effort and struggle covering my face. Then I stagger towards the second set of closet doors at the very end of this so-pleasantly decorated corridor.

As I open this second set of doors, I know I have come close to ruining everything. My pounding heart is filled with fear and self-contempt. All of this could have been destroyed by weakness!

Behind the second set of doors is not another corridor leading to some fetish Narnia, but two tall parallel towers of drawers and a smaller wardrobe space containing a truly delightful selection of lingerie and foundation wear. I stare at the array of petticoats and slips – all silk – in a range of colours, but mostly white, black and red, in a darkly aroused astonishment and then run my hands through them. Warm, excited flesh meets a mist of pure silk and I cry out my helpless unyielding desire.

My eyes travel beyond the slips and petticoats to an amazing collection of foundation garments. Hanging from a variety of specially designed hangers are at least eight panty girdles and four panty corselettes. I imagine my Aunt's ample form imprisoned in one of these sensual straitjackets of feminine restriction and swoon with pleasure. Like the slips and petticoats, they too are presented in a variety of colours, again mostly black and white. I take one of the panty girdles from the metal rack and run my hands over its shimmering elastane surface. I place it by the skirt and blouse and then return to the drawers. I open a drawer at random and gasp with delight. Before me are two rows of beautiful silk panties, all white, all beautifully embroidered with precise rose patterns and frilled with French lace at the waist and legs. I take out one pair and it is as if my hands have descended into a stream of liquid silk. I place the panties with the other clothing and then add one of the white silk slips, the vision of my changing sharpening in my mind with each new gorgeous addition.

I open a drawer in the second tower and find myself looking at a series of rows of carefully folded nylon stockings, all black. A thought crosses my mind and I return to the opposite tower of drawers. I open the drawer beneath the one containing the wonderful white panties and discover yet more panties, their design almost exactly the same as the ones above, but these coloured light pink. Further exploration of this tower reveals that each drawer contains a number of pairs of the same type of panties, each drawer a different colour! The obsessive care and attention applied to this intimate storage is both disturbing and arousing!

I return to the 'stocking tower' and discover drawer after drawer of sexy, expensive, finely styled hose – stockings and tights. I moan with a dreadful, utterly uncontrollable pleasure and run my hands across this sheer nylon cornucopia. I am in fetish heaven!

I extract two pairs of nylon tights. First, a semi-opaque, tan-coloured pair, and then a much sheerer, black pair. I carry them to the other clothes, teased to tears by an almost helpless love, as if transporting holy relics of an external and cosmic desire. I place them by the skirt and swallow down a terrible urge to cry out in semi-orgasmic pleasure. I know I could spend all day here exploring these wondrous delicate secrets of my Aunt's dazzling femininity, but time is of the essence and I am on a mission years in the making.

I take the clothes from the rack and then go back out into the bedroom. I place each item neatly on the silk-sheeted bed, creating a strange feminine form by placing the skirt beneath the blouse and the tights beneath the skirt, with the slip, girdle and panties in a separate arrangement.

Then the first stage of the dressing begins. My heart pounds against my chest with fear and furious arousal. This is surely the moment of no return. As I remove my jacket, I know I am stepping into a world I will never leave, that this is the next step towards my full feminisation, my all-powerful and permanent consumption by the great and irresistible power of the Feminine.

Within a few minutes, I have stripped down to my underpants. Now, more than ever before, I am aware of my male physique. My long hard cock strains over the top of the black cotton and presses into the pit of my slight, almost perfectly flat stomach. I run my hand across its hot angry length and gasp loudly, the sex ache deep in the heart of me, a need so profound that it has consumed every inch of my physical being.

Looking down at the bed, at the beautiful, elegant and deeply erotic clothing of Aunt Emma, I feel, once again, a sense of happiness. Here, I am becoming the person I have always wanted to be; here, I am finding complete self-realisation.

I remove the underpants and watch my crimson cock pop upwards with a savage determination. This is all there is and can ever be.

I step out of the underpants and lean forwards, my hands shaking once again. I take the soft, firm panty girdle from the bed and press it against my cock. I cry with pleasure and agonised expectation. Then, my heart beating like an insane toy drum, I step into the girdle and slowly, with a care that is both caution and ignorance, draw it up my legs.

I notice the light, thin layer of golden-coloured hair that covers my legs and feel a sense of disappointment and fraud. Here is the brutal physical confession of a masculinity that I have always felt uncomfortable with, a masculinity that is invading the truth I am trying so very hard to reveal. Eventually, my legs will be shaved, they will be silken smooth; eventually I will be the she-male of my dreams. Yet the journey to making that dream a reality is a long one, and it begins now.

I pull the tight elastane front of the girdle over my rampant aching sex and feel the boiling, furiously hard sex organ pushed back and held firm in the most feminine of embraces. I haul the rest of the girdle over my always pert backside and up around my waist. Then I am lost in a strange detached space of pure masochistic ecstasy. A feeling of intense and joyous envelopment consumes me: this is the first amazing step towards my debut transformation.

I run my hands over the panty girdle, I feel its taught second skin pressing so precisely against my backside, shaping and re-shaping, creating an ideal feminine contour. Yet this is just the beginning. Next, there are the astonishing delights of the tights. I pick up the tan-coloured pair and feel a shiver of fetishistic delight shoot through my body. I stretch one of the long, electric-soft legs against my arm and feel the warm scented nylon tease the sex-sensitised skin of my arm. I feel a charge of powerful sexual excitement and imagine a future enveloped in sheer, sensual hose.

I sit down on the bed. I feel the panty girdle tighten around my waist and press between my buttocks and place a deeply erotic pressure on my balls. I take the tights and carefully roll the left leg into a gently bunched bowl, remembering a moment of pure erotic bliss when I had watched my mother dress a few years before, a moment secretly snatched through a crack in her bedroom door, a moment branded onto my tormented transvestite consciousness. My dream had been to repeat her elegant, graceful gestures as she had sat on her dressing table stool and slipped into a pair of ultra-sheer black nylon tights, as she had so carefully and yet easily guided the soft shimmering nylon over her long silken legs, the slightest smile of pleasure on her strawberry lips, a smile that betrayed a simple joy in her gorgeous femininity, a joy I have yearned to feel myself for so long – a joy I am now finally experiencing.

I guide my left foot into the bowl and squeal with a dreadful pleasure as my skin makes first astonishing contact with the soft nylon fabric. Its impact is amazing. Suddenly, it is as if I can feel a tidal wave of the Feminine crash across my body and envelop my soul. As I guide the nylon over my foot, I feel each gesture, each tiny movement, each beat of my heart become so much more feminine. I find myself pointing my toes downwards in exactly the same manner as my mother, a gesture of profoundly feminine grace. I pull the leg of the tights up over my foot and then begin very slowly to stretch it up to just below my knee. Then, carefully, with a teasing precision, I repeat the process with the second leg. Then, my legs together, my cock struggling with an erotic desperation and futility against the tight elastane wall of the panty girdle, I stand and ease the tights up my legs. As I do so, tears of a dark, harsh and most unforgiving pleasure trickle down my red cheeks. This is all I have ever wanted. This is all I am.

I find myself wiggling my erotically oppressed bottom and hips in a helplessly feminine manner as I pull the tights up over my thighs and the patterned surface of the panty girdle. A sense of pure elation fills me like a huge white light. Yes, I am in heaven!

Then the tights are positioned and I look down at my legs with new eyes. I run my hands over the second skin of soft nylon and fight a sudden dizziness, the pleasure fierce and utterly irresistible. The electric pulse of the nylon teases my hot, desperate flesh and I am consumed by feelings of hyper-erotic femininity. I step forwards, taking small, girlish steps, watching the way my legs move with a tormenting elegant sway. I marvel at the way the tights accentuate and demonstrate the feminine curvature and length of my legs and thus begin to reveal in the most striking fashion the simple fact of my instinctive feminine being.

Then I slowly return to the bed and sit down. I cross my legs and gasp with renewed pleasure. I stretch my toes and feel astonishingly transformed, the girl at the heart of me exploding forth, an eruption of graceful femininity. I take up the second pair of tights, black and slender, a maximum of twenty denier. I run them across my hands and sink my hot face into the silky, semi-transparent gusset. Then I breathe deep, hoping for some pungent hint of my Aunt's most intimate secrets.

Then I pull the tights over my already hosed legs and the desired effect is made immediately apparent. Suddenly, my legs are truly feminine: the combination of the semi-opaque tights and the black tights ensure that any sign of masculine hair is completely removed. Yes, these are now the legs of a beautiful young woman, of the beautiful young woman in *me*.

I walk across the room, trapped for a few seconds in a strange sex delirium, lost in a world previously beyond comprehension, a world of pure, unrefined and utterly unforgiving pleasure. For a moment or two, all sense of self is lost, as if I have been wrapped in a fine film of sensual black nylon and plunged into a gorgeous void of fetishistic nothingness.

It is a struggle, but eventually I manage to pull myself from this pure, tormenting ecstasy and return to the bed. Here I slip – with an increasingly helpless feminine grace – into the shimmering white silk panties. The fine, slightly slippery material brushes against my nylon-sheathed legs with an electric tickle and I gasp with shocked desire. Then I pull the panties gently into place and take up the equally delicate and sensual white silk slip. I pour it over my slender shoulders with a moan of pleasure and let it fall down my chest like a stream of pure arousal. As it envelops my body, I feel even the slightest trace of masculinity crushed and suppressed. The victory of the Feminine is total, a victory I embrace with an addict's desperation.

I smooth the shimmering silk fabric over my body and then lift the check mini-skirt from the bed. I widen its elasticated waist and very delicately step into it, each movement – never mind how slight – gorgeously exaggerated and precisely enhanced by this heavenly feminine attire. I position the skirt around my waist. It barely covers my black nylon-sheathed upper thighs and adds to the deliberate and intensely erotic revelation of my elegant, long and very shapely legs. I stare down at the shocking reality of my femininity and it is as if I am looking down at someone else, at the legs of a beautiful, sexy young woman.

Then I take the plastic bag from the bed and pull out a grey-coloured cardboard box. From the box I extract the pair of black patent leather court shoes, classic in design, sensual in intent. I stare at them with hungry, yet also nervous eyes. I have never walked in heels, and these shoes have five-inch stilettos that end in sharp metal tipped points – severe, sado-erotic and utterly amazing!

I place the shoes at my hosed feet, bending forwards with knees drawn tightly together in a suitably demure and intensely feminine manner. I stand up and stare down at the shining, almost teasing shoes. Then, carefully, nervously, I slip my right foot into the corresponding shoe, feeling the sudden elevation and the erotic elongation of my leg. I gasp and quickly – almost panic-stricken – slip my left foot into the other shoe, pulling myself upwards and forwards as I do so and suddenly launching myself five inches into the air, where I sway with a momentary terror and a definite and desperate ungainliness.

At first it is merely a matter of maintaining my balance, of preventing an embarrassing and pathetic collapse. Panic is the main emotion. But then there is another feeling: relief; the shoes fit and, after a few minutes, there is at least a sense of slight confidence in my balance. I will remain upright for the time being! But then I try to take a step forwards and what little confidence I have managed to retain is immediately put in terrible doubt. The step becomes a stagger and I feel myself fall helplessly forwards. The only way to prevent myself pitching into oblivion is to take another step and thus double the chance of collapse. But it is a risk I must take, and suddenly I find myself tottering helplessly forwards, my arms waving at my sides like some insane robot, my bottom wiggling uncontrollably, the electric nylon enveloping my thighs creating a fear-framed sex static as my legs are forced together by the tiny steps demanded by the heels. Then, suddenly, I am walking. A point of balance is attained. The crisis is past.

And, within a few minutes, I am lost in the pure ecstasy of an instinctive and rather beautiful feminine movement, a modest ballet built upon the basic principles of counterbalance. My steps tiny, my bottom wiggling, my hips swaying, I achieve the truth of a girlish locomotion and moan with pride and pleasure. And for a further five minutes I totter eagerly around the room, each high-heeled step a further confirmation of the glorious reality of my natural femininity.

Then I move towards the dressing table. Carefully, with a renewed nervousness, I lower myself onto the red leather-backed dressing table stool, legs again close together, my cock burning with a blind, animal fury, my heart pounding with a sex-fuelled intensity into my ribs.

Then I am staring at myself, at the pretty young man in the female attire, at the shocking ambiguity of my reflection, at the fact that even before make-up, padding and the gorgeous silk blouse, I more resemble a girl than a boy.

I take up a blood-red lipstick and carefully unscrew its long, phallic length. Using the mirror to guide its progress, I place the stick against my upper lip and rather shakily run it across the length of soft, sensual human flesh. With my lips painted, the transformation is even more intense and realistic.

After the lipstick, I apply a light, heavily scented tan foundation powder with a pink-coloured puff, across my cheeks, forehead and neck. Then I use a light-blue eye-shadow to decorate my eyelids, followed by mascara, a final touch of feminine decoration that leaves a smile of excitement and triumph on my painted lips.

The face before me is now surely that of a young woman. Everything I have always suspected is here revealed as truth. I am a creature of the Feminine, and its dreadful, beautiful power emerges in my smile and the sparkling light at the heart of my astonished gaze.

I cover my neck and shoulders in a powerful rose perfume and only just stifle an embarrassing sneeze. Then I totter joyously back to the bed and add the final piece to this lovely, life-changing jigsaw – the beautifully cut and designed white silk blouse. I hold it up before me like an expensive antique, with an eroticised care. My sex-filled eyes pass across its perfect form and I know all my secret dreams of feminine envelopment will very soon be realised.

I guide the right sleeve over my narrow, girlish wrist and then up my slender right arm. The kiss of gravity-defying and very expensive silk is almost unbearably pleasurable and by the time I have managed to slide the other sleeve up my left arm and gently tease the blouse over my shoulders, I am fighting the very real threat of a resounding premature ejaculation.

But I survive this further test of my will to dress, and manage, after struggling with the pearl buttons, to button the blouse up all the way to the high be-frilled neck. Then, very gently, as if handling sex dynamite, I tuck the blouse deep into the skirt.

I run my hands over my elegantly feminised body and feel a briefly blinding sense of absolute triumph. I have created myself anew, or rather I have freed a long-suppressed and profound facet of my personality. I make my way with some trepidation towards the full-length mirror fixed to the inside of one of the closet doors knowing there is now no turning back, that, even after I have carefully replaced all this wondrous feminine attire, I will be unable to put this new feminine me away. Today I have opened a box of delights and identity that will never be closed. And this fact is made even more apparent when I face my reflection, the reflection of a very boyish, but also beautiful teenage girl, whose wide, deceptively innocent eyes betray fascination and a fundamental, inescapable need for more of this forever and ever.

I am lost in my reflection. Indeed, it is as if I have stepped into a mirror universe where I am the pretty girl I have always dreamed of being. I am so lost in these first moments of deep and overwhelming self-fascination that I fail to hear the bedroom door open and my Aunt, my lovely, imperial, buxom Aunt, enter the room.

And it is only when she steps into the range of my reflection that I am suddenly, shockingly and awfully aware of her. I freeze solid. Suddenly, desire turns to the most intense terror and then a dreadful, soul-crushing sense of inescapable humiliation.

But then I look into her eyes and see not the expected anger, horror or outrage, but a surprised amusement and something else: consideration of a new and fascinating opportunity.

I turn and face her, struck dumb with embarrassment and fear, yet even now gripped by the need to retain femininity, grace, care of movement. Yes, the reflection has broken free of the mirror, whatever happens.

'Well, well,' my Aunt whispers, her bloody, glistening lips curved into an ironic, yet also potentially cruel smile, a light of desire and fascination burning in her golden-brown eyes. 'What have we got here?'

– *Chris, North London, UK*

Payback

My story goes back to when I met two friends I hadn't seen in ages, but who had been really close when the three of us always went on holiday in the same place. I've changed the names and places, for obvious reasons, but everything else is as it happened.

It started in London, and I had to look twice before I could be sure it really was Becky walking towards me down the street. She looked so different, so smart. She'd cut her riot of brown curls short, and, in place of the jeans and jumper I was used to, she wore a black skirt suit, designer cut and obviously expensive. Glasses, patent heels, and most of all the leather briefcase she was carrying made her look a million miles from the vivacious hoyden who'd always teased the boys so outrageously back then, on those endless summers near Yarmouth on the Isle of Wight.

Eight years had passed, but it was still like yesterday: the three of us, Becky, Sarah, and I, always together, on the beaches, down at the clubs, just walking on the open hills above the holiday park in which our parents had owned chalets. Becky had always been the noisy one, extrovert, brash even, the one who got us into trouble. Sarah had been our siren, sultry and sexy, with her huge brown eyes and envy-making chest, the one who drew the boys, always. Me, I'd been the quiet one, little, mousy Jo, although I'd had my moments.

She was heading for Moorgate tube, and I was going to be lost if I didn't hurry. A frantic dash across the street, earning a rude remark from a passing cabbie, and I was pushing through the crowd behind her, and calling out. She turned, looking puzzled, then surprised, then delighted. Ten minutes later we were in Jack's, laughing together over a bottle of chilled Pouilly-Fuissé, and I was calling Sarah.

From Jack's the three of us went to the Pack Rat, for a bite to eat and another bottle, of Chilean Shiraz this time, and a third, which left us giggling together with our arms linked as we walked back towards the station, just like the old days, only in the City instead of along the beach. We made the station, but we were having far too much fun to head home separately. Becky's flat was the nearest, a top floor conversion in South Islington, where we crashed out with another bottle of wine we'd picked up along the way.

We'd started reminiscing, inevitably, about the times we'd had together: our all girls team in the local raft race; pinching my parents' car to drive into Cowes; and boys, most of all boys. That left me a little quiet. Every boy we'd met, just about, had fancied Sarah first. Becky had been quite capable of putting herself forwards, which had often changed their minds. I'd had to put up with the leftovers.

Becky was in full flow.

'. . . of and that French guy, Patrice, so cute . . .'

Sarah gave a snort of pure contempt.

'. . . and so arrogant with it! Do you know what he said, on our last night? "Sarah, *mon petit choux*," he says, "you know I am a – how do you say –

a free spirit, that I must love other women, but, for me, you will always be my English girlfriend, and I will be first in your heart".'

Becky and I laughed, for the memory, and for her phoney French accent. I could well remember Patrice, a slim boy with a wistful expression and tousled brown hair. He'd been attractive, but not the most attractive. Oh no, that had been Mark Calderdale; dark, mysterious Mark, with the cool smile and ever-present shades, Mark who every girl fancied. He'd had his own caravan. He'd had a motorbike. He'd had everything.

He'd had Sarah, and inevitably he was the one she moved on to.

'. . . and that Mark, he was something else. I'll never forget him . . . The first night, after a beach party, we walked up to the Downs, along that little sandy track between the tall hedges, you must remember, to that place we used to meet for picnics, looking over the Needles . . .'

She finished with a long sigh. That was not enough for Becky.

'Did you?'

Sarah nodded.

'My first time.'

'Tell.'

'Becky! I . . .'

'Tell, Sarah.'

I wanted to know. Like Becky, and every other girl around at the time, I'd fancied him rotten. He'd been so horny, just the way he was, and because of the rumours of the things he'd done, the people he knew. I added my voice to Becky's.

'Tell us, Sarah, come on. This is us.'

Sarah smiled, a little shy.

'OK, OK, if I have to.'

'You do.'

'Yes, and we want the juicy details.'

Sarah was more than a little flushed, but she took a good swig of her wine and began, with Becky and I listening entranced.

'He'd really got to me . . . you know that, obviously, and you know the way he was, too. I felt I was ready, and that he was the right person, because . . . because he was so experienced, and he knew how to be gentle, and . . . and he made me feel special. We were standing by the fire, a little back, and he just put his finger to his lips, to hush me, and took my hand. I let him lead me, up the track, with a band of stars visible between the tops of the hedges, and so silent, and his hand warm in mine. I don't think I've ever felt more protected, and I knew I could simply give myself to him and everything would be all right . . .'

Becky interrupted.

'Never mind that, what about the dirty bits? Did he make you suck his cock?'

'Becky! No, he did not, he didn't *make* me do anything. He was very gentle. When we got to the picnic site he spread that long leather coat he used to wear down on the grass and laid me down. We were kissing for so long before he did anything heavy. He spent ages just stroking my hair and neck, kissing too, until it was like I was in a dream world. There was nothing crude about him, nothing, not like most boys . . .'

Becky interrupted again.

'Yeah, like that bloke Pete who was always trying to get girls to show their knickers. Now there was a dirty bastard.'

'You went out with him!'

'Oh yeah! He'd do anything I wanted, for hours, and I mean hours.'

Sarah gave a meaningful cough.

'Mark was not like that. He was the perfect man – my perfect man, anyway, maybe not yours, Becky – very strong, but very gentle. It was as if he could read my mind too, because he only began to undress me when I was truly ready, and he did it for me, not for himself. He kept telling me he loved me too, and how special I was, and how privileged he was . . .'

Becky made a face, pretending to be sick.

'Becky! If you don't want to hear . . .'

'No, no, I want to hear. Sorry. I'll shut up now.'

'Good. Where was I? Oh yes, he really took care of me, made me feel I was the most important person in the world, and that he really understood how special the moment was to me. He took all my clothes off, every stitch, and I can still remember what he said, "to show the full, tender bloom of your beauty". It was so lovely, and . . . I just melted into his arms, and . . . and I was crying as we did it, just a little sad, maybe, but mainly for joy.'

She shrugged, embarrassed, and hid her face in her wine glass. Becky looked a little surprised.

'That's it?'

'Yes. What more do you want?'

'I don't know, some dirty details maybe . . .'

'I told you, he wasn't like that. It was a wonderful, fulfilling experience.'

'Tame, more like! He wasn't like that with me.'

A look of serious shock appeared on Sarah's face.

'With you? What do you mean, with you?'

Becky went on blithely.

'When he had me. He was rough, well rough. It was in that club, the Monkey's Nuts . . . not your sort of place, maybe, but you remember, where the bikers used to go. He was always down there, and even those guys, really hard guys, Hell's Angels and all sorts, they used to respect him. One night these two guys were giving me a hard time – like fucking bears, they were, big and hairy, and they stank of fags and booze. It was getting nasty, and they wouldn't let me go, saying if I wanted to hang out there I had to be gang-banged. So Mark comes over, so cool, and puts his arm around me and just says, "Hey, guys, she's my girl, OK?" They backed off, just like that. Now, I mean, you know what he was like, and I was not fighting, but I tell you, I don't think it would have made any difference. He keeps his arm around my shoulder, right, and just steers me towards the loos. Everyone sees, and everyone knows what's going to happen. In we go. He sits down, unzips and pulls out his cock. "You can give me a blow job," he says, not like there's a choice, but like he knows I want to. Oh that was good, so good. I go down on my knees, and he's already half stiff, and rolling his foreskin up and down. I take him in, and, oh, just the feel of him in my mouth, and his taste, all man . . .'

She paused, gave me a knowing looking and took a swallow of wine. I was beginning to get seriously horny, and feel something of the envy which had always been there in the background on our holidays. I wanted to listen, though, because I could remember the club, which I'd hardly dared go near, never mind into. Becky's view of Mark was rather more as I remembered him too, and I knew that if he'd demanded I suck his cock I'd have been down on my knees in a flash. She went on, a little breathless, her neck flushed pink.

'I was happy just the way we were, with his lovely long cock to suck on, and all those hard guys outside knowing what I was doing. Not Mark. He decided he wanted it all, and what he wanted, he got. He told me to sit in his lap, told me, not asked me. I did it, straddled on him with my knickers off and my skirt up around my waist. He made me take my top off too, so I was showing everything. There were even holes in the walls, you know, like gay guys suck each other off through, and I'm sure we were watched, but I didn't care. It was just too good, to be with Mark that way, with him in control . . .'

She finished with a little shiver. Sarah had listened wide-eyed and staring. When she spoke it was in an awed whisper.

'He didn't, really?'

Becky was smiling as she answered.

'Oh, yes, he did.'

'Yes, but . . .'

Sarah didn't get a chance to finish, Becky interrupting her with a sigh.

'He was the best, wasn't he? You fancied him too, didn't you, Jo? Shame you missed out.'

I shook my head.

'No. I didn't miss out.'

Sarah had been looking thoughtful, or maybe just drunk, but her head jerked up sharply. Becky nearly dropped her glass.

'You are joking!'

'What, serious, you fucked Mark?'

They'd answered in chorus, their voices full of doubt. I lifted my chin a little.

'Yes, I did, as a matter of fact.'

'Tell!'

'Yes, what happened, Jo? And when?'

I had their full attention.

'What happened was that right at the end of one summer, when you two had already gone back, and so had just about everyone else, I met Mark in Yarmouth. We went for a walk together, talking and joking about all the fun we'd had, you know, a bit melancholy, because summer was over. I remember we could feel that autumn was coming as we walked through the woods, along by the shore. He let me wear his coat, and when he put it around my shoulders he kissed me, and . . . and well, it just seemed so natural.'

Sarah gave a weak nod.

'And this was the same summer he went out with me?'

I realised I'd made a mistake.

'I . . . yes . . . shit . . . it was a long time ago, and he said you'd had this big row on your last night, and . . .'

'No we did not have a big row! We were writing love letters to each other for months! I've still got them somewhere, and all the time, with my friend . . .'

'Sorry, Sarah, I really thought . . .'

'I'm sure you did, but . . . but really! And what a two-timing rat he was! And hang on, hang on. If you and Mark were together at the Monkey's Nuts, Becky, that must have been . . . ninety-five. Because it got closed down, didn't it?'

'Yeah, ninety-five sounds right . . . ninety-four maybe?'

'No. We didn't know him in ninety-four. So, what you're telling me you and he . . . shagged, while he was going out with me?'

Becky answered quickly.

'Before, I think. That beach party wasn't until . . .'

'It was the day after you arrived, I remember. You'd just got your driving test and you drove us around the island.'

'Oh, right . . . OK, OK, I didn't want to say this, because I know you liked him, but he told me he was going to dump you, and . . .'

'And you believed him? Becky, how could you, and you, Jo?'

170

I spread my arms helplessly. Becky was more practical.

'Let's put it behind us, yes? It was years ago, and when it comes down to it it was his fault. He told me he was free, and the same with Jo.'

Sarah nodded, although she still looked angry.

'Yes . . . OK. I'm with Jon now, I shouldn't worry . . . Sorry, both of you. But if I could just get my hands on the bastard, right now! I'd wring his neck, I'd . . . oh, never mind. I bet he's married now . . .'

'. . . and divorced . . .'

'. . . twice, with eight kids . . .'

'. . . and two mortgages . . .'

'. . . and a crappy old car instead of his bike . . .'

'. . . and a crappy old job too . . .'

Becky broke in on Sarah's and my soul-soothing exchange.

'No, he owns a car showroom, in Barking, apparently.'

'Bastard! How do you know?'

'Because I ran into his mum, in Portsmouth, maybe two years ago now.'

'Oh . . . I wonder if he's still there?'

'I'll find out. How many Calderdales can there be in Barking?'

'No, Becky . . .'

Becky had picked the phone up, and ignored Sarah. As somebody who was obviously male answered, her voice changed from loud, drunk and boisterous to a honeyed purr. After a few questions she put the phone back in its cradle.

'He lives above the premises, Calderdale Cars, in Redbridge Lane. Here's his number, Sarah. Call him up and give him a piece of your mind.'

'No! I couldn't do that!'

I agreed.

'Nor could I. What if he's married, and you got his wife or something?'

'Good. Tell her what a shit he is.'

'That's a bit harsh . . . on her, I mean.'

Sarah gave a wistful sigh.

'You're right, best let it be, but it would be fun, wouldn't it? Just to get him back.'

Becky shook her head.

'It would be more fun to go round there.'

'Oh yes, and tell him to his face! I'm not sure I'd dare . . .'

'I would! Just let me at him . . .'

Sarah shook her head.

'He'd just laugh at you.'

I couldn't agree.

'No, he wouldn't, not if you went alone. He'd try and get off with you, that was Mark's style.'

Becky gave a thoughtful nod.

'Yeah, you're right . . . but . . . but what if he didn't know we'd found him out? What if Sarah went round, pretended her car had broken down, whatever. He'd try it, he would, and then when he's fit to burst, you could tell him, and just walk out!'

Sarah laughed and so did I.

'Great! Imagine his face!'

'I wouldn't dare, not with Mark, but still.'

'I would, and I'm going to. Let's get a cab.'

'Becky!'

'You're not serious?'

'I am.'

'You're not! What if his wife answers the door or something?'

'Then I make my excuses and go, leaving her wondering who the gorgeous brunette in designer gear was calling for her husband.'

'Becky!'

She'd picked up the phone again, but I still thought she was messing about until she'd ordered a cab to take us to Barking. Ten minutes later it had arrived, and I had to go, if only to watch what happened, and to back my friend up. Sarah very nearly didn't, but drink and curiosity got the better of her, and off we went.

Calderdale Cars sounded grand, and it was, or at least flashy, a double front of curving glass within a compound, with Mercs, BMWs, Jaguars and more, both outside and in. The flat above was obvious, with the lights still on and a door to one side. I'd have chickened out, so would Sarah, but not Becky. She went and rang the bell.

Sarah and I scarpered, giggling as we hid around a corner, and expecting Becky to join us. She didn't. I heard the door open and a man's voice, a voice that took me back in an instant to when I was eighteen: Mark Calderdale, the one boy everybody wanted. He sounded just the same, confident but full of humour, and if it was hard to make out his actual words, there was no mistaking the tone of his voice, or the honey in Becky's as she responded. Then the door closed with a click. For a moment there was silence, before Sarah spoke.

'You know what's going to happen, don't you?'

'No?'

'He's going to shag her, that's what. We'll be left standing in the street like a pair of idiots while he talks her out of her knickers in about five minutes, and he'll shag her.'

'Do you really think so?'

'Yes! Who could ever resist Mark? I couldn't, you couldn't, and Becky sure as hell couldn't.'

I shrugged, not wanting to believe it. More than once when Becky could have gone off with

173

a boyfriend she'd stuck by me. Sarah had always gone. I knew what she meant though, because just the sound of Mark's voice had been enough to make me start to melt.

Five minutes passed, and ten, with both of us growing slowly more agitated. It wasn't a particularly nice area, and I couldn't help but wonder what people would think if they saw Sarah and me standing together on the street corner. To be approached by some kerb crawler would be embarrassing, and creepy. To be hauled in by the police for soliciting would be awful.

Fifteen minutes passed, and twenty. Sarah wanted to ring the bell and I was going to agree with her when a soft thump sounded from above us, then Becky's voice, spoken in an urgent hiss.

'Catch!'

She threw something down, which landed with a metallic clatter on the pavement: a bunch of keys. I picked them up, found the right one on the second go and we were in Mark Calderdale's flat, running up the stairs together. I'd given up all thought of telling him what I thought of him, and I didn't know what to expect at all, but it certainly wasn't what we saw when a giggling Becky let us through the second door at the top of the stairs.

Mark Calderdale's flat was more or less what I had expected: very masculine, a touch flashy, with black leather furniture and an obviously expensive deck set against whitewashed walls beneath the wooden beams of what would originally have been an attic. There were a lot of CDs, a fair few videos, a couple of magazines, a carpet patterned in a glaring black and white zigzag.

Mark Calderdale was not at all what I would have expected. Not that his looks had changed. If anything he was more handsome than I remembered him. He even had a leather jacket on, a very smart one, and designer jeans. What was unusual was his being bent double with hands tied behind his back.

A strand of thick cord tied off on the beam above him kept him completely helpless, while his face was set in an expression of wild-eyed consternation. He didn't say anything, because a tie patterned with broad silver and yellow stripes had been tied around his mouth, leaving a wisp of pink material sticking out over his lower lip.

My mouth had fallen open, but I managed to speak, just about.

'How . . .'

Becky was grinning.

'Simple. Mr Macho here started his old routine and I told him I was up for it if I could give him a bit of tie and tease.'

Sarah came back like an echo.

'Tie and tease?'

'You know, bondage and that. My Ricky's well into it.'

'You mad cow!'

'Be cool, will you? And stop panicking, Mark, we're only going to have a little fun with you.'

He'd begun to thrash about a little, and her words didn't do anything to calm him down. When her hands went to his belt buckle he really began to struggle, but it just made her laugh.

'What a baby! Who'd have thought, eh? Big bad Mark, and he can't even handle a little bondage, with three cuties too. Most men would be privileged!'

Mark didn't seem to be and, although I was fighting not to giggle, there was a tiny spark of common sense trying to talk to me inside. Sarah clearly felt the same.

'So . . . so what are we going to do? And what's he got in his mouth?'

Becky answered as she pulled his broad leather belt from his jeans.

'My knickers. I had to shut him up somehow. We're going to teach him a lesson, like we said. OK, Markie baby, do you remember the summer of ninety-five? Nod if you do.'

Mark's crazed stare didn't change, at first, except to grow more crazed still as Becky undid the buttons of his trousers, which fell down. He had on purple briefs, very tight around his neat, muscular buttocks, on which Becky brought the doubled belt down with a meaty crack. Suddenly he was nodding, as if his head was about to come off. Even Sarah giggled. Becky gave a happy crow of laughter.

'Good boy! There, you see, Mark, you've just learnt rule one. Never fight it, because it only gets worse. Next question: did you go out with Sarah?'

He nodded, but the belt smacked down anyway, making him jerk in his bonds. I was telling myself that it was because he had such a cute bottom that I was getting so turned on, and not because he was helpless and being given a belting, but I knew I was lying. It felt good.

Mark obviously didn't agree, if the look of consternation on his face was anything to go by, and Becky had to wait until her laughter had died down before she could speak again.

'That one was just for fun, Mark. You're a good boy really. Now, girls, what do you think? Shall I?'

She'd taken hold of his briefs, pulling them a little way down. He shook his head urgently. She gave him an arch look.

'Nobody's asking you, Mark. What do you think, girls?'

176

Sarah wasn't certain.

'I'm not sure, Becky . . .'

I was.

'Go on, Becky, pull them down. I want to see.'

Becky nodded.

'Jo's right. After all, what would he do if it was one of us? He'd pull our knickers down, wouldn't he, so . . .'

She tugged, taking his briefs right down, to the level of his knees, to leave his fine buttocks naked, and everything showing between. He was quite big, and very smooth, while I could smell his male scent. His skin was marked where she'd hit him with the belt, and again I couldn't helping giggling, both from nervousness and excitement. Becky was far cooler, standing back a little and measuring the swing of her arm against his buttocks as she spoke.

'Yes, Mark, you went out with Sarah, and that's OK, that's cool, but you went with me, too, didn't you? Didn't you, Mark, at the Monkey's Nuts that night?'

Her voice was full of honey, but it changed as he began to shake his head again, to pure venom.

'Liar! You bastard! Right, that's twenty hard ones!'

The belt cracked down on his buttocks, much harder than before, and his eyes opened wide with shock and pain, a reaction that sent a little guilty jolt right to my pussy. Becky didn't stop, or even pause, laying in the next stroke, and the next, to set him kicking his legs with his balls and cock jiggling between his legs, and, as the beating continued, slowly changing shape. He was getting excited.

Becky stopped, laughing and clapping her hands in glee as she saw.

'He likes it! He's getting hard! What a dirty little boy!'

Mark had gone bright pink. Sarah had her hand to her mouth, her eyes wide in delight. I was having trouble not putting my hand to my pussy. Becky applied another smack, now talking.

'What was I on, eight, nine maybe? Oh, never mind, I'll just have to start again, won't I, Mark? Yeah, twenty for lying, and another twenty for two-timing Sarah with me, and another twenty for two-timing Sarah with Jo, and no, don't you go shaking your head, Mr Casanova, because we know the truth! Oh, and twenty for two-timing me with Jo, so that's ... that's eighty ... no, let's call it a hundred, starting now!'

She'd been using the belt with a will as she spoke, and with every smack of the leather across the hard flesh of Mark's buttocks his cock had been growing a little bit stiffer. As the next stroke fell Becky began to count, one ... two ... three ... each smack punctuated by a muffled grunt from Mark and a little writhing. I joined in, and Sarah, calling out the numbers and clapping in time to his beating, until at forty strokes, Becky stopped, now flushed and dishevelled, with her face glowing with excitement and her nipples poking up through the silk of her blouse.

'You have a go, Sarah!'

Sarah took the belt, her face set in delight and determination as she measured up her stroke and laid in, just as hard as Becky. I began to call the count again, and to clap, watching Mark's now rigid cock bob beneath his iron-hard belly. Becky joined in, calling out the numbers as she walked around in front of him and sank into a squat. Extending one painted fingernail, she began to tickle him under the chin.

'Ah, poor little baby Markie, does it hurt ... does it hurt? Yes, I bet it does, but not that much, no, because a certain naughty little boy is getting ever so excited because he's having his botty smacked, isn't he? Isn't he?'

Mark held out for just a moment, and then he was nodding frantically. Becky laughed, right in his face, and rose again.

'Harder, Sarah, go on, give the bastard what he deserves!'

Sarah didn't need telling. All her reserve was gone, and all her ill-feeling from her long-passed holiday betrayal was coming out, the belt smacking down on Mark's now-blazing red buttocks. She didn't stop when we got to thirty either, but kept right on, her eyes blazing as she thrashed him. I had to speak up.

'Hey, it's my turn, Sarah!'

She stopped. She passed me the belt. She stepped away.

'Go on, Jo, give him hell!'

Sarah was almost in hysterics as I laid the first smack across Mark's bottom, jumping up and down with her fists clenched and her eyes shining with a truly wicked joy. Becky was no better, cackling with laughter, bent double with one hand over her mouth and the other clutching her tummy. It was funny too, the way he squirmed his body and kicked his legs about, with his erect cock waving wildly under his belly. I was laughing as well, having trouble aiming, but getting him, smack, smack, smack across his buttocks, not bothering to count any more, completely out of control . . .

Until he came.

It just happened. I'd caught him a cracker, right across his cheeks, and it was as if I'd knocked the stuff out of him. Thick white come erupted from the tip of his cock, all over his carpet, and again with my next blow, and again. Sarah gave a gasp of shock and delight. Becky tried to duck down to look and fell over, laughing so hard she couldn't get up again, and wailing: 'He's come! He's come! What a dirty, dirty, dirty little boy! He's come, all over his own fucking carpet!'

I'd stopped. My whole body was shaking, and the scent of Mark's sperm seemed to fill my head. Dizzy with drink and dizzy with need, I just had to do it, there was no choice. I didn't even care what my friends thought as I ran to his bathroom and slammed the door. Two quick motions and my skirt was up and my hand was down my knickers, rubbing in the moist groove of my pussy and the thoughts tumbled over in my head.

Mark ... cool, handsome Mark, the original caveman, Sarah's gentle rogue, and we'd tied him up and whipped him ... tied him up and whipped him with his own belt ... tied him up and bared his bottom and whipped him with his own belt ... tied him up and bared his bottom and whipped him with his own belt until he'd come in helpless ecstasy ... which was exactly what I was doing, with my teeth clamped tight to my lower lip as wave after wave of climactic bliss swept over me, until at last I could stand no more, and stopped. I opened my eyes to find Becky standing in the doorway, smiling.

'Bad girl, Jo! Fun though, wasn't it?'

'Great fun.'

She went to the loo as I tidied myself up, and may also have sneaked a frig once I'd gone. Certainly she took her time. Back in the living room, Sarah was looking remarkably pleased with herself. Mark wasn't. He looked thoroughly fed up, but I didn't have much sympathy. A man like that needs to be taken down a peg or two occasionally. Besides, as Becky had said, how many guys get sex from three girls at the same time? Well, sort of sex ...

Our one little problem was how to let him go safely. Not that he knew where any of us lived, but it wasn't fair to just leave him, after all. I solved the problem. While Becky phoned for a cab, we tied his ankles together and to the leg of his couch, then undid his wrists when the cab was in the street. We scarpered, and my last glimpse of Mark was of him tugging desperately at his bonds, with his trousers still around his ankles.

We couldn't stop giggling all the way back to Islington, and the cabbie obviously thought we were mad. Becky got dropped off first, and Sarah and I went on together, as we only lived a few streets apart. I still needed to calm down, a lot, and asked if she'd like to come in for coffee. She accepted, and we set off for my flat, arm in arm and silent, until she spoke up, suddenly.

'Hang on a minute . . . Becky was lying. She never went with Mark.'

'No? How do you know?'

'Didn't you see? She mentioned his foreskin. Mark's circumcised, isn't he, and he always was. I should know.'

'You're right! So she was making it all up?'

'She must have been. Anyway, he never fancied her, and she was always jealous.'

'Well . . . yes . . .'

'The lying little cow!'

She paused before speaking again.

'I always wondered what turned him on. Not me, that's for certain.'

'How do you mean? You . . .'

'No, it wasn't . . . it wasn't quite like I said with me either. The first bit, yes, but when we got up on the cliffs he couldn't do it. He said it was the wind, which was quite cold, but he couldn't get hard. I did everything I could, sucked him, let him put it between my breasts . . . He just couldn't. It was the same all the time we were going out. He just couldn't do it.'

'So you never had sex with him at all?'

'No, and nor did Becky. Looks like it was just you.'

I nodded, unable to bring myself to tell her I'd made it all up as well.

– Jo, Cambridge, UK

What We Did On Our Holidays

I've always known that my wife is out of my league, really. I'm older than she is and I'm very average looking, while she's a true beauty, bright and clever, and an obviously sexy woman. I suppose a lot of people would say she only married me because I have a bit of money, and I can give her a good life in material terms. But I know that my Ginny isn't like that. She doesn't have a mercenary bone in her body. And, despite the difference in our ages and the fact that I'm not the world's greatest sexual performer, she still loves me for myself and would never leave me.

For many years, though, I felt guilty about my deficiencies and, even though Ginny never complained, I would shower her with gifts and clothes and holidays to try and compensate for our less-than-dazzling sex life. Ginny's no fool, though, and I could tell she knew what I was doing. She always accepted everything I lavished on her with genuine sweetness and gratitude, and responded lovingly in bed in order to make me feel better about myself.

However, just recently, during our last holiday, I found a new way to give her everything she needs, both materially and sexually. A way that satisfies some new needs of my own at the same time.

It all happened when we booked into a secluded luxury hotel, miles from anywhere, for a short break to celebrate a recent financial success. A business colleague had recommended it to me, after I'd noted how fit and contented he was looking when I hadn't seen him for a while.

'You ought to try it, David,' he'd said, giving me a heavy wink, which surprised me, as I'd always thought of him as a sober, no nonsense sort of chap. 'It'll give you a new lease of life, man. Really spice up your love life, if you know what I mean?'

Despite the fact that there isn't a hotel on earth that can give me a bigger dick and a longer-lasting erection, I booked a few days there for Ginny and myself the following week. Even if it didn't do anything for us in the sexual department, I was still looking forward to the superb gourmet food, the elegant suites, and the beautiful landscaped hotel grounds that my friend had also highly praised.

The place certainly wasn't a disappointment in terms of décor and facilities. It had a fantastic Art Deco look, understated yet stylish, and I could tell that Ginny was thrilled with it. She was in high good humour and gently flirtatious with waiters, barmen and fellow male guests alike, and seeing the way that they all admired her and lusted after her seemed to put a bit more lead in my pencil for a change. On the morning of our first full day there, we had our best and most satisfying fuck in ages. Years in fact . . . I didn't last quite as long as I would have liked to but, even so, I got Ginny part-way there, and I thoroughly enjoyed watching her finish herself off afterwards with a vibrator. I've always loved the way that she's so natural and uninhibited in the bedroom, even though in company she always behaves like a lady.

Later on, with me feeling pretty pleased with myself, we went for a swim in the hotel's large, well-appointed pool. It was obvious to all around that Ginny had recently had an orgasm. She had a deliciously sensual and seductive look to her. A real glow. Her cheeks were pink and adorably rosy, and she had a naughty sparkling twinkle in her eye. In her tiny bikini her body looked like that of a goddess, with stiff nipples crowning her lovely rounded breasts. Her long thighs, her flat belly and her sumptuous peachy bottom were all beautifully displayed too in the minute cotton thong of her abbreviated swimsuit.

There were lots of men around the pool, including a very tall, beefy, and darkly handsome lifeguard. I was sure that every single one of them was checking her out, ogling her charms and noting that one or two frisky little pubic hairs had escaped the confines of her thong. As we took in the sun I was forced to lie on my front because the idea of her taking the tiny little garment off altogether and showing more than a dozen men her silky beautiful pussy had me unexpectedly hard again, even though we'd recently had sex. Even a few cocktails didn't spoil the effect. In fact they helped.

As I got slightly tipsy, my imagination got wilder, and I pictured Ginny being fucked by all the men around the pool. One after the other they put it to her, ending with the big, well set-up pool attendant, who made her howl and squirm with the pleasure of a string of wild, intense orgasms.

I was just considering throwing a thick towel over myself and seeing if I could get away with having a swift wank underneath it when a ripple of interest seemed to cascade around the edges of the pool like a silent Mexican wave. Heads went up and there was a muted mutter of sound as a man and woman came down the steps from the hotel and made their way towards a couple of sun loungers adjacent to where Ginny and I were lying.

The new female arrival was dark haired and statuesque, nowhere near as pretty and shapely as my Ginny, but still vibrantly attractive in an obvious, tarty way. She had enormous breasts and a very big, slightly sagging bottom, but even so she was still pretty much sex on two legs. And, despite her generous figure, her bikini was of the 'dental floss' variety and even more minuscule than the one my slender wife was wearing. I could see that the eyes of all the men were as good as glued to this woman's every movement – especially when she lay down on her back, without her bikini top. Her breasts slid sideways a bit but, even so, her nipples were the biggest and darkest I've ever seen, crowning her ample curves like a pair of perky Black Forest cherries.

We knew that the guy with her was her husband as we'd seen them sitting together at dinner the night before and heard the waiter refer to them as Mr and Mrs So and So. He was a pretty average guy, slightly younger than me, and from the state of his trunks I could see that he found the sight of his wife as good as naked in public a tremendous turn-on.

I must admit that I found the dark woman arousing too, and that made me feel more than a little guilty when my own lovely wife was right beside me, just inches away. But, to my surprise and relief, when I glanced at Ginny, she seemed amused rather than cross, and she just gave me a grin and shook her head in mock despair. This reaction – so generous and understanding – just made me realise all over again what a fabulous woman she is and how bloody lucky I am to be married to a gem like her.

After a few minutes spent fantasising about Ginny and the big-breasted newcomer getting it on together, I was just considering a swim to cool off my rampant thoughts when one of the other male guests strolled across to the lounger next to the dark-haired woman. He sat down on the opposite side from her husband and nearest to us and immediately began to chat her up, totally ignoring her spouse's existence.

No, that's not quite right. He didn't ignore the husband completely. In fact he actually looked straight at the guy once or twice, with a pitying, almost sneering expression on his face. I couldn't quite hear the conversation, but the brunette obviously liked what her admirer had to say and soon they were laughing and joking together in an openly sexy way.

Then, as I – and the rest of the assembled guests – watched closely, the new man, who was really quite middle-aged and balding and in much worse shape than either me or the brunette's husband, reached out and started fondling one of her big round breasts.

And then it was as if that wave went round the pool again. There was a sort of collective grunt of appreciation as if an entertainment that everyone had been waiting for was just about to start.

The big brunette, for her part, seemed delighted by the new turn of events. As the balding guy squeezed and rolled her ample flesh around, using his fingers and thumbs pretty vigorously, she started wriggling on her lounger and scissoring her thighs together in obvious arousal. A second later, she was squeezing her other breast herself with one hand, and had slid the other hand inside her tiny bikini bottoms. She was clearly playing with herself and it looked as if there was a small animal burrowing around beneath the abbreviated triangle of fabric.

I could barely believe what I was seeing but, on glancing quickly around, I discovered that the other guests didn't seem surprised at all. Some of them were even getting up in order to move closer and get a better view of the floorshow. Obviously this was what my friend had meant when he'd said that a trip to this hotel would spice up the love life. Uninhibited sexual behaviour was clearly one of the special attractions not listed in the lavish brochure.

I couldn't help wondering what the husband thought of all this and, when I managed to tear my eyes away from the voluptuous sight before us, I stole a quick glance at him. He was gazing fixedly at his writhing wife, and the man still feeling her up, and there was a strange combination of lust and shame on his face. What's more, his hand was firmly clamped to his crotch, kneading furiously at his cock through his nylon trunks.

Oh God, I knew exactly how he felt!

Fortunately Ginny and I were near enough to the 'performing' couple to get a grandstand view of the proceedings, and the guests who were gathering around them were considerate enough not to block our line of sight.

It didn't take long for the dark-haired beauty to whip off her thong and spread her legs wide open for the delectation of her hypnotised audience. Given her obvious predilection for displaying her charms, it didn't surprise me that her pussy was completely shaven and, when she drew her legs right back and literally opened herself up like a clam shell, every last detail of her sexual topography was clearly visible. She was dripping wet, and she began to tease her clit in slow, circling strokes. Her admirer was still handling her breast pretty enthusiastically, but he had his cock out of his trunks now and, as we watched, entranced, he knelt down beside his paramour and began to rub himself against her breast, mashing her soft flesh against his erection and masturbating with it.

All this was honestly the hottest thing I had ever seen, far more sizzling than even the most explicit porn video, not least because it was taking place as Technicolor live action in front of us. And not only was the woman groaning and the man panting and muttering profane encouragement to her, I could swear I could smell the raw, pungent scent of cunt over the tang of chlorine from the pool, my own sun lotion, and Ginny's familiar floral perfume.

By now I *had* to have a wank and, sliding my hand between my stomach and the surface of the lounger, I grasped my aching tool. I thought I was being pretty daring but, on looking quickly around, I realised I was probably the most circumspect man in the entire assembly. Several blokes now had their cocks out of their trunks or shorts and were openly masturbating. And it didn't take long before a guy right next to the naked woman let out a loud cry, jerked his hips, and came all over her. The spunk jetted out in an arc and landed right on her glistening pussy, as I guess was his intention. I saw her smile in a slow, sluttish way and massage it lasciviously into her own juices as she continued to rub herself.

A moment later, as another man stepped forwards to stand over the writhing hussy, I experienced a huge pang of guilt.

I was simply loving the sight of all this . . . but what was my Ginny thinking of it?

I hardly dared look at her but, when I snuck a quick glance her way, I got the surprise of my life.

Ginny was masturbating too. She'd slid her hand in between her tummy and the lounger's mattress and her delicious bottom was lifting very discreetly beneath the towel that was spread strategically across her lower body.

Great minds think alike!

I'd expected her to feel a bit uncomfortable seeing all this licentious behaviour in broad daylight but, even though her cheeks were an even prettier pink than before, I could tell that it was from arousal not embarrassment. I caught her eye and gave her a quick wink, which she instantly returned, and then a moment later she continued her secret fun. I expect that if the brunette and her swains hadn't been putting on such a spectacular – and by now very loud – performance, some of the gathered men might have noticed what Ginny was doing and clustered around her instead. But, as it was, all eyes remained locked on the main event. Including Ginny's. And even as I saw her shapely little toes curl up, and her face flush even brighter, she nodded towards the ménage and bade me observe it too.

Oh Christ, what I've done to deserve such a sweet and sexy wife, I really don't know!

By now there were several more active participants. Our writhing amateur porn star had abandoned her own breasts and pussy and now held a sturdy, gleaming cock in each of her hands. She was rubbing away enthusiastically at the one in her right, while the guy whose dick was in her left had his fingers folded around hers and was more or less just using them as a masturbation aid. Several other guys were simply wanking in her general direction, and one enterprising fellow now had one hand between her legs and was diddling her enthusiastically while he played with himself with the other.

Until then, I'd never seen quite such a scene of debauchery in my life. Not even in my fantasies. And

I wondered what the dark-haired woman's husband was thinking and feeling. What emotions did the sight of his wife being used and played with and wanked over by so many other men inspire in him?

Tearing my eyes away from her bucking body, I looked over at him. He was puce in the face, panting like a racehorse, and just about to come himself. His trunks were round his ankles and he had his fist clamped around what looked like an alarmingly tiny dick. Even as I watched, he let out a whimpering cry and ejaculated, his rather sparse emission not even reaching his wife's body, but just spattering unnoticed on the muscular calf of one of the men who was gathered around her.

I could really feel for him. I'd experienced some of those same ambiguous desires and yearnings myself.

The thing was, he was getting off on the lurid sight of his woman being pleasured by men who were much younger, more handsome and far better endowed than he was. Putting myself in his place, I imagined the strange turbulent sensation of both dying of shame and mortification and the sensation of inferiority . . . and at the same time experiencing exactly the thrill I'd been craving for a long time.

At that moment, I had a sudden huge desire to see Ginny being groped and fondled and serviced by the same band of studs that were enjoying the buxom brunette. I wanted to see her throwing herself about, her pussy glistening with come while she shouted and cursed and climaxed in a state of ecstasy that my pathetic equipment and performance were never likely to induce.

It was illogical. It didn't make sense. But I longed for it. God, how I longed for it!

And just that longing was the thing that finally tipped me over.

Beneath my towel I shot my load into my trunks.

When I finally got my breath back and was able to think straight again, events had escalated over on the adjacent sun lounger ... and the sight that met my eyes would have stiffened me all over again, if I hadn't just emptied myself so comprehensively.

The brunette beauty was being fucked now. Well and truly rogered. One enterprising fellow had hauled her bodily right to the end of the lounger and then kneeling on the stone flags, had inserted himself into her and slung her legs clean over his shoulders. Holding her securely by the hips he was shoving and thrusting hard, in a fast, furious rhythm. And judging by the way her heels were flailing, she was having the time of her life.

She wasn't able to express her delight in vocal terms, however, because another man's cock was stuffed into her mouth.

This guy was kneeling beside the lounger, hips angled forwards, and had drawn her head and upper body towards the side of the mattress, allowing her to suck him. I could clearly see her cheeks hollowing and her throat undulating as he worked himself in and out between her stretched and salivating lips.

The entire tableau was both grotesquely animal and simultaneously an astonishing, searing turn-on. Three bodies jerking and thrusting and pumping and writhing. Sometimes they achieved a bizarre state of perfect syncopation. At other times they were just an ugly jumble of limbs, cocks, arses, breasts and pubic hair.

I was just on the point of starting to touch myself again, to see if I could rouse my own sticky semi-interested cock into another full erection, when I felt the soft touch of a hand upon my shoulder.

'Come on, David, let's go,' whispered my Ginny.

She was crouching by my lounger, and had already gathered up her few belongings.

For a moment I felt another surge of guilt. Despite her previous show of interest, the orgy that was going on a few feet away had obviously become just that bit too much for her to cope with. She is a sexy, broadminded woman and never criticised anyone for their sexual preferences, but there is a limit to what even the most liberal person could tolerate. And she'd just reached it . . .

Right, time to go. I'd had more than enough fun for one afternoon. I mustn't be greedy.

But then I looked into her eyes. And what I saw there made my cock leap to full, miraculous attention. She had a bright, wild expression on her face and her lovely cheeks were still furiously flushed. 'Let's go back to our room,' she continued huskily. Her smile only widened when I stood up and she saw the damp patch on the front of my trunks and the newly rising bulge.

She didn't have to ask again and, despite the increasingly frantic activity on the nearby sun lounger, I'd suddenly lost interest in the brunette and her multiple lovers. Ginny and I as good as ran back to our room and, almost before the door was shut, we'd stripped off our suits and were fucking.

And, boy, was it amazing! Because I'd already come, I managed to last a fair while – for me – and coupled with Ginny's own state of high excitement we managed to achieve a more or less mutual orgasm. Something I dreamily counted as a bit of a triumph, considering it'd never really happened before in all the years of our marriage.

Afterwards, relaxed and still dreamy – perhaps a bit too dreamy – I confided my fantasies to Ginny. The ones I'd had about seeing her fucked by the guys around the pool.

Of course the minute I'd voiced them, I immediately regretted it, and could have kicked myself for spoiling the perfect mood. But, God bless her, my Ginny confounded me all over again.

'I've been thinking about the same thing,' she admitted shyly, 'and imagining it was me out there made me hotter than the actual sight of her being fucked did.'

To say my heart skipped a beat is a huge understatement and, screwing up my courage, I very tentatively asked if she'd ever do something like that for real.

'Yes,' she said, sounding a lot less shy now. 'It's something that I've always secretly wanted to do, but never really admitted to myself ... But I wouldn't want to upset you ... I mean ... fantasy and reality are two different things, aren't they?'

I agreed, and we talked for a while, and I tried to explain these weird feelings of mine. To explain the peculiar combination of shame and excitement that I feel when I think about my Ginny being screwed, in public, by other men. I'm not sure that my words made a whole lot of sense, but somehow, because she's an intelligent, intuitive woman, I realised that Ginny understood me perfectly. And understood how intensely I wanted the fantasy to be real.

The way she did ...

After we'd been talking for around fifteen minutes, I realised that she was shifting her bottom around in the bed, and moving in that sort of uneasy, excited way that always told me that she was acutely turned on. When I touched her between the legs I found she was dripping wet and engorged. I was just about shagged out after all the fun I'd already had and, even though the spirit was willing, the flesh was temporarily weak, so I rubbed her to another orgasm whilst describing the filthiest group sex scenario I could possibly imagine – with my beautiful Ginny as the star attraction.

Later, when we'd had a sleep, it was time to dress for dinner.

How can I describe the sense of anticipation that sizzled between us? Neither one of us had tacitly come out and said anything, but we both knew that something was going to happen and we were going to make our fantasies real. And sooner rather than later . . . The idea of it seemed to make a young man out of me again. I kept getting semi-erections while we were getting ready, despite the fact that I'd already come several times that day. I felt as if I had a spring in my step, and that I was ready for anything. Anything at all . . .

And as for my glorious wife . . .

Wow! is all I can say. She's a beautiful woman, even when she's wearing the scruffiest of work-out gear, or baggy old jeans to work in the garden, but tonight she'd made herself into even more of a stunner than usual. She'd piled her lovely chestnut hair up into a flirtatious confection on the top of her head, with sexy little tendrils tumbling to her shoulders, and put on a little more make-up than usual around her eyes and on her lips.

And the dress she was wearing was amazing. One I hadn't seen before. A saucy little slip of a thing in red satin that clung to her gorgeous curves and stopped short well above her knees to show her exquisite, immaculately toned thighs. The top was held up by the thinnest of spaghetti straps and there was no way she could wear a bra with it. Not that she needed one. Her breasts are nowhere near as big as the brunette from the pool orgy's were, but they're firm and high and rounded, with pertly prominent nipples, and well able to hold their own without support.

With this delightful garment, she wore a pair of black patent high-heeled shoes that did wonders for her already superb legs, accentuating the graceful turn of her delicate ankles, and the smooth, shapely line of her calves and knees.

She was a picture. A goddess. Sex incarnate. As we made our way down to dinner, I could hardly believe that such a sublime creature was married to me, and every lustful glance she got from male guests and staff alike only made me more proud and excited.

The evening was mild and balmy and, along with a small group of other diners, we were seated out on a spacious but secluded terrace to eat. To reach this area, we had to walk through the main dining room, and it wasn't my imagination that there were one or two genuine gasps of admiration as Ginny passed by. My own attention, however, was firmly locked onto her lush little bottom as she preceded me.

There was no indication whatsoever of underwear beneath the clinging red fabric of her naughty little dress, so it was obvious that she'd left off her panties for the occasion.

It was difficult to look anywhere other than at the vision sitting in front of me but, as we settled at our table, I realised to my surprise and excitement that many of the people on the terrace with us were the same ones who'd been around the pool earlier on. The star of the show was there, with her podgy husband, but there were more other women around now too. Maybe these wives had been at the beauty salon and in the gym earlier on when the bout of exhibition sex was going on?

The *first* bout, I thought to myself, feeling my rejuvenated dick start to rise beneath the table.

I was even more pleased when the wine waiter came around, and I discovered that he was actually the lifeguard from the pool, moonlighting for some extra money no doubt. We hadn't actually seen him fuck the buxom brunette earlier, but he'd certainly been in the group around her. I could tell my Ginny was attracted to him from the way she kept casting sly glances at his crotch and at his backside in his tight waiter's trousers. I could feel myself willing her to flirt with him, and lure him, and make him her own . . .

My perfect Ginny in her divine little red frock and killer heels was far, far more than a match for the siren from the pool, who now looked overblown, overweight and somehow a lot older than she had earlier. Her skin-tight leopard print sheath dress made her look ever so slightly like a pantomime seductress rather than a real one.

Throughout the meal, I could feel myself getting more and more keyed up and turned on. Ginny was flirting outrageously with the wine waiter-cum-lifeguard, and also casting encouraging smiles at all the other men who kept glancing her way too. There was a sort of electricity building in the air. An awareness that something was going to happen . . . I've no idea what pheromones smell like, but I could swear that the atmosphere was thick with them. By the time we'd finished the dessert course, my dick was like a miniature battering ram beneath the tablecloth, and I could see that Ginny's nipples were as hard as cherry stones inside the flimsy bodice of her dress. And our pet waiter couldn't seem to look anywhere but at them every time he came to the table to serve us.

Finally, by unspoken agreement, my darling wife decided it was time to take action and, when her chosen swain came to ask us if there would be anything further, she said, 'Yes . . . this,' softly and huskily.

Then, before his greedy but somehow not entirely surprised eyes, she peeled down the straps of her dress and bared her sensational breasts.

A ripple went round the room, just like the one that had circled the pool earlier in the day. Ginny sat there proudly, her gorgeous tits on show, and even garnished the delightful view by lifting a hand and slowly and sensuously fondling one of her nipples. A moment later, she reached for the waiter's hand and closed it around her breast.

Just as I'd expected, he didn't waste any time, and began to knead and caress her enthusiastically, rolling the teat between his fingers and tweaking it in a way that made Ginny gasp and shift uneasily in her seat. Her colour was rising and I could tell that between her naked thighs her excitement was rising too.

Still manipulating her, the waiter bent down to give her a long, wet kiss, his tongue clearly plunging into her mouth and exploring and possessing it.

Beneath the table, I clasped my fingers around my aching tool.

They kissed for a long time, hungrily and messily and, all the while, Ginny made little groaning and mewing noises in her throat. She was like a delicious she-cat, supremely on heat, dying to be serviced. And to encourage her prospective mate, she was now openly fondling his crotch.

When the kiss ended, he pulled her to her feet, pushed away her chair and, with no further ado, thrust his hand up her skirt. His hungry smile broadened when he discovered what she and I knew already, and others probably suspected . . . the fact that she wasn't wearing any undies.

'No knickers? God, you're a horny little slut, aren't you?' he said, his voice, deliberately loud, carrying across the terrace. Any diners who might not have noticed yet what was going on were certainly alerted to it now. And, just as earlier, they began to gather around our table, men and women alike.

Ginny moaned softly as he began to play with her. It was impossible to see exactly what he was doing to her but, judging by the way she swayed and shifted from one foot to the other, and caught her breath from time to time, it was clear that he was manipulating her clit with a fair degree of skill.

And how was I feeling?

Well, again, it was that strange melting pot of emotions. A peculiar sense of shame and jealousy that my wife was being handled in the most intimate way by another man, and so very obviously getting a lot of pleasure from it. But, at the same time, an intense sexual excitement that was like a delicious drug ... The degradation of being a spare part in all this, a fifth wheel, made my prick tingle and pound and, without stopping to think, I unzipped myself and pulled it out. I was beyond caring what anyone thought of me. I mean, who would tear their eyes away from the horny sight of my wife being felt up by a total stranger in order to notice that I was openly masturbating too?

And I wasn't the only one. Several of the men were rubbing themselves through their clothes now, and one or two had already unzipped too. In readiness ...

Slack of jaw and still tugging at my dick, I watched the waiter whip off Ginny's dress and bare her completely to their audience. Several men reached out to grab her, gripping her tits and her bottom, squeezing and assessing her flesh.

'Let's get a better look!' called out someone. A moment later, our table was hastily cleared of china and silverware and she was hoisted on top of it, laid on her back, and her thighs roughly parted to expose her glistening sex.

'You're really ready for it, aren't you, gorgeous?' said the waiter, his hand already between her legs again. Ginny didn't answer. She just wriggled slowly, twisting and bunching the tablecloth beneath her, her beautiful body asking silently to be fucked.

'Well, you're going to get a damn good shagging, baby . . . A real seeing-to, better than anything you'll get with hubby.' He glanced my way, his grin contemptuous and sleazy. It should have mortified me, and made me feel like the lowest worm, but somehow it just excited me more than ever. My dick might not be as big as the one he was whipping out even as he spoke to me, but I'll swear that I was equally hard.

I could barely breathe as he took her by her hips, hitched her forwards on the table and then stepped between her thighs and positioned himself at her entrance.

'Ask for it, baby,' he crooned, holding himself and rubbing the tip teasingly around her pussy, 'Beg for it, you horny little pro. Beg me to fuck you.'

Ginny didn't need any encouragement. 'Fuck me! Please fuck me!' she groaned, grabbing the table and trying to force herself onto the waiter's probing dick, 'I want to feel you in me,' she continued, really getting into her performance, 'I want your giant dick rammed right into my pussy.'

The sound of her voice made *my* dick throb and burn. I was right on the edge, ready to spunk at any second, but there was a part of me, somewhere in the back of my mind, that seemed like a detached observer. And an observer who was laughing and applauding Ginny's outrageously sexy act, and who knew that, in spite of appearances, it was all done for me.

'Right you are, baby,' her prospective lover said. He sounded triumphant, but also a little ragged around the edges as if he too was in awe of her, 'Here you are . . . You're gonna get it . . . And when I've had you, these lads want a bit too.' He nodded to the men gathered around and, as if by silent agreement, one clasped Ginny's hands and held her arms back across the table, while another began playing with her tits.

The waiter thrust into her, and she moaned in delight, shifting her bottom about, thrusting herself back against him. She was straining against her makeshift restraint, her superb body flexing and bucking, while not one, but two men now kneaded and squeezed her sweet, rounded breasts.

She was so aroused that it took but moments for the pleasure to become too much for her, and she squirmed like an eel, locking her ankles round her lover's hips and shouting 'Yes, oh God, yes!' as she came.

A moment later the man inside her was overcome by her wild erotic writhing, and obviously by the intense contractions of her gloriously tight pussy around him. He ground out, 'Fuck, fuck, fuck!' and almost before he'd finished, one of the other blokes grabbed him by the shoulders, pulled him off her, and took his place.

But my sweet Ginny was more than a match for them. She was only just hitting her stride. Still held by the hands, she threw herself around lasciviously on the tablecloth, still groaning with pleasure, and quickly milked her second stud to orgasm.

'She needs to get some doggy style,' growled a third man, stepping forward as Stud Number Two staggered clear and almost fell.

Several pairs of strong eager hands lifted Ginny bodily and placed her face down against the cloth, her delightful bottom pertly raised up. Her third lover stepped forward, nudged apart her ankles, and then inserted himself into her from behind. More hands scrabbled beneath her to fondle her boobs, and another man began to play with her bottom, pulling her buttocks this way and that and rudely stretching open her anus.

She wriggled. She flexed her beautiful thighs. She shoved herself bodily back onto the cock inside her.

'For God's sake, someone touch my clit,' she commanded, her voice that of a goddess of sexuality, completely in control of all the slavering studs around her despite her superficially submissive position. Almost instantly, someone sprang to obey her and, the moment he touched her, she shouted hoarsely and came again.

In an almost delirious haze, the orgy went on and on and on, my glorious, inexhaustible wife wearing out man after man, and taking cock after cock into her pussy, her mouth, and even into her butter-smeared anus. After a while, those swains of hers who had recovered their erections began to seek out other sources of relief, some of them wanking, and others approaching their wives and girlfriends and coaxing them into action too.

Me? What did I do?

Well, I pretty quickly lost control and shot my load, blown away by the magnificence of my Ginny. And even though I thought that in all the madness of being fucked and fucked and fucked she might have completely forgotten my existence, she hadn't, bless her. As my hips jerked, she caught my eye and, to my astonishment, her semen-smeared lips formed the precious words, 'I love you.'

Eventually, after what seemed like a bacchanalian dream that had lasted well into the small hours, everyone, even the youngest and most athletic of the men, was knackered. Even Ginny seemed to have finally run out of steam. I retrieved her dress from under the table, gently helped her into it, and then flung my arms around her waist and half-supported, half-carried her off the terrace, along the path and to our room.

After a long, shared shower, we fell into bed, too exhausted to do anything but sleep. Ginny nodded off a few moments before me and, as I listened to her gentle breathing, I began to drift myself, lost in wonder at the magnificence of my sweet and beautiful young wife. And marvelling at the way a really very average middle-aged guy like me had managed to be lucky enough to win her.

No matter how many men she'd been with back on the terrace, it was my arms she was sleeping in that night.

The rest of our holiday was in a much lower key. Ginny didn't participate in any more orgies, even though we did observe at a few more frolics – usually involving the big-busted brunette and one or more admirers. We did, however, spice up the sex in the privacy of our room with plenty of dirty talk about Ginny's outrageous exploits, and that really boosted my performance. I might not be the horniest young stallion any more, but I think I acquitted myself pretty well for the rest of our stay and managed to satisfy my sweetheart.

You won't be surprised to learn that we've just booked another stay at that hotel in the very near future!

– *David, Worcestershire, UK*

Lesbian Longing

The pub was quieter than usual on that fateful Wednesday evening, and I thought we might stand a chance of winning the quiz for a change. My best friend, Dianna, and I had come second on many occasions but gaining those few extra points to win had seemed impossible. There were a dozen or so teams and we were known as The Golden Pussies. But the top team, The Night Girls, always beat us by a couple of points. Little did I know that we were going to win that night. And I had no idea that my life was about to change dramatically.

Sipping my vodka and tonic, I checked my watch and smiled. The Night Girls hadn't turned up and the quiz was about to begin. The problem was, Dianna hadn't turned up either. As the minutes passed, I wondered whether to call it a day and go home. I really didn't want to sit there alone for a couple of hours. Besides, I wouldn't have done at all well in the quiz without Dianna's help.

Had I known then what I know now . . . Would I have left the pub? Would I have gone home to my loving husband? I was 35 years old, I didn't want change. I was happily married to a wonderful man. I had a beautiful home, a home that we'd built together. A home built on love and trust. I didn't want the very essence of my life ripped out.

'Hi, Sarah,' Dianna's eighteen-year-old daughter said as she approached my table. 'Mum's twisted her ankle so I'm here to take her place.'

'Is she OK?' I asked, concernedly.

'She was in a hurry to get here and she slipped on the stairs. She'll be all right.'

Tanya bought herself a glass of white wine and joined me at the table. She was extremely attractive with long blonde hair cascading over her shoulders and she had a figure that any woman would die for. Her blue eyes sparkled with life, her glossed lips were full and succulent, and her smile was enchanting. She was delightful company and, to top it all, she was academic. But, despite all this, her boyfriend had recently dumped her. What more could a man want in a girl? I wondered. She didn't go into the details, but she did say that he'd gone off with some other girl.

Tanya was wearing a turquoise mini-skirt, and the men in the pub couldn't take their eyes off her. The tight material of her white blouse faithfully following the contours of her petite breasts, her nipples clearly defined . . . She radiated an air of sensuality. It was no surprise that the men had never taken an interest in me, I reflected. Thirty-five years old with lank brown hair, my days of turning heads were far behind me.

Not only did we have a great evening, but we won the quiz. I answered the music questions and Tanya went for general knowledge. We were a good team, and I suggested that she join her mum and me each week. As we walked back to her house, we chatted about this and that and got on really well together. Although I'd known her since birth, I'd never had a chance to spend any time alone with her. Having spent the evening together, I realised what a delightful girl she was.

'I'd better check up on the invalid,' I said with a giggle as she opened her front door.

'I'll put the kettle on,' she said. 'You go and find Mum in the lounge and I'll bring the coffees in.'

Dianna had gone to bed so, rather than disturb her, I sat in the lounge with Tanya. She put some music on and, again, we chatted and laughed and got on like old friends. Her father was working away, and I knew how much she missed him. What with her boyfriend dumping her and her mum in bed, I got the impression that she was pleased to have some company. Although I had to get back to John, my husband, I chatted to Tanya for over an hour. John and I hadn't had kids, and I realised that I was envious of Dianna. If only I'd had a daughter . . . It was no good looking back.

'I'd better go,' I finally said, finishing my third cup of coffee. 'John will be wondering where I've got to.'

'I've really enjoyed this evening,' Tanya said, following me to the front door. 'I've not had such a good night out in ages.'

'Me, too,' I breathed, turning and facing her. 'You'll have to come along to the quiz next week.'

As she placed her hand on my shoulder and leaned forwards, I thought that she was going to kiss my cheek. But, pressing her full red lips to mine, she kissed me passionately. I was shocked, stunned, confused . . . She finally moved back and smiled at me. I didn't know what to think, what to say. Her blue eyes sparkling, she brushed her long blonde hair away from her pretty face and thanked me for a wonderful evening.

Walking home, I tried to convince myself that Tanya's kiss had been nothing more than a friendly gesture. She'd always been a cuddly, demonstrative girl, and I was sure that there'd been nothing more to her kiss. John was asleep when I slipped into bed beside him, but I couldn't sleep. I lay my head on my pillow and stared into the darkness for hours. I was thinking about Tanya, how attractive she was, how well we got on together . . . And the way she'd kissed me.

Dianna rang me the following morning. Her ankle was a lot better and she asked me whether John and I would like to go round to her place that evening for a drink. I was a little hesitant and said that I wasn't sure what John had planned. I knew that Tanya would be there, and I didn't want to face her. There'd be an awkwardness, we'd gaze at each other and . . . Was I making something out of nothing?

'You have to come,' Dianna insisted. 'I didn't see you last night and Tanya is looking forward to it. In fact, it was her idea.'

'I'll see what John says,' I breathed.

'I suppose you don't need me now that you have Tanya,' she quipped.

'What do you mean by that?'

'The quiz, you won the quiz.'

'That was only because The Night Girls didn't turn up. I'm not saying that Tanya was no help. It's just that, without The Night Girls . . .'

'You made a good team,' Dianna cut in. 'Tanya told me how much she'd enjoyed the evening and she's going to come along every week.'

'Oh, right,' I murmured. 'Well, that'll be nice.'

'You ask John about this evening, OK?'

'Yes, yes I will.'

'Great, I'll see you both later.'

Replacing the receiver, I realised how silly I was being. Tanya had kissed me, a simple kiss to say goodbye. Why couldn't I face her? I knew that John had nothing planned for the evening, so why was I making excuses? But, something deep in my mind was nagging me. Tanya's kiss ... It wasn't a simple goodbye gesture. So, what was it? I felt confused again as I tried to busy myself with housework. But, no matter how I tried, I couldn't push thoughts of Tanya out of mind. I could almost smell the perfume of her hair, taste the saliva on her lips ... I had to stop acting like a silly teenage girl and compose myself.

John was more than happy to go round to Dianna's place for the evening. Although I went to the quiz every Wednesday and he met up with his friends in the local pub on Fridays, it made a nice change to go out together. I grabbed a couple of bottles of white wine from the fridge and we walked the short distance to Dianna's house. I was looking forward to the evening, and decided not to ponder on Tanya's kiss.

We sat on the patio with the evening sun warming us as we laughed and joked and drank wine. Tanya was wearing a loose-fitting white blouse and a red mini-skirt. Although her skirt was very short, she had beautifully long slender legs and didn't look at all tarty. She didn't catch my eye or flash me a knowing smile and I felt a lot easier as we chatted. Everything was normal, and I knew that I'd read more into her kiss than was there.

'I think she's in love,' Dianna said as I followed her into the kitchen.

'Who, Tanya?' I asked her as she took another bottle of wine from the fridge.

'All the signs are there. I asked her about it but she won't tell me his name or what he looks like or how old he is. But I know that she's in love.'

'Oh, right,' I breathed. Was I jealous? No, I couldn't be. 'So, has she said anything at all about him?'

'All she said was that she's met the most wonderful person ever. I got the impression that he's quite a bit older than her. I just hope he's not a married man.'

Or a married woman? I mused anxiously. 'I'm sure she'll tell you more when she's ready,' I said, forcing a giggle. 'You know what teenage girls are like.'

We returned to the patio and drank more wine and I began to feel quite light-headed. Was it the alcohol or the thought that Tanya was in love with me? I wondered. Something was happening to me, but I didn't know what it was. Unable to take my eyes off Tanya, I finally went into the house and stood in the kitchen. I had to free my mind of silly thoughts, I knew, as I gulped down my wine.

'Alone at last,' Tanya said as she joined me.

'Yes, I . . . I was just . . .' I stammered.

'Waiting for me?'

'No, I . . . I wanted a glass of water. The wine has made me feel quite thirsty.'

'It's made me feel quite sexy,' she breathed huskily. 'Do you feel sexy?'

'Tanya, I . . .'

As she held my head and pressed her glossed lips to mine, I felt my stomach somersault. This couldn't be happening, I thought, as she slipped her tongue into my mouth. This was unreal. My husband was on the patio with Dianna, my best friend, Tanya's mother . . . I had to push Tanya away but, as much as I tried, I couldn't do it. I could hear John and Dianna laughing. They wouldn't be laughing if they knew what we were up to. My eyes closed, my head spinning, I breathed heavily through my nose as Tanya explored my mouth with her tongue. I could feel her hand squeezing my breast, her fingers pinching my nipple . . .

'Tanya,' I finally gasped as I managed to step back.

'I'm sorry,' she said softly, licking her full lips provocatively. 'I couldn't help myself.'

'For God's sake, I'm not a . . .'

'A lesbian?' she cut in, cocking her head to one side and grinning at me.

'Yes, no, I mean . . . Tanya, you're my best friend's daughter.'

'I know that, Sarah.'

'And John is my husband.'

'I know that, too. Now that we've established who we are and our relationships with others, let's talk about our relationship.'

'We haven't got a relationship, Tanya.'

'Haven't we?'

'No, we haven't. Let's go back to the patio before . . .'

'Before you change your mind about me?'

My hands trembling, my heart banging hard against my chest, I felt my womb contract as I lowered my eyes and gazed at her long legs. The heady taste of her mouth lingering on my lips, I wondered what was happening to me as I lifted my head and locked my eyes to hers. I was a happily married woman, a heterosexual woman . . . I wasn't a lesbian, was I?

As Tanya opened another bottle of wine, I recalled my school days. I'd had a silly crush on a girl in my class. Holding hands, we'd walked across the common after school one afternoon and stopped behind some bushes. We kissed and fondled and I'd thought that I'd fallen in love. I could think of nothing other than her, the perfume of her hair, the taste of her mouth, the feel of her hand between my thighs. I was a silly teenage girl with a silly crush. What was I now?

'There you are,' Dianna said as she wandered into the kitchen. 'Has Tanya told you about her new boyfriend? Has she told you that she's in love?'

'Mum, do you have to?' Tanya sighed.

'Sorry, but I'm intrigued.'

'As it happens, I have told Sarah that I'm in love.'

'Really?'

'Yes, and I told her who I'm in love with.'

'Come on, spill the beans,' Dianna trilled, turning and facing me.

'I . . . I think I'll keep out of this,' I said. 'It's a mother-daughter thing.'

Leaving the kitchen, I went out to the patio and sat with John. Things were getting out of hand, I reflected, as he asked me what the trouble was. I giggled and said that I'd had too much wine, but he frowned at me. He obviously sensed that something was wrong. I then feigned a headache in an attempt to conceal my guilt. But he again asked me whether anything was wrong.

'I'm fine,' I said. 'I've just had a little too much wine.'

'Dianna was saying that Tanya's in love.'

'Yes, apparently so,' I breathed nonchalantly. 'It's beginning to get dark. Shall we head back soon?'

'It's early, Sarah. Surely, you don't want to go already?'

'No, I suppose not.'

'Are you sure you're all right? You were fine before you went into the house and now you seem edgy.'

'I've told you,' I returned. 'I have a headache.'

It was unlike me to snap at John, and I knew that I had to put a stop to the nonsense with Tanya before he suspected something. Deciding not to go to the quiz the following week, I also thought it best to stay away from Dianna's house for a while. She could call on me for a chat over coffee, which wouldn't involve Tanya. Things would be all right once Tanya had got over her silly crush, or so I thought.

212

Within minutes of John leaving for work the following morning, the doorbell rang. I'd just had a shower and was still in my dressing gown and wasn't going to bother to answer the door. But, when the bell rang again, I thought I'd better see who it was. I should have looked out of the lounge window before opening the door, but it was too late.

'Hi,' Tanya said. 'I was just passing.'

'Tanya, please . . .' I began as she walked past me into the hall.

'It's all right, I got the message last night,' she sighed. 'You're not interested in me. You made that plain enough.'

'It's not that I'm not interested. I'm a married woman and . . .'

'Yes, so you said last night.'

'Come and sit down for a minute,' I sighed, leading her into the lounge. 'I think we need to talk.'

Making herself comfortable on the sofa, she smiled at me as I sat opposite her in the armchair. Her long blonde hair framing her pretty face, her blue eyes sparkling, she was incredibly attractive. She was wearing her red mini-skirt, and I couldn't help but cast my eyes over her naked legs. I had to muster up my willpower to resist her. But, why was I having to resist her? There shouldn't be a battle raging in my mind, I reflected. I had no lesbian desires to quash, did I?

'I know what you're going through,' she said. 'I went through the same dilemma.'

'Dilemma?' I echoed.

'Male or female, which is your preference? I've had several boyfriends, as you know. And I've discovered that I prefer my own sex.'

'Tanya, I'm not going through a dilemma,' I stated firmly. 'And I certainly don't have to discover my sexual preference. I'm a happily married woman. A happily married heterosexual woman.'

'I tried to convince myself that I was heterosexual,' she said, leaving the sofa and kneeling at my feet. 'I fought it for as long as I could, and finally gave in. Don't fight it, Sarah.'

I stared in disbelief as she moved my dressing gown aside, parted my legs and kissed the smooth flesh of my inner thighs. I wasn't sure whether it was shock or curiosity, but I was unable to stop her as she moved dangerously close to my naked pussy. What the hell did she think she was doing? I wondered. What the hell was I doing? A thousand thoughts careering through the confusion in my mind, I was powerless to halt the imminent act of lesbian sex.

The feel of her hot breath against my outer lips, her wet tongue running up and down my sex crack, I gripped the arms of the chair and tried to deny the immense pleasure she was bringing me. Again and again, her tongue ran up my valley of desire, waking sleeping nerve endings, sending quivers through my rhythmically contracting womb. In a dreamlike state, I felt as though my mind was blowing away on clouds of lust. Had I found my sexual heaven?

My sex life with John wasn't particularly good, the flame of passion having inevitably diminished over the years. Oral sex had become a thing of the past, the days of licking and sucking were over. We made love once a week, usually with John entering me from behind as we lay in bed. He'd come, fill my vagina with sperm, and then we'd fall asleep. Rarely did I enjoy an orgasm, but that was marriage.

'No,' I breathed as Tanya stretched my sex lips wide apart and encircled the bud of my erect clitoris with the tip of her tongue. She ignored me, licking and sucking fervently on my pleasure bud as I gripped the arms of the chair. I could feel my juices of arousal seeping from the gaping entrance to my vagina as she worked expertly on my ripening clitoris. I couldn't allow this, I thought, doing my best to fight my inner desires. I had to stop her before I reached my orgasm. I was a married woman, a heterosexual . . . I couldn't come in a teenage girl's mouth.

As if aware of my imminent coming, Tanya moved down my gaping sex valley and licked the pink cone of wet flesh surrounding the entrance to my vagina. My vagina, John's vagina . . . It should have been my husband's tongue there, I thought anxiously. It should have been my husband's penis there, not a young girl's tongue. What the hell was I doing? Why had I no power to resist? What the hell had happened to me?

Pressing her full red lips hard against the open entrance to my vagina, Tanya pushed her tongue deep into my sex sheath. I shuddered as my clitoris swelled and my nipples became erect and brushed against the material of my dressing gown. Aroused as never before, I was desperate for the relief of orgasm. But this was my best friend's teenage daughter, I reminded myself. Her long blonde hair tickling my inner thighs, my lower stomach, her nose pressed hard against my solid clitoris, she sucked out my juices of desire. I could hear her swallowing, gulping down my creamy offering. My best friend's daughter. This was so very wrong, and yet . . .

'Tanya, no,' I breathed as she moved up and again sucked my clitoris into her hot mouth. No matter how I tried, I couldn't hold back as she repeatedly swept her tongue over the sensitive tip of my clitoris. I was going to reach my orgasm, I was going to come in another girl's mouth. Slipping two fingers deep into my contracting vagina and massaging my hot inner flesh, she sucked and mouthed deftly on my clitoris. I arched my back, my knuckles whitening as I gripped the arms of the chair harder and waited for the inevitable explosion of pleasure.

'God,' I cried as my orgasm erupted within the solid nub of my pulsating clitoris. 'Tanya, no.' Again and again, waves of pure sexual bliss crashed through my trembling body. My clitoris pulsating wildly, my orgasmic cream flooding her thrusting fingers, my breathing fast and shallow, I tossed my head from side to side as she sustained my incredible climax. Dripping in confusion, drowning in pleasure, the stark reality of the situation hit me as my orgasm finally began to recede. I'd committed an act of lesbian sex with a teenage girl.

Shuddering as Tanya slipped her fingers out of my inflamed vagina and lapped up my flowing juices, I tried to blame her for what had happened. She'd seduced me, she'd forced me . . . I only had myself to blame, I reflected, as she sucked out my hot milk. I should have pushed her away. The minute she'd parted my thighs, I should have been strong and pushed her away. Why hadn't I?

'Was that nice?' she asked me, her pussy-wet face beaming as she looked up at me. 'Did you enjoy that?'

'Yes, no . . .' I murmured, pulling my dressing gown together to conceal my wet sex crack. 'Tanya, this is wrong.'

'Wrong?' she echoed, her blue eyes frowning. 'Why is it wrong to bring you sexual pleasure?'

'Because we're both female. I'm not a lesbian, Tanya.'

'That word worries you, doesn't it? Lesbian. Lesbian sex.'

'Yes, it does worry me. I'm a married woman and I enjoy sex with my husband.'

'Does he lick and suck you the way I did? Does he bring you as much pleasure as I did?'

'Well, no . . . Yes, yes, he does. I mean, not exactly the way you did but . . . I don't know what I mean.'

'It's all right, Sarah,' she breathed. She flashed me a knowing smile. 'I know exactly what you mean.'

What did I mean? I pondered as she climbed to her feet and settled on the sofa. Did I mean that she'd brought me far more pleasure than John had? I couldn't deny it, I mused anxiously. A teenage girl had taken me to the most fantastic orgasm I'd ever experienced. I had difficulty admitting it to myself, let alone Tanya. I had to end this, I decided. End it now. Rising to my feet, I walked to the lounge door and turned.

'You'd better go,' I said coldly. 'And I think it best that you don't come here again.'

'You're in denial,' she said, leaving the sofa. 'After a day or so, you'll come to terms with your true feelings. When you've done that, ring me.' She walked past me into the hall and opened the front door. 'Ring me when you're ready,' she said, before leaving the house.

I breathed a sigh of relief as the door closed. She'd gone, my ordeal was over. Ordeal? I mused. I could feel my vaginal milk streaming down my inner thighs as I went into the kitchen and filled the kettle. A stark reminder of my lesbian-induced orgasm, I thought uneasily. Pouring myself a cup of coffee, I pondered on Tanya's words: *You're in denial*. She was right, of course. But I wasn't a lesbian.

I spent the day doing housework and clearing out the kitchen cupboards. I'd cleaned the shelves and put the tins and food back in the cupboards and then emptied them and started again. I was trying to occupy myself, kill time, clear my mind of thoughts of lesbian sex. When John came home from work at six o'clock, I had a nice meal ready for him. His favourite: roast beef and boiled potatoes and ... I tried to come across as normal, but he knew that something was bothering me.

'Anything interesting happen today?' he asked me during the meal.

'No, no,' I murmured. 'I've just been doing house-work.'

'Didn't Tanya call in this morning?'

'Tanya?' I felt my hands trembling, my heart racing. 'No, no she didn't.'

'I saw her hovering down the road when I left for work this morning. I thought she might have come to see you.'

'No, she ... she must have been going to college or something.'

After the meal, I cleared the dishes away while John went for a shower. I felt like a nervous wreck, and I knew that I couldn't carry on like this. The anxiety, the lies, the guilt ... A dreadful thought struck me as I poured a glass of wine. I'd committed adultery. Was it true adultery? I pondered. I'd not had full-blown sex with another man. But I had been licked and sucked to orgasm by another girl. Male or female, a tongue was a tongue. Male or female ... I'd committed adultery.

Trying to calm myself, I drank far too much wine. John settled in his favourite armchair, the very chair where I'd opened my legs and Tanya had ... More guilt, more shame. I did my best to avoid John during the evening and finally went to bed early to escape his questioning. He was worried about me, he cared for me. I couldn't face him, I couldn't even face myself. I couldn't hide my guilt, my shame.

When he slipped into the marital bed and cuddled up behind me, I knew that he wanted sex. I could feel the hardness of his penis against my bottom as he kissed my neck. As his swollen knob slipped between my thighs, trying to gain access to my sex sheath, my guilt swamped me. Finally driving his solid penis deep into my vagina, he told me how much he loved me. Love? What was love? Tanya loved me, my husband loved me . . . Who did I love?

I squeezed my eyes shut as John withdrew his shaft and drove into me again. Finding his rhythm, he breathed heavily and murmured his words of love. With every thrust of his manhood, I thought about Tanya's tongue. She'd licked me there, pushed her tongue deep into my vagina and sucked out my juices of arousal. And now John was fucking me there. I'd committed adultery.

John came quickly and then fell asleep. I could feel his sperm oozing between my inner lips, trickling over my thigh. I lay awake for what seemed like hours. Worrying, riddled with guilt, swamped by shame, I must have fallen asleep at some stage. John was up and about long before I woke. It was Saturday, he had no work. He must have thought it best to leave me sleeping. Why had he thought it best? What did he know? Had he discovered my dark secret? I was being ridiculous, I knew as I slipped out of bed and took a shower. There was no way anyone would ever discover my dirty secret.

I enjoyed the weekend. We went out for a pub lunch and pottered in the garden, doing things together as we always had. John obviously noticed that I was more relaxed and I thanked God that his questioning was over. We talked about having a break, perhaps going away for a weekend. I liked the idea and we decided on Devon. A small cottage away from it all. Away from Tanya?

Dianna rang me on Monday morning. She was excited about the quiz and reckoned that, now we had three in our team, we'd beat The Night Girls hands down. I finally managed to get a word in and told her that I wouldn't be going. I said that John and I were going out for a meal Wednesday evening. I lied to her, lied to my best friend. But my lie was nothing in comparison to what I'd done with her daughter, I reflected guiltily.

After the phone call, I paced the lounge floor for half an hour. Dianna had obviously sensed that something was wrong with me. I had to talk to her, I decided. Leaving the house, I rehearsed my lines as I walked down the road. *Tanya came on strong to me, tried to seduce me.* No, I couldn't tell Dianna that her daughter was a lesbian. *I'm keeping out of Tanya's way because we had words.* By the time I'd reached Dianna's house, I was more confused than ever. I had no idea what to say to her and came to the conclusion that it was best to say nothing.

'Come in,' Tanya invited me as she opened the front door.

'Thanks,' I breathed, hanging my head so as not to catch her eyes. 'It's a lovely day,' I said stupidly, following her into the lounge.

'It's a beautiful day now that you're here. So, you've come to terms with your true feelings. I knew you would.'

'I've come to see your mother,' I returned, settling on the sofa.

'She's gone out. Didn't she tell you when she rang? She's gone to the doctor about her ankle.'

'No, no she didn't. In that case, I ... I think I'd better be going.'

Tanya sat beside me and placed her hands over my ears and turned my head to face her. I gazed into her blue eyes, her sparkling blue eyes, as she leaned forward and kissed my lips. Why hadn't I stopped her? I wondered as she slipped her tongue into my mouth. Why had I allowed her to trap me, yet again? Or had I trapped myself?

I felt her hand fondling my breast, squeezing me there, as she kissed me and tongued my mouth. Unable to move, unable to halt the lesbian loving, I felt my womb contract as she slipped her hand up my skirt and pressed her fingertips into the swell of my panties. I didn't want this, I wasn't a lesbian, I was a happily married woman ... Our lips still locked in a passionate kiss, her fingers pressing into my panties, massaging my erect clitoris, I pushed my tongue into her mouth and tasted her saliva. What on earth did I think I was doing? I didn't know what I was doing.

Tanya took my hand and slipped it between her slender thighs, and I knew that she wanted me to reciprocate. I felt the warm swell of her panties, the softness of her pussy lips through the thin material. I was about to reach the point of no return, I had to stop ... She parted her legs wide as she continued to massage my clitoris through my panties. I could feel her sex crack, but, could I give her what she wanted?

My mind swirled with confusing thoughts. I should have been with a man, my hand should be grasping the solid shaft of a penis. A teenage girl, panties, vulval lips rising either side of a sex crack ... I had to stop myself but my clitoris was erect in arousal and my juices of lust were flowing. As Tanya pulled my panties to one side and massaged the solid nub of my sensitive clitoris, I again knew that she wanted me to reciprocate.

My fingers moved almost involuntarily, pulling her panties to one side and exposing the swollen lips of her young pussy. I felt her there, ran a fingertip up and down her open crack. She was wet with desire, lesbian desire. Her clitoris was solid, waiting in

221

expectation for my caressing fingertip. I massaged her there and she shuddered and gasped as her mouth left mine. Her eyes were closed, her succulent lips parted sensually. She continued to massage my pleasure bud, and I knew that I was nearing my orgasm. I'd passed the point of no return.

Moving my hand down her valley of lust, I slipped a finger into the wet heat of her teenage vagina. She gasped again, her head lolling from side to side as I massaged deep inside her tight sex sheath. We kissed again, our mouths locked as we masturbated each other. I seemed to have no control over my actions as I moved my finger up to the swollen bulb of her clitoris.

We reached our orgasms together, shaking uncontrollably as we pumped out our juices of lesbian desire. I felt drunk on lesbian sex, delirious in my coming. The battle between right and wrong raging in my mind had ceased, for the time being. Revelling in my lesbian orgasm, I pushed my tongue deep into Tanya's mouth as we kissed passionately. I was lost in my coming.

No words passed between us as our pleasure began to wane. Slowing our clitoral massaging, our lips parting, we finally lay back on the sofa gasping in the aftermath of our loving. I had nothing to lose now, I mused dreamily as I slipped off the sofa and knelt at Tanya's feet. Pulling her wet panties down her long legs and tossing them aside, I parted her thighs and gazed longingly at her vulval crack. To my amazement, she had no pubic hair. She whispered to me as I gazed at her pussy. She said that she'd shaved for me. The swollen pads of her outer lips rising alluringly either side of her creamy-wet sex, she looked so young and alluring.

Burying my face between her naked thighs, breathing in the scent of the most intimate part of her young

222

body, I pushed my tongue into her sex crack and tasted her there. Lubricious, tangy, slightly bitter, girlie . . . She writhed and gasped as I repeatedly ran my tongue up her crack. Trembling uncontrollably, she whimpered incoherent words of sex as I sucked the solid nub of her clitoris into my hot mouth and swept my tongue over its sensitive tip.

'Yes,' she breathed as I drove two fingers into the hugging sheath of her teenage vagina. In my sexual frenzy, all thoughts of John and my marriage faded into oblivion as I sucked and mouthed on the girl's bulbous clitoris. Had I found my niche, my sexual preference? Was I in love with Tanya? Raising her legs and placing her feet on the sofa either side of her hips, she allowed me deeper access to her tightening vagina.

'Coming,' she announced shakily as I increased my thrusting rhythm and sucked harder on her solid clitoris. Slurping, mouthing, licking, fingering . . . I felt elated as she shook wildly and let out a cry of sexual pleasure. I sustained her climax, sucking out her orgasm as she thrashed about on the sofa and pumped out her girl cream. Slipping my fingers out of her inflamed vagina, I pressed my lips hard against her wet hole and sucked out her lubricious cream. Drinking from her teenage body, I massaged the last ripples of sex from her pulsating clitoris until she begged me to stop.

'No more,' she breathed, her young body convulsing. 'God, no more.'

'Was that all right?' I asked her, sucking my pussy-wet fingers.

'It was beautiful,' she murmured, her blue eyes rolling as she gazed at me. 'It was heavenly. I've never had an orgasm like it.'

Rising to my feet, as she sat up and grabbed her wet panties from the floor, I straightened my clothes and ran my fingers through my dishevelled hair. Where to from here? I pondered, as she left the sofa and swayed on her sagging legs. Adultery, lesbian sex with a teenage girl . . . No one would ever discover my dirty secret, I consoled myself. Tanya would hardly go blabbing to her mother and I'd never tell John. But, I knew in my heart that I couldn't live a lie. Lies, deceit, adultery . . . I couldn't do it. Tanya rushed upstairs to her room as her mother's car pulled up in the drive. Wiping my sex-wet mouth on the back of my hand, I tried to calm myself as Dianna called out from the hall.

'In here,' I said, sitting on the sofa.

'Sarah,' she trilled, standing before me. 'I didn't know you were coming round. Where's Tanya?'

'Upstairs,' I replied softly. 'Dianna, I . . . I have to talk to you.'

'What is it?' she asked concernedly as she joined me on the sofa. 'You look pale. What's the matter?'

'I can't live a lie.'

'What? What do you mean?'

'I . . . I've discovered that I'm a lesbian,' I blurted out.

'All right, calm down,' she said softly. 'Just relax and tell me about it.'

'God only knows what you're going to think of me. But I can't harbour secrets. And I was never any good at lying.'

'You don't have to tell me that,' she quipped. 'I remember when we were at school your face would turn bright red and . . .'

'Dianna, listen to me. What I'm about to tell you will probably put an end to our friendship. All I ask is that you don't tell John.'

'OK, I promise.'

'The girl, the woman . . . I've known her forever. It's only now that I realise . . .'

'I know, Sarah,' she cut in. 'You don't have to tell me.'

'You know?' I gasped, staring hard at her.

'Yes. I was hoping that . . .'

'You don't mind?' I interrupted her. 'I mean, you're not going to have a go at me?'

'I've prayed for this day to come, Sarah,' she whispered as she leaned forwards and pressed her lips to mine. Her hand slipping between my thighs, she pulled my wet panties aside and slipped her finger deep into my very wet vagina. 'I've wanted you since we were at school together,' she breathed huskily.

– Sarah, Oxfordshire, UK

One Snowy Night

It was a snowy Friday night and I was working at the front desk of a small motel. Because of the weather, business was slow, the motel was almost empty and I felt as if I was the only one in the entire city – not even a car passed on the normally busy street. I was just relaxing, watching the small black-and-white TV that my boss was kind enough to have left for days like this one, when I noticed someone trudging through the snow towards the door. I'd gotten so comfortable just sitting enjoying my slow evening that it felt like an intrusion to have a customer check in.

Tall and dopey-looking, the man had mulatto skin, the biggest Afro I'd ever seen and he spoke with a slur. 'Great, another nut,' I remember thinking.

He tried to negotiate a better price for the room, but I was firm – I guess as payback for interrupting my TV programme. The entire time he was standing at the desk, his eyes remained fixated on my cleavage.

The way he leered at me was almost to the point of creepy: the way he would lick his large lips before each sentence and how closely he leaned in when I spoke. There was something very sordid about him and even desperate. While I'm not one to turn my back on male attention, I was quick to help him and send him on his way.

Within minutes of his check-in, the telephone charge printer started; he was making quite a few phone calls. I'd been with the motel for a while and recognised the numbers he was calling – all escort services. It wasn't a surprise that he was horny by the way he stared at my tits during check-in.

The callbacks started to roll in and, whether out of boredom or just plain feeling naughty, I decided to listen in when I transferred the next call, all the while thinking to myself, 'Of course this winner has to pay for sex!'

'Hi there, my name is Pam. I hear you're looking for some company,' she said seductively.

His slurred broken English asked almost frantically, 'Do you have big brrreasts?' He rolled his Rs and I tried desperately to hold in my laughter. As their conversation went on I became stunned to hear him describe the type of girl he was looking for. 'I want one girl with big brrreasts, big bum and brown curly hair,' he insisted.

He had described me! He received several other callbacks and with each requested the description.

Though he was not at all attractive to me or even remotely charming, I began to get excited thinking of how badly this man wanted to fuck me – or a reasonable facsimile. He had stared at my cleavage almost hungrily when he'd been in the office and, when I went around the counter to shut the door behind him, he looked my entire body up and down and licked his lips. He seemed a bit pervie but no more, and I hadn't thought anything of it at the time. Being a pretty, petite and curvaceous girl usually got me a double take or two.

I began fantasising about what he'd said and picturing the escort entering his room – just imagining what they might do. I became wet as the face in my thoughts became mine. Poor guy turned down all of his callbacks as each offered girls of the wrong description. I couldn't believe how turned on I was becoming. I'd always been a good girl by most standards, yet here I was picturing being fucked by this large clumsy guy. My clit was so hard, it was dying to be touched. I contemplated going into the back room and fingering myself, but then I got a better idea. I dialled his room number, my hands trembling at the idea. 'Hi, it's the front desk calling,' I began, 'I hear you want some company.'

'I want to fuck,' he said with no hesitation. 'I like big brrreasts.' He paused.

I had a feeling he hadn't understood that it was me calling, so I went along with it.

'I have brown hair, big breasts and a round bum,' I said, trying to make it as simple for him as possible.

'Come here now. I pay you two hundred dollars.' He practically yelled with excitement. The other girls had been asking for three hundred and fifty, but I wanted to fuck, so the two hundred he offered was an added perk.

Still amazed at myself, I knocked on his door. 'You want me?' I smiled nervously.

He grunted and led me into the room. 'Take off your clothes,' said the already-shirtless giant as he undid his jeans, revealing a very long hard cock.

I complied, first removing my sweater, then my skirt and stockings. I finally stood pantiless in just a bra, my cunt throbbing – aching to be played with. He didn't waste any time; he wanted me bad. He gently pushed me onto the bed. I lay back with my ass at the edge of the mattress, he parted my legs, then leaned over me and grabbed the tits he'd wanted so much. He sucked and licked, taking almost an entire breast into his mouth, groaning with delight.

He began licking quickly downwards. I sat up just enough to see him put his large lips over my glistening cunt. He went to town on my clit, sucking me like I had never been sucked before. He put two, or maybe it was three, fingers into me and pumped in and out in a frenzy.

My body started quivering – I knew I was about to come harder than I had ever come before when he pulled his now-wet face away from my clit and moved upwards, pushing his weight on top of me.

He used his hands to raise my legs up and wrap them around himself. In one quick movement he thrust his hard, now-purple cock into me. His thick member slid in and out of me quickly, almost sloppily.

He fucked me like he'd not had a woman in years. This excited me even more. With every thrust I could feel how badly he needed a cunt. I felt like his dirty whore and I loved it. The sensation of his balls slamming against my ass when he lifted my legs into the air and farther apart made me even hotter – it was all it took to push me to come, and come I did. I could feel my juices dripping out of my pussy and down my ass and couldn't do anything to contain my moans of pleasure. Within seconds he came too, pulling his cock out and blowing his load all over my belly, grunting loudly. I rested for a moment and tried not to look at him for fear that I might feel awkward for what I had just done, but he got up right away and walked over to the dresser. He returned, handed me a small stack of bills, my clothes, and grunted out a 'thank you'.

I dressed quickly as he stood watching me and left without another word, went back to the desk and put away my money. Seconds later I saw him again outside trudging through the snow, this time away from the motel. I leaned back into my chair, turned the TV back on and enjoyed the remainder of my best and most lucrative shift ever.

– *P. J., Ontario, Canada*

231

nexus

The leading publisher of fetish and adult fiction

TELL US WHAT YOU THINK!

Readers' ideas and opinions matter to us so please take a few minutes to fill in the questionnaire below.

1. Sex: Are you male ☐ female ☐ a couple ☐?

2. Age: Under 21 ☐ 21–30 ☐ 31–40 ☐ 41–50 ☐ 51–60 ☐ over 60 ☐

3. Where do you buy your Nexus books from?

☐ A chain book shop. If so, which one(s)?

_____

☐ An independent book shop. If so, which one(s)?

_____

☐ A used book shop/charity shop
☐ Online book store. If so, which one(s)?

_____

4. How did you find out about Nexus books?

☐ Browsing in a book shop
☐ A review in a magazine
☐ Online
☐ Recommendation
☐ Other _____

5. In terms of settings, which do you prefer? (Tick as many as you like.)

☐ Down to earth and as realistic as possible
☐ Historical settings. If so, which period do you prefer?

_____

☐ Fantasy settings – barbarian worlds
☐ Completely escapist/surreal fantasy
☐ Institutional or secret academy

- ☐ Futuristic/sci fi
- ☐ Escapist but still believable
- ☐ Any settings you dislike?

_____

- ☐ Where would you like to see an adult novel set?

_____

6. In terms of storylines, would you prefer:

- ☐ Simple stories that concentrate on adult interests?
- ☐ More plot and character-driven stories with less explicit adult activity?
- ☐ We value your ideas, so give us your opinion of this book:

_____

_____

_____

7. In terms of your adult interests, what do you like to read about? (Tick as many as you like.)

- ☐ Traditional corporal punishment (CP)
- ☐ Modern corporal punishment
- ☐ Spanking
- ☐ Restraint/bondage
- ☐ Rope bondage
- ☐ Latex/rubber
- ☐ Leather
- ☐ Female domination and male submission
- ☐ Female domination and female submission
- ☐ Male domination and female submission
- ☐ Willing captivity
- ☐ Uniforms
- ☐ Lingerie/underwear/hosiery/footwear (boots and high heels)
- ☐ Sex rituals
- ☐ Vanilla sex
- ☐ Swinging
- ☐ Cross-dressing/TV
- ☐ Enforced feminisation

☐ Others – tell us what you don't see enough of in adult fiction:

_____

_____

_____

8. Would you prefer books with a more specialised approach to your interests, i.e. a novel specifically about uniforms? If so, which subject(s) would you like to read a Nexus novel about?

_____

_____

_____

9. Would you like to read true stories in Nexus books? For instance, the true story of a submissive woman, or a male slave? Tell us which true revelations you would most like to read about:

_____

_____

_____

10. What do you like best about Nexus books?

_____

_____

11. What do you like least about Nexus books?

_____

_____

12. Which are your favourite titles?

_____

_____

13. Who are your favourite authors?

_____

_____

14. Which covers do you prefer? Those featuring:
(Tick as many as you like.)

- ☐ Fetish outfits
- ☐ More nudity
- ☐ Two models
- ☐ Unusual models or settings
- ☐ Classic erotic photography
- ☐ More contemporary images and poses
- ☐ A blank/non-erotic cover
- ☐ What would your ideal cover look like?

_____

15. Describe your ideal Nexus novel in the space provided:

_____

_____

_____

_____

16. Which celebrity would feature in one of your Nexus-style fantasies? We'll post the best suggestions on our website – anonymously!

_____

THANKS FOR YOUR TIME

Now simply write the title of this book in the space below and cut out the questionnaire pages. Post to: Nexus, Marketing Dept., Thames Wharf Studios, Rainville Rd, London W6 9HA

Book title: _____

NEXUS NEW BOOKS

To be published in January 2008

BLUSHING AT BOTH ENDS
Philip Kemp

Funny, full of surprises and always arousing, this is a brilliant collection of stories about innocent young women drawn into scenarios that result in the sensual pleasures of spanking. It features girls who feel compelled to manipulate and engineer situations in which older authority figures punish them, over their laps, desks, or chairs.

£6.99   ISBN 978 0 352 34107 5

To be published in February 2008

WEB OF DESIRE
Ray Gordon

Mandy is struggling with life, especially with money and men. And when she bumps into Paula, an old friend from school, she immediately envies Paula's glamorous lifestyle – the luxury, the travel and the affluent boyfriends in tow. Competing with Paula's success and sexual encounters, Mandy begins to dress, act and behave as she has never done before. Single-minded in her reckless pursuit of her friend's conquests and triumphs, the naïve and inexperienced Mandy is soon indulging her most salacious fantasies. And it's not long before Mandy is on a par with Paula's professed indulgences. She's slipped so far down the slope to depravity she hardly recognises her former self. But then Mandy discovers a shocking truth about Paula – something that will rock her to her core.

£6.99   ISBN 978 0 3 523 4167 9

If you would like more information about Nexus titles, please visit our website at www.nexus-books.co.uk, or send a large stamped addressed envelope to:
Nexus, Thames Wharf Studios,
Rainville Road, London W6 9HA

NEXUS BOOKLIST

Information is correct at time of printing. To avoid disappointment, check availability before ordering. Go to www.nexus-books.co.uk.

All books are priced at £6.99 unless another price is given.

NEXUS

☐ ABANDONED ALICE	Adriana Arden	ISBN 978 0 352 33969 0
☐ ALICE IN CHAINS	Adriana Arden	ISBN 978 0 352 33908 9
☐ AQUA DOMINATION	William Doughty	ISBN 978 0 352 34020 7
☐ THE ART OF CORRECTION	Tara Black	ISBN 978 0 352 33895 2
☐ THE ART OF SURRENDER	Madeline Bastinado	ISBN 978 0 352 34013 9
☐ BEASTLY BEHAVIOUR	Aishling Morgan	ISBN 978 0 352 34095 5
☐ BELINDA BARES UP	Yolanda Celbridge	ISBN 978 0 352 33926 3
☐ BIDDING TO SIN	Rosita Varón	ISBN 978 0 352 34063 4
☐ BLUSHING AT BOTH ENDS	Philip Kemp	ISBN 978 0 352 34107 5
☐ THE BOOK OF PUNISHMENT	Cat Scarlett	ISBN 978 0 352 33975 1
☐ BRUSH STROKES	Penny Birch	ISBN 978 0 352 34072 6
☐ CALLED TO THE WILD	Angel Blake	ISBN 978 0 352 34067 2
☐ CAPTIVES OF CHEYNER CLOSE	Adriana Arden	ISBN 978 0 352 34028 3
☐ CARNAL POSSESSION	Yvonne Strickland	ISBN 978 0 352 34062 7
☐ CITY MAID	Amelia Evangeline	ISBN 978 0 352 34096 2
☐ COLLEGE GIRLS	Cat Scarlett	ISBN 978 0 352 33942 3
☐ COMPANY OF SLAVES	Christina Shelly	ISBN 978 0 352 33887 7
☐ CONCEIT AND CONSEQUENCE	Aishling Morgan	ISBN 978 0 352 33965 2

----------✂----------------------------

Please send me the books I have ticked above.

Name   ....

Address   ....

                ....

                ....

                .... Post code ....

Send to: **Virgin Books Cash Sales, Thames Wharf Studios, Rainville Road, London W6 9HA**

US customers: for prices and details of how to order books for delivery by mail, call 888-330-8477.

Please enclose a cheque or postal order, made payable to **Nexus Books Ltd**, to the value of the books you have ordered plus postage and packing costs as follows:

UK and BFPO – £1.00 for the first book, 50p for each subsequent book.

Overseas (including Republic of Ireland) – £2.00 for the first book, £1.00 for each subsequent book.

If you would prefer to pay by VISA, ACCESS/MASTERCARD, AMEX, DINERS CLUB or SWITCH, please write your card number and expiry date here:

....

Please allow up to 28 days for delivery.

Signature ....

Our privacy policy

We will not disclose information you supply us to any other parties. We will not disclose any information which identifies you personally to any person without your express consent.

From time to time we may send out information about Nexus books and special offers. Please tick here if you do *not* wish to receive Nexus information.   ☐

----------✂----------------------------